PRAISE FOR HUSH, NOW FORGET

Forget Batman and Robin! This dynamic duo will blow your mind!

— JANET, BARNES AND NOBLE REVIEWER

Frost, Eva and their Aunt Maggie are wonderfully drawn, feisty women.

— IND'TALE MAGAZINE

With ghostly legends, mystery, heartbreak, murder, and possession—this book will keep you flipping the pages desperate to find out what happens next.

— VANESSA, BOUND AND BREWED

Fans of Sam and Dean Winchester will definitely get a kick out of this book.

— CLAIRE, THE COFEEHOLIC BOOKWORM

The bond between the sisters felt genuine and just seemed natural.

— BOB, PLATYPIRE

Thrilling and captivating.

— CARL, AMAZON REVIEWER

Once you start reading this book you will not want to put it down even for a minute.

— BRITTANY, TEEN LIBRARIAN

I will definitely be getting the sequels. I like the different twist on ghost mythology in the story, the teenagers are authentic, and the humor is sly to add a little fun, the occasional smirk.

— GLENNA, GOODREADS REVIEWER

A good blend of mystery, paranormal, and romance. It is a clean read, nothing crude in it. I feel good about recommending it to my friends – a quality that many books in this genre don't possess.

— LORNA, AMAZON REVIEWER

I love the way each chapter is from a sister's point of view.

— BRENDA, KOBO REVIEWER

Totally fun and imaginative read. The sisters are relatable, the supernatural is thrilling, and the settings are true-to-life. I am so excited to have a new series!!!

—JENNIFER, AMAZON REVIEWER

HUSH, NOW FORGET

Sisters of Bloodcreek #1

GRAY, LARSEN

Read a FREE short story prequel about our favorite Blurred One turned hunter friend, Leo, by visiting BookHip.com/PWSHNX.

For fans of Sam and Dean

The cradle rocks above an abyss, and common sense tells us that our existence is but a brief crack of light between two eternities of darkness.

— VLADIMIR NABOKOV

CHAPTER 1 - FROST

Bloodcreek Road twists and squirms like the water moccasins in our creek back home. Usually, I have to watch the road to not get carsick, but not today. Today, we've got a mission in the crosshairs.

Prepping for our Spanish class' field trip to San Antonio.

I scan today's news for a particularly juicy headline on my phone. I need something Maggie, our pseudo-aunt hunter friend, can't ignore. Something violent, something unexpected. . . and something that was *definitely* caused by the supernatural.

"How about this one?" I tap the shiny new screen of my phone. "'Newlyweds Found Dead After Eating Each Other's Faces Off While Honeymooning in Chicago.'"

Maggie's aged eyes crinkle at the sides as a bulky tractor slows our progress on the road. "Now that's not the most romantic way to begin one's nuptials."

Behind me, Eva, my younger sister by just thirteen months, is already doing "phase-two" of Mission Get-To-San-Antonio—hiding any and all weapons Maggie loaded us up with before we hopped in the car. Maggie may be a gem by all intents and purposes, but she tends to forget that things like switchblades and hunting knives can get both of us expelled from school.

Eva conceals the last pair of salt grenades, but by doing so, she noisily rattles a cup holder.

Maggie's experienced hunter eyes narrow, and it's only a matter of seconds before she realizes we ditched the majority of her contraband back at the house. Maggie will *never* support the school's policy of zero weapons—not when there are things like banshees and wendigos on the loose—so, in an effort to mask my fear with affection, I seize my friend's meaty arm. "Think you'll go?"

Maggie's slow smile tells me she appreciates the gesture and she *pat-pats* my hand with her calloused fingers. When she peers through her newly cracked windshield, it's like I can hear what she's thinking: *I could* escape the humidity for a while. But Chicago will be even farther away from my girls. . . .

With Eva and me gone, though, we all know she'll be bored. No shooting lessons or reminders of how to do CPR. No lectures on putting on temporary tattoos to prevent the possession of demons or ghosts. Maggie's never been good at sitting around, so it doesn't come as much of a shock when she ultimately huffs. "Might as well."

We veer around a cluster of hail-damaged mobile homes, and I'm so excited, I grin at a pair of bikini-clad mannequins someone's posed atop a cherry-red convertible. It won't be long till Eva and I are neck-deep in *all* the answers regarding our "special brand" of the supernatural.

When we make a sharp turn to the left, though, Eva

lurches from her seat to hide what must be the last of Maggie's stockpile.

"Just what are you doing back there?" Maggie quasi-growls.

Eva's lies are as smooth as baby oil. "Looking for Mentos."

But now, Maggie's eyes are narrowed at my fingers, which have somehow wrapped around the "oh-crap-bar" above my head. My saving grace comes in the form of the mother of all potholes.

We've arrived at our school.

Too-thin siding houses a library and a biology trailer, and tobacco cans line the sidewalks like rope lighting at a fancy hotel. There's a shack for baseball gear, too, but that's where all the pot-smokers go when they're tired of bettering themselves.

After sailing into a parking spot a few cars over from the bus, Maggie throws her Buick into park and flings her door wide open with the gusto and flair of a bull-rider. "You girls all packed up and ready to go?"

Eva and I stumble onto the asphalt, scrambling for our essentials.

"Got your switchblades?" Maggie's hopeful gaze lingers on Eva's fringed bag that matches her maroon-blitzed fingernails.

I laugh, loud, because Maggie has the sort of voice that travels. Hopefully no one overheard. While Maggie refuses to show us what's inside her fanny pack—her mysterious "Pack o' Wonders"—she was a little too generous with her silver bullets before we left the house.

Eva and I side-eye each other, her dramatically eye-lined charcoal eyes to my blue.

Got rid of it all? I tilt my head like our orange tabby, Gato.

Her eyes twinkle as she gives an almost imperceptible bow. The sun glitters off the dozen or so rings on her fingers, reminding me of her biggest pair of fuchsia headphones. Truth is, we're the complete inside-out of each other—Eva's the fun one, while I'm the one who typically follows all the rules.

Now, though, Maggie keeps tapping her fanny pack like it's her prized rodeo buckle. Like she's tempted to pull out something else—handcuffs with devil's traps? —but she must see that there isn't enough time. One of my camouflage-wearing classmates has moseyed over and is already sniffing around the knife-tipped railroad spike jutting out from the side pocket of Maggie's cargo pants.

Besides, it's not like we didn't just spend all night going over how to barricade ourselves in our rooms and the proper thickness of salt lines for keeping out ghosts. Eva and I may not be hunters, but Maggie's always armed us with these sorts of details.

Opening her arms like we're a pair of diapered toddlers, Maggie says, "I'm going to miss my girls."

Eva and I snuggle up, because Maggie's been our homiest home for years.

Her paisley shirt is like silk to my fingers. Her shoulders are soft, but layered by muscle. There's the ever-present scent of bug spray, Dawn soap, and engine oil. She's our Mama Bear, our Hagrid of Hogwarts. Parent without actually being a parent. Lifeline when our parents are being impossible.

To my embarrassment, Maggie's already blinking furiously when she lets us go. She fumbles for her eyeglasses perched atop her short brown curls before swiftly planting them on her nose. Maybe it's easier not to cry when she's "the scholar," Maggie Darrow.

Wiping her nose on the back of her rolled sleeve, she clears her throat. "Call me when you get there?"

Eva places a bejeweled hand over the front ruffle of her shirt. "When the cat's away, the mice won't play."

Maggie furrows her brow. "I'll pretend that's how it goes. Frost, you'll look after her?"

Yes, I very nearly say, almost wishing Maggie could chaperone. But who would look into those newlyweds who ate each other's faces off in Chicago?

Maggie rests a hand on my shoulder, still awaiting my answer, and guilt churns in my stomach like a hungry spider. I'd like to reassure her that everything will be okay, but no one can really know. Taking care of Eva is sort of like taking care of a bumblebee—she's a little precarious and flies wherever she wants to go.

So, I give Maggie the best answer I can. "I suppose."

Pacified, Maggie drops her hand as my heart slows. She doesn't mention the Almond Joy brownies she snuck into my satchel, or the peach cobbler she crammed inside Eva's duffel bag between her lip-gloss and headphones. No, instead Maggie holds up a stubby finger, and in her low, authoritative voice, says, "Don't forget to take notes."

Eva rolls her eyes. "Like Frost's capable of *not* being a nerd."

Maggie's already rosy cheeks darken with pleasure as she shifts in her hiking boots. Her collection of knives and pepper sprays makes her our Maggie. Our Jesse James, Carrie Nation, and Annie Oakley all balled up into one.

"Just promise me," she says, wiping the tears shining in her eyes, "that you'll carve those sigils into the doors. And don't forget to say your prayers."

She only said that because our parents must have reminded her to tell us before we go. Our family may not be hunters—we're a little higher on the totem pole—but we all know the necessity of arming ourselves.

Maggie doesn't have to state her "other" rules. The ones she's been drilling into us ever since we told her our Spanish class was going to the Alamo. She knows Eva and I have always been too curious for our own good.

No EMF readers. And no *ghost tours.*

When we broke it to her that we were actually staying at the Gunter—one of America's most famously haunted hotels, and where, incidentally, resides one of our hidden horrors—Maggie grabbed an Aleve before rolling out the white board.

No searching for ghosts of blonde girls, she wrote, because Albert Knox, a particularly horrible supernatural being, is a collector of those.

No taking baths, because that's where Knox put his victims after shooting them while they were in their underwear.

No shoes that make your feet look small.

No Sixties music.

And, absolutely, positively *no meat grinders.*

Like we're going to lug one of those to San Antonio.

Now, though, Maggie doesn't drag up any of her addendum rules, and I'm pretty darn glad, because I'm about done drawing undue attention to ourselves.

It isn't long before Eva and I are hunkered low in our shared vinyl seat, our fellow residents of Bloodcreek stringing together their most inspiring curse words. Twangy guitars and tambourines serenade us over the radio. Something splatters my cheek as someone tries to discard their tobacco out the window, and I wipe it off with the back of my sleeve.

A girl quips a clever joke about something anatomical, and in the back one of the boys moons the highway patrol.

Our driver jerks around a possum. One of the band geeks makes a fart noise, and we're just bouncing over a neat little collection of Missouri's potholes when Eva breathlessly turns to me.

"I packed a blonde wig."

I pull a purple plastic bottle from my satchel. "I brought bubble bath with chamomile."

CHAPTER 2 - EVA

ind your *Tejas Hombre*, everyone," Mrs. Sanders shrills, waddling in her neon purple crocs toward the sloped roof of the Alamo.

I throw my arms like a giant windmill around Frost's bony shoulders. My ride-or-die sister from the same mister.

Reaching up, she pats my hand with her always cold one in solidarity, and we watch our twenty-something classmates scramble over the burning cobblestones to find their travel buddies. I force myself to not quirk an eyebrow at their bad teeth, Wranglers, and the hottest designers from ten years ago. I know it makes me a snob, but I can't help wishing Frost and I were part of a group with *less* hunter-flage and more style.

Double-decker tour buses, cars, trucks, and horse-drawn carriages crawl past us with the infamous Alamo standing behind them. It's kind of majestic, but sad at the same time, with its still visible cannonball dents.

We totally look the part of one of many high school tour groups, but the bad dye jobs and tobacco can-lined back pockets separate us from the prep school polos, pressed khakis, or otherwise washed and well-nourished groups. I have to remind myself there's more to people than looks, although after almost a year with these people, for most of them, I'm not sure how much more.

"Maybe we can find some guys here who actually shower," I mutter to Frost below a giant oak tree, hesitant to move into the beating sun.

She gives a small snort, and her movements have that jerky tendency she gets when big sis Frosty is stressed. Is she wondering if maybe we *should* have put on one of Maggie's temporary warding tattoos in case of an emergency? Quiz each other on the Latin Maggie taught us in case we have to exorcise a ghost?

"This is gonna be awesome." I nudge her lean, tan calf with my flip-flop. "Finally out of the house, ready for answers."

With a quick glance at her calf to make sure I didn't make it dirty, she flashes her perfect white teeth in a genuine smile. "Yes! Plus, we haven't had to pick up any rocks for like thirty-six hours now!"

"Ain't that the truth." But the mention of home reminds me how we left Maggie's contraband behind. She's gonna be pissed. "Did you remember to ditch the Reaper?" I murmur in Frost's ear.

Frost's head bobs. We'd found that in Frost's duffel beneath her nerd stash of history books and highlighters. Nice try, Maggie. We can probably get away with vials of holy water and salt, but no security guard is going to think kindly on Maggie's favorite blade. Fittingly nicknamed for its sick, silver curved blade. "Better for hackin' a banshee's head off," she likes to say. A small banshee, but a banshee just the same. Course, if the parentals caught any wind of us even dabbling in hunting, they'd crap a giraffe.

Not that we've ever used the blade, ourselves.

"Okay, are we ready, *hombres?*" Mrs. Sanders says, drawing out her best Spanglish accent. She claps her wrinkled hands, making her plastic bangles clatter. "Let's go over our plans for the rest of the *dia!*" She sings that last part and I stifle a laugh, not wanting to wet blanket her enthusiasm. She's probably frazzled, since all the other chaperones flaked. I'm just glad no one cared enough to make us cancel.

One of our classmates who has most likely never brushed his crooked teeth in his entire life pumps an arm, whooping, and Frost and I look at each other, her half-rolled eyes mirroring my own. Did I hear a snicker from the Khaki Yale Brigade?

The sickly sweet smell of bathroom cologne assaults my nose as one of our classmates, Wade, brushes my arm with his gangly one. He nudges me hard enough I feel his wiry arm-hairs. I desperately want to wipe off my arm.

"Hey." He winks his way-too-blond and too few lashes at me and jiggles his leg like he's struggling with a wedgie.

"Hey . . ." It comes out like a question, and I'm taking shallow breaths to help me not gag. This. This is the difference between being country and being hick, hillbilly, or redneck. Country still has class. Country knows about hygiene.

"You oughta be my old lady." Wade reaches his heavy, damp arm around my suddenly very tense shoulders.

"Okay, buddy. Okay. Your mullet is looking extra curly today." I simultaneously want to laugh and vomit, but I don't actually know what he means, so I look at Frost, but she's already scribbling something in her notepad. So much help. I'd love to punch him in the stomach for touching me, try out some defensive moves in the real world, but I mind my manners.

"Let's talk later. I don't want to miss our plans for the *dia* with my Tejas hombre!" I duck out from under his arm—not enough cologne to mask that body odor—and drape my own over Frost's shoulders. "Time to gooooo." I steer Frost toward the Alamo's entrance. Thankfully, Mrs. Sander's speech was short this time, and the students are clambering through the mission's thick white-washed archway.

Wade runs one hand through his neck curls and reaches the other into his back pocket to feel for his snuff. "Aight! I'll catch you'ns later then! Bye, sexy lady!" he shouts after us just as we reach the gate.

"Dodged that mullet." I chuckle, extra pleased with my pun. I breathe in the cigarette and cumin flavored air. "See what we were missing out on riding to school with Dad all these years?" I've seen Wade float around girls before, but this is my first close encounter. He probably smelled fresh meat—a rarity in the redneck center of the world, where everyone has dated everyone and some chlorine could definitely be used in the gene pool. Mom and Dad transferred us this year away from the "big city influences" of Salem, Missouri—population whopping five thousand—after Dad found out one of his students had been on probation once.

"You sure know how to pick them." Frost pokes me where she knows I'll squirm, right between the ribs, so I pull back my arm.

"I know, I know. Wade Pinkman, my next flavor of the week." Shaking my head, I notice several pods have fallen from the tree into my dark hair. I set to picking them out. So dignified. When I'm satisfied I'm pod free, I turn to take in the mission more completely.

It's actually more peaceful than I would have expected from such a war-torn landmark. A string quartet plays "Deep in the Heart of Texas" in the big shady, tropical park while a group of kids play "soldier" with muskets near a babbling fountain.

Frost begins to listen to an audio tour through headphones, dutifully taking notes on her small blue notepad. I have no desire to be stuck in a notebook and instead enjoy the moment of freedom and just breathe. She can help jog my memory for my paper later. Does that make me selfish?

I lift one side of her headphones so she can hear me. "I'm glad you're a history buff, Frosty. Makes writing research papers way easier." I wait for a semi-annoyed look, but something must catch her eye, because she nearly drops her notepad to grab my arm.

"Camo bogie, eight o'clock!" she hisses into my ear. I'm shocked her fingers are still cold in this heat, but I'm turning around to spy the intruder when suddenly, someone takes a giant grab of my rear.

"What the—!" I leap and turn toward my assailant.

"Hey, ol' lady!" My long-locked admirer, Wade, has already returned. "How you likin' the Alama? I seen a spot o'er yonder I wanna show ya."

Utterly confused, I look to Frost. Does she have any idea why he just took license to my behind? She must be lost, too. Her hazel eyes are wide as pancakes, darting from me to Wade and back, probably waiting for me to try out Maggie's maneuvers now.

"Uh, we've been here two minutes. And, Wade? Why are you touching my butt?"

"Shoot." He spits a thick yellow blob from his tobacco, and I don't think he's even trying to be discreet. Also, it lands way too close to my sandal. "'Cause you're my old lady."

I'm a China doll, my big eye-lashed eyes capable only of blinking.

"Ya know, we're goin' steady, right?"

A snort escapes Frost, and I have to look away from his ruddy cheeks. A tidal wave of his breath mixed with B.O. reaches my nose. I absolutely love flirting and kissing here and there, but my *assets* are very protected. My stomach lurches again. I don't want to be rude, but this ain't happening.

A set of strong shoulders emerges from behind a tree—shoulders no one in Bloodcreek could possess, and I swear a light bulb just appeared above my head.

"Oh, Wade, I think there's been a misunderstanding." Awkwardly stooping, I extricate his hand that's taken up residence in my back pocket and dash toward two guys examining a plaque a few feet away. I grab the dusty blond's arm, instantly attracted to the muscles underneath his well-worn leather jacket. Unseasonable, but attractive. I plaster pure innocence across my face and look up a couple of inches into my diversion's scruffy face. Yay—he's taller than me.

"I already have a boyfriend," I tell Wade. "He came here to meet me. Isn't that right, honey bunches of sugar plums?" I hope he doesn't notice my voice is a little tight and my hands are shaking—and that he might possibly find me charming and not crazy.

I lay it on thick so he'll know what I'm doing. I reach one arm around his back, put my other hand on his perfectly sculpted chest, and rest my head on his shoulder. I look at Wade while holding my angelic expression. I bat my lashes up at this complete stranger and then steal a glance to Frost for reinforcement. She just hangs her head, shaking it a bit. She's not going to be joining in anytime soon. Too bad. Making her play along would be a high of its own.

The tall drink of water looks from me to Frost to his own friend for a clue as to what is going on. He starts to pull away when Wade winningly spits another wad of yellow gunk. My heart leaps as my man-candy stops moving away and settles into my arms.

"Hi, uh, pookie."

Oh my gosh, his voice is raspy and low. My stomach does

that sinking feeling I get when I'm about to fall crazy in love or go down a steep rollercoaster.

His friend is also handsome, in a more sophisticated, old soul way, wearing suspenders like he stepped off a 1920s movie set, with a perfectly placed widow's peak and a dimple you just have to touch.

"I think you're saving a damsel in distress." The friend grins at me, and I instantly like him. He turns his gaze on Frost, and something like relief washes over his eyes. His grin widens to Cheshire cat degree. "Raylan has been looking forward to this all day." He nudges "Raylan" in the side.

Raylan clues in but isn't entirely thrilled by the ruse. With a straight face, he deadpans, "This guy bothering you?"

He focuses on the bulge of chew protruding from Wade's big pink lips. Wade frowns at me for a long moment, a dog who didn't get his bone. But then, looking around, he sees a different stick he likes—Frost.

"How 'bout you? Wanna be my ol' lady?" He winks at Frost, who isn't hearing any of this conversation anymore. She's staring at Raylan's friend.

The stranger is still smiling at her like they're long lost buds, and it lights up his whole face. Her cheeks flush the way they do on the rare occasion that she sees a boy she likes. She is suddenly intensely trying to find something in her purse and ends up dropping her brand new cell phone straight on the asphalt.

"Oh no!" She's immediately on the ground, squatting like a child but somehow doing it gracefully, examining the phone. The boy steps forward, I'm assuming to help, but then stops. They start talking, oblivious to the three of us, but I tune them out, focusing on my conquest.

"Wade." I shift, settling more into Raylan's side. "I heard Jenny say you're cute the other day, and she's right over there." I nod to the tall strawberry-haired girl standing over a small group of shorter, frizzy, badly blonde friends. Her limbs are long and awkward as she tries to make herself smaller instead of owning her model-like beauty.

"Yeah?" He spits again. "Well aight, I'll go give her a holler! Thanks, Elena!" He saunters off and shakes his legs a little. I do believe the Wranglers have given him a wedgie. I turn my attention back to my hottie at hand.

I clear my throat and say as sultrily as I can, "It's Eva, actually." I back off a bit so there are a few inches between us. Don't want him thinking I'm a complete psychopath.

He's not looking at me, however. He narrows his intense eyes and lowers his brows. An odd chill covers me. He reaches behind his back and removes a dark, black object. A gun?

On instinct, I look for his target, and my blood runs cold. A woman. Blonde, beautiful, but oddly dressed in a flowing white nightgown, and not wholly there. As in, I can still sort of see the tree behind her. She parts her lips in a sneer when the blast of the gunshot shakes the square. I gasp and choke on an awful smell—rotten eggs? Sulfur!—and gunpowder. My eyes water. I blink and she is *gone*. Not run away, not dead or bleeding before me. Just gone. My mind tries to rip through everything Maggie has taught us about the supernatural. Maybe she's a ghost, and he just shot her with salt? I saw her face, so I'm pretty sure she's not a—

A little girl screams and points at Raylan.

I look to Frost, hoping she saw what just went down, but panic grips the square and she's busy helping a man pick up his cane. A pair of security officers are running toward us. Fire crackers pelt the air and I know it's part of some sort of reenactment, but it sounds like more gunshots and people are screaming, shouting for their loved ones.

Raylan, concealing his weapon as fast as he pulled, shouts something to his friend. My brain is too full to hear what.

They need to leave. But he doesn't wait. He takes off for the exit. After a half second of hesitation, I'm running through the crowd after him. One day into our trip and we run into a pair of hot hunters? Has to be fate.

"Eva! Eva!" Frost yells, looking the other way.

I'm sure she doesn't want me disappearing after this guy. It's reckless. I should stick with the plan to lure out Mr. Knoxy, but sometimes you gotta be reckless when opportunity strikes. Safe hasn't worked. Patience, asking questions about what these creatures actually are, hasn't worked.

Raylan turns to glance at Frost as she yells, and as he does, we lock eyes for the briefest of moments. I don't know what I see there, but it's not evil. Conflict? Sorrow? I know I should be horrified. Well, I am. Partly. But a real-life hunter? Maggie would be so impressed and Dad would turn Mr. Hyde. Plus, hello muscles. I can't let this be my last interaction with him.

So I do my best to not run like a Tyrannosaurus Rex while trying to keep my boobs from falling out of my shirt. See, Dad? I'm not childish, I'm spontaneous!

He disappears into the exit of the Alamo shrine. I push my way through a group of petrified exiting tourists in neon green "Florez Family Fun" shirts and keep running after Raylan. I'm not especially fast, but Maggie's always said I have good instincts for tracking. Thank you, Capture the Flag.

He's slipping through the gate and heading past the cinnamon fumes of a pretzel cart toward the busy street. It's hot and loud and there're so many people, but his leather jacket stands out in the bright San Antonio atmosphere.

"Raylan, wait!" I yell, but if he hears me, he doesn't show. Thankfully the road is full of cars and horse-drawn carriages, so he has to hesitate, allowing me a few precious seconds to almost catch up. The panic inside the Alamo hasn't reached out here yet.

Just as I'm almost to him, a pocket of space opens up and he darts across the street. But I'm right on his tail, and I grab a handful of smooth leather as he reaches the other curb.

Angry eyes slice onto my face, and he jerks his arm out of my grasp. Were I a lesser—smarter?—woman, I would take that as my final warning and let him go. But I have a death wish and I think with my hormones, so I still follow him as he speed-walks away. He darts into a small space between buildings and grabs my arm, pulling me with him.

"What are you doing?" His words are like a volcanic explosion. His intensity reverberates from my head to my toes.

"What am I doing? What are *you* doing? You just shot someone!"

"You have no idea what you're talking about."

"Uh, gun went boom at someone right over there." I gesture toward the violence-prone monument. "Was that a ghost?"

A beat passes before he replies. I fold my arms, feeling slightly smug that I know about ghosts. He levels his cool blue eyes at me, brow furrowed. "Right."

"Seriously?" I blurt. "That's awesome! Who was she?"

He looks away, scanning the area. Uniformed police now dot the street and sidewalk.

"Go back to your friend. I need to go."

"Sister," I correct. "But seriously, who was she? Are you really a hunter?" I can't settle on which question is most important. Maybe he knows about Mr. Knox and his meat grinder.

But there isn't time for him to reply. Police radios squawk right around the corner. Across the street, an officer's gaze lingers on Raylan as he reaches for a radio. There's nowhere to run. He's going to get his butt hauled off to jail. But I need time. I need answers.

So I grab Raylan by the lapel and push him against the mossy cement wall and kiss him with all I've got. He's stiff and surely surprised but knows the police are coming too, and suddenly this kiss turns into something else entirely. Dude's got instincts. He wraps his arms tightly around my back, smashing me into him. I have no choice but to slip one leg between his or I'll lose my balance, and dang if I am not on another planet.

The police, tourists, Wade, classmates, all disappear from existence. His scruff is rough but not painful, and he tastes like a man. Maple and apples? I slide my hands back to his hard chest, then shoulders once more because I need to feel those full muscles again. I can hardly breathe in the best way, and every inch of me tingles.

He nibbles my bottom lip just a tad, and now I have to have more, so I reach one hand into his soft blond hair and pull him even harder into me. Just when I think I will melt and he will have to catch me before I am a pool of molten lava on the ground, he freezes.

He unlocks his vice-like grip on my back, puts his hands on my waist, and pushes me back, looking me in the eyes. I am void of any ability to communicate, just trying to stop my head from spinning. Softly he says, "Thanks," before running out of our niche and slipping away down the street.

CHAPTER 3 - FROST

'm ready to say it.

Our category of the supernatural.

Here goes.

Deep breath.

The Blurred Ones. And that's what Knox is.

That's pretty much all we officially know.

Mom and Dad will nod a little when Eva and I bring them up—scramble for grapes or orange juice at the breakfast table —but mostly they do everything in their power to avoid the topic. We know Blurred Ones are spirits and translucent— like regular ghosts. But they're a sheen of black when regular ghosts are white. Not that I'm an expert. Well, not anymore. The one and only Blurred One I knew when I was little has been, from my mind, inextricably banished.

That white shadowy figure in the square? She was a ghost.

Eva and I have been too curious. Instead of exploring the minefield that was my childhood, the only thing I knew how to do was to take two giant leaps forward and pretend my past didn't exist. But we shouldn't have brought the blonde wig and bubble bath with us, because all that's happened now is my sister's revved up. Next thing I know, she'll run off with this new hunter, and Mom and Dad will disown me for not protecting her well enough. Not to mention the conniption fit Maggie will have.

College and my impending acceptance letter? I can't focus on them until all of this is sorted. Eva deserves that. Still, it doesn't help that I had to pretend she was already on the bus when Mrs. Sanders asked me where she was.

Pistachios and cucumber water mock me from where I hunch at our room's desk. I'm supposed to be writing my paper on the Alamo, but she could be dead in some sewer somewhere or—no. The girl's probably got the guy buying her drinks and chauffeuring her around the hippest parts of town.

The flashier of us Abram girls, she's got a pattern.

There's my ex-boyfriend, Ricky, who actually liked her first. We once went over to our friend's to play hide-n-seek in the dark, and Ricky so happened to hide wherever Eva was.

There was Nick, who drove the Mustang and was at least twenty years old. Derek, *my* chemistry partner. Louis—who I thought was too old for me until Eva admitted they liked to kiss when they were supposed to be in class. Not that I wholly blame her; Bloodcreek doesn't have a lot of options.

My sister has a gift for luring men out to satisfy her own devices, but what if her gift gets the best of her before she can actually ever settle down?

The card reader clicks, and my shoulders tense. What if it's another ghost or one of those hunters? I glance to the corner of the room where I very nearly carved a sigil like Maggie taught us, warding all demons. But I didn't have the heart, what with losing Eva the moment we stepped off the bus.

Pulling the heavy door open, though, is Eva, flip-flops in

one hand, dark hair windblown. Her ruffled top's a little off-kilter, though she's *safe.* I hunker down over my book, forcing myself not to throw myself over my chair and run to her.

Where were you? I bite my tongue.

You could have gotten yourself killed.

What are you going to do when I leave you?

Instead, I murmur all casual-like, "Look what the cat dragged in." I barely look up from my line of pistachio shells so she can't read my panic.

Tossing one of her flip-flops to the corner where it *thwaps* a floor-lamp, Eva sighs her most impressive, dramatic sigh— just like Mom's, but a couple of decades younger. One of the flip-flop's toes meets my gaze, and I shudder, because that flip-flop used to be white.

"Hey, that's *my* sandal!" I can't believe I didn't notice she was wearing them before.

"Yeah." She sighs Mom's monster-sigh again. "Sorry about that."

I open my mouth to argue, but seeing how she's actually ridden with guilt, I stop myself. Last thing we need is a blow-up the first night we're free from our folks.

So, I take a dainty drink of my ice-cold cucumber water and decide to go back to skimming a heading about Santa Ana conquering the Alamo. But I can practically feel Eva's large eyes bulldozing mine.

"What is it?" I glance up. I act like I'm not worried, but it's getting harder to do—especially with the way she's looking at me. Sad eyes. Sagging shoulders, head tilted down. She's feeling vulnerable. Like the time Dad slapped her for not cleaning the garage fast enough.

I close my book. "Talk."

She takes in the pasty white floorboards and the bed, all made up in perfect lines with a starched comforter. Looks like we'll be sharing tonight, but that's nothing new.

I don't mind. Just as long as she doesn't steal all the covers.

"He's cute," Eva says, voice small. And I should have known she'd have to talk about the boy at the Alamo.

"Not very inconspicuous," I say, because maybe she'll clue in to the fact that she was chasing after a *hunter* when Maggie's the only hunter we're supposed to know.

"A great kisser."

I open my mouth only to snap it shut. We had our very first supernatural encounter—true—but is this how it's going to be when I'm gone? She makes out with every boy she meets in every far-off town?

I push out of my seat. She needs to be reminded of her options. "We should call Maggie." I stare at her to encourage her to pull out her phone, but when she doesn't, I seize my own, only to stare at the newly cracked screen. When I hit the plastic Home button, it doesn't flicker on.

"For her to lecture us?" Eva digs around in her bag for her blonde wig, which she settles on her head, making her look like a gaunt Marilyn Monroe. "I *thought* we had a plan."

"We do." I look from her wig to my satchel, which still conceals the bubble bath. I should have dumped that down the drain hours ago. "Maybe we should put those away until we figure out why that ghost woman appeared in broad daylight." I say "broad daylight" like it's a clue.

Eva snorts. "It's not like we're staying in the *real* room where Knox killed everyone. Relax." Still, Eva tosses her wig to the top of her bag, where it lands with a *splat*. Thankfully, she hates conflict as much as I do. She adds a little too softly, "I thought you'd be excited that we got our first clue."

I watch my sister's large eyes trickle over the room. I wish I could say, "Let's just enjoy researching the Alamo!" But Eva's no longer so docile. I used to be able to lure her away from busy streets, the water moccasins that like to lie in wait in our creek back home. Then, as she got older, I was able to fortify my shield with Mom's and Dad's fear of the supernatural. Always carry temporary tattoos. Wear silver barrettes.

I'm only a year older, but a lot happened when I was seven years old.

Eva's eyes scour the heavy brocade curtains, TV, and mini fridge, where her gaze lingers. I'm sure she's tempted to see if I, in fact, stocked the tiny appliance with her favorite Diet Coke, which I couldn't *not* do. But Diet Coke must be her last worry, because she's sinking into the edge of the manicured bed, looking to the floor again.

"Look," she says. "We've actually found someone with answers. Someone who won't punish us for asking what the Blurred Ones really are. I don't know about you, but I'm *really* tired of shoveling manure."

We've never actually shoveled manure, but I get what she's saying. Since the age of two, Eva's and my middle names have been Slave and Labor.

"Still. That hunter guy?" He doesn't follow our rules. "He had a gun!"

"So would we if Maggie had her way."

"But with Maggie there's always a double-standard."

"With *you*, there's always a double-standard."

I break from her gaze, as she's obviously got me there. I was all about looking into Knox and figuring out what makes him a Blurred One just to get her all settled, but at the first hint of danger, I planned to hit the brakes. Brick walled.

No wonder Eva's the one who's interested in law enforcement and all I want to do is something relatively safe and ambitious. Like be a doctor.

Sinking onto the edge of the bed next to Eva, I try to think logically. Like I'm reading what happened today from the paper. "Okay. If Maggie were here, she'd warn us to be wary of the hunters." Especially cute ones. "Even she doesn't like to shoot in broad daylight."

"He was shooting because that ghost woman was a threat."

"Even so." I wish I could open a book in Maggie's study or pour over a tome of the occult at the bookstore. Still, Eva has a point. For the first time, we actually saw a ghost. Soon, she'll understand just as much as I do.

My sister absently ties knots in her own hair, and she looks so crestfallen, I reach over and unknot a silky strand. Last thing she needs is to think I don't care—that I'm the enemy now. "We let the hunter boys be, but if they show up again—we reassess our plan."

"Really?" She squeals like I've just bought us two tickets for Depeche Mode. She's just about to give me a hug when her hands drop to her lap. "You're hoping we don't see them."

I arrange my face into a falsehood.

Narrowing her eyes, Eva tries to look stern, but ends up jutting out her lower lip. "You are an evil one."

Mom and Dad are always warning us to protect ourselves from being evil, which makes me laugh, diffusing all traces of worry or anger. Eva joins me, too, so I know all's forgotten. *Say your prayers*, Mom and Dad have always warned. *Read God's word, because vessels are far less vulnerable to Blurred Ones' possession if they arm themselves*. We're pretty good at keeping up the habits. We should pull open the scripture app on our phones, but more than ever, I need sustenance. The both of us do.

Eva watches as I dig the eight-by-eight pan of Almond Joy brownies out of my satchel.

"NO!"

She dives for her duffel bag, which I dragged up here with a little of Jenny's help, and woots when she finds the peach cobbler Maggie secretly stashed in there.

Eva pulls out her phone. "THANK YOU SO MUCH

FOR THE DELICIOUSNESS." She texts Maggie and her phone goes *whoop* right before she scrambles across the room for a fork. I already saw that our room didn't have any, though, so from the restaurant downstairs, I grabbed a pair.

Lucky for us that Mrs. Sanders was only willing to take us on this trip if we stayed in a nice hotel. Some of our class-mates have been doing fundraisers for years to pay for it. Of course, Eva and I slaved at home.

Skewering a juicy peach in the center of the pan, Eva enthusiastically sails her newfound romance into her mouth. "Urnnng." She moans, closing her eyes. Food is my best weapon for getting Eva to forget about boys.

Taking a nibble of my brownie's corner, I murmur, "Do you think that ghost woman was connected to the Knox murders?"

Eva scoops another forkful while shrugging her shoulders. And before she thinks to ask, I offer her some of mine, which she gleefully accepts. I'd eat cobbler, too, but eating too much before bed gives me nightmares.

No doubt from comparing the sweet coconut flavor with the more bitter dark chocolate Maggie tends to use, Eva gets this stupid dreamy smile on her face. She can't forget about the hunter dude for one minute.

"What's his name?" I lose my inner resolve and end up stabbing a peach when Eva passes her cobbler pan over.

"Rrr-raylan," she says like she's part tiger.

Sugar pumping through me, I can't help laughing. I could bring up the other boy that was with him in the square, but I'm pretty sure I don't want to dig around for that romance. He was cute—don't I know it—but if he's who I think he is, I better pray he never shows up again. I'm here to help my sister. Pulling on that thread could quickly make me unravel.

Stomach sufficiently sated, I reach for my sister's pan o'

peaches as she flinches backward like I'm threatening to whack off a limb.

"You're going to be mad at me if I don't make you stop," I explain. "You'll want some tomorrow."

Silently nodding, she allows me to take it before I set both pans on the fridge and click off the floor lamp.

Hooking my bra loose and slipping it through my armhole, I hang it over the corner of the big screen, since it's not like anyone else is coming in here.

A streetlamp from outside lights my murky path back to our bed, and I'm just about to ask Eva to scoot when she snores and flips over—smack-dab into the center of the bed. So I curl into my quarter of the mattress, telling myself not to think about the boy—the one with the widow's peak and earnest smile I've forced myself not to picture for years.

---

*L*ike a screwdriver's scraping granite, the bedside table slides open with a soft creak on even softer wood. Something moves from inside the drawer. Long, slender fingers curl out from the opening, fastening to the top of the table like an upside-down arachnid.

"Eva?" I sort of whimper. I totally forgot about carving those sigils—the common triquetra with the three pointed ovals that intersect like we always use on our house. We didn't even say our prayers. We came here looking for Knox, but Eva and I? We haven't exactly been trained in combat.

The fingernails are painted. Just like the girl's in the story before Knox severed her hand. Maggie made sure we didn't bring fingernail polish.

The tint is blood-red. Fire red. Red Delicious.

What if this ghost wants to possess us? If so, Maggie taught us what to say. *Eieci te ad infernum.* I banish you to hell.

But I don't exactly want to banish this lady before she has the chance to tell us what makes Knox a Blurred One.

Maybe the hand won't move? It'll just sit there.

The fingers fly toward me like a deranged hermit crab. Icy fingers fasten around my bicep. Fingernails dig into my flesh and shake me so hard, my teeth jumble in my eyelids.

"Eva!" I squawk, recalling the vial of holy water I keep in my satchel front pocket as I spot the blonde wig Eva put on before going to bed. The hand releases my arm and digs its pointed nails through my T-shirt and down the baby-soft flesh of my back. The pain is sharp and cold, and I shriek, "Hide the wig!"

Eva belly-flops over the side of the bed. She *hrrumphs* as she frantically starts stuffing the wig back in the duffel bag, but when she pulls the zipper, it snags on the inner lining of the wig's cap. "IT WON'T CLOSE."

The hand clings to my back like newly peeled carrot skins. So I flop over the side of the bed, too, as the hand whirs through the air in a blur of white, securing its pasty fingers around my sister's esophagus.

Eva's already large eyes stretch even wider. She swats at it like it's a baby tarantula.

I grab the phonebook from the end table and start whacking like the time we found a nest of spiders outside Maggie's shed. I manage to smack Eva's boob, her milk-white neck. The side of her cheek splits open from a papercut, which makes me feel pretty bad. But this is collateral damage. She'll thank me later, yes?

The hand drops from Eva's neck and lies limply on the bed like—like I killed it. But instead of five fingers, there's four, which reminds me of the guy on *The Princess Bride*. The one with six fingers on his hand. I'm thinking we just might have survived our first ghost attack when a wrist emerges like a snake from the hand. Bones shimmer and pop. An arm and laced bodice trickle into the shape of a human from dust. Blonde hair sprouts from a previously bald head.

The ghost woman whimpers, "He hurts us."

I stare into the ghost woman's defeated milk-white eyes. Is she talking about Raylan? Or Knox? Or me? I hit her with that phone book pretty hard.

Typically, ghosts only linger when they have unresolved business. So maybe we hurt her feelings for staying in her room. Maybe she's here to warn us. But this isn't Knox's room. He stayed in the room that's the sign of the devil—six-six-six. Eva and are in six-three-six. We're not idiots.

The woman's full and swollen lips twist like she's often been kissed. High cheekbones top a pale, slender figure, and her torn, laced bodice writhes like baby copperheads.

Eva scoots closer to the woman. Maggie told us once about a ghost who threw her thirty feet out of a barn, so maybe Eva has a death wish. "D-do you need help?"

The lady extends a shaky hand. Chopped fingers exude a trail of rusted floating blood.

Her figure blinks like the light's going out, and the TV clicks on, blaring static.

The room's door bursts open. Wind blows in a gust straight back to the curtains as two figures emerge. Black shadows, but corporeal—shoulders back. They shoot the ghost woman. The menacing stance like before tells me it's Raylan shooting, but there's a silencer on his black pistol now. I hope it's loaded with rock salt. That will slow her down.

As his bullets hit their mark, dust shoots from the woman's body, so it is. It flies into my eyes, coating my sleep-crinkled contacts.

The flesh and bones below my butt hint that I've sort of halfway landed on Eva's lap, and she's got her arms wrapped around me like we're about to ride Mr. Freeze again.

The boys stand in front of us—arms hanging powerfully at

their sides, feet shoulder-width apart like they're from the Magnificent Seven. The one with the widow's peak and long, full bangs grins that heartbreaking, earnest smile of his, and he's not supposed to be here. *He isn't real.* I glance away to the retro floor-lamp.

CHAPTER 4 - EVA

*R*aylan is here. In my room. We kissed. And it was *uh-mazing*. I shove Frost's bony butt off my lap and start to scramble off the bed. Because we just saw a freaking ghost and Raylan's here to chitty-chat.

Frost paws my arm, murmuring in a panicky little voice, "Did *you* let them in? I didn't let them in." I don't know why she's freaking out, but I'm ecstatic. I'd already been planning how to hunt him down and here he is, fallen into my lap. It just took a ghost attack to get him here, but my knight in shining armor. Is. *Here.*

I'm sure Frost and I could have gotten rid of the ghost lady eventually—I was totally about to reach that holy water —but I'll play damsel for this guy any ol' day.

I give him my biggest, most flirtatious smile. "Hey, hon," I say, bobbing one shoulder playfully.

Raylan barely registers my existence while holstering his pistol. "Looks like she's gone." He looks around our room of discarded bras and strewn bags. Well, my. Isn't he observant. He has to know the cute pink lace one is mine. Also, hooray for a small bladder since I got up to pee and changed into my cute jammies earlier. And he's eyeing my cobbler I may have forgotten to put away like it's sewage. Or delicious. I honestly can't tell.

"She'll be back," his friend says, fiddling with his suspenders while glancing around the room—the discarded phonebook on the floor and Frost's open books on the study table. Her disarray of pistachios and old cucumber water gives our room a nice "lived in" appearance. Better her than me making the mess, for once.

Now, though, Raylan's friend's icy blue eyes are roving over Frost's, and her cheeks are burning so red, she might need to be doused with a little ice water.

I don't know what it is, but I would bet my britches from the way Frost is looking at this suspender-wearing boy that she knows him. Heck if I know where, though, 'cause he sure ain't from any town around us.

A construction truck beeps, backing up outside, and the nighttime crew's yelling for it to stop, which only highlights the sound stretching over the room.

Quiet.

Raylan's friend rests his hand on his hip next to a super cool old-school revolver. I almost point this out to Frost, but now she's scooting off the bed looking all white and pasty like —well, like she's just seen a ghost.

I look from Imma-Gonna-Marry-You Heartthrob to Suspender-Wearing Heartthrob before settling my gaze on my favorite eye candy. "Couldn't forget about me, huh?"

Raylan strides across the room in this quasi military or cowboy strut. He peers out the curtains to stare at the construction going on below. He wordlessly moves to the bathroom, eyeing my cobbler again. Clicks and taps sound from the bathroom, and it isn't until the shower curtain squeaks that Frost apparently decides to pretend that the other boy isn't obviously checking her out.

She turns Martha Stewart and starts making the bed, of all things.

Raylan saunters back, skirting his gaze from Frost to me, like I'm the *last* thing he wants to see. Is he just playing hard to get? "Either of you know how to use one of these?" He pats his holstered weapon.

"Yep," I'm happy to say. "But yeah, we sort of left ours at home since our school frowns upon carrying around deadly weapons."

Raylan's jaw pulses, giving me all kinds of encouragement.

Truth is, even though, yes, Frost and I know how to shoot guns, we're not exactly snipers. We glance at each other as I picture our last semi-successful lesson from Maggie of root beer bottles and watering cans. Not my best day. But Raylan is giving me this annoyingly skeptical look, so I decide he doesn't need to know.

"We left our Glock and Sig at home." I lift my chin in false confidence.

He still looks doubtful as his friend rifles through what looks like a military supplies duffel they brought with them. "Guess we left it in the other room," the friend decides.

With a huff, Raylan brushes past his friend and stomps from our room. Gosh, he's even sexier when he's angry. I sort of want to follow him.

Frost and the other boy are sizing each other up again now, but I can't really register what mojo is going on between them, because—Raylan.

He reappears with a ridiculously large salt canister and opens the top spout. He bends over—oh, he's bending over—to shake a thick line around the door's entrance. No ghost can cross that barrier. We didn't do it before since we kinda sorta wanted this visit, but yeah, we possibly bit off more than we can chew.

"They should stay in here until the spirit is dealt with,"

Raylan says to his friend, as if Frost and I aren't standing right here. "We'll use salt lines to keep it out."

"Hold on," I say, not liking where this is going. I'm not about to get caged up right now. Plus, I've got to give Frost some room for whatever it is she's got going on. "You're not serious, are you?"

Raylan doesn't even bother to look up. "Yep."

No one is going to take away my new sweet, sweet freedom. If he thinks he can make me with his cool little authoritarian thing, he's got another thing coming.

"How long will that take," Frost interjects. "Mrs. Sanders will be expecting us in the lobby in the morning."

I don't love bringing up the fact that I'm still very much in high school, but she's got a solid point.

Raylan straightens and looks at us both, his face still that maddening mask.

So I hedge. "We can protect ourselves. And I'm sure you'll have her taken care of by tomorrow night, right?" Stroke the ego, get what I want. He silently moves to the windows to line them with salt too. My heart is back to normal, but now I'm just trying any tactic to get through to him. "We'll carve sigils on the doors."

Still nothing.

"Enough with the salt already!" I fight the urge to yank the canister from his hands.

His friend seems to remember he is part of this situation, too, and gracefully joins Raylan at the window. In stark contrast to Raylan, this boy has an open expression. So honest.

His bangs hang in his eyes as he shyly looks at Frost for the billionth time. The corners of his mouth seem eager for a smile, but pain stabs his eyes and oh my gosh. She *does* know him. Because she's fidgeting with the bottom cuff of her pants and her shoulders are *so* tense.

"What made you want to stay in room six-six-six?" he says, voice hushed.

"Six-three-six," I correct him.

One side of the boy's mouth twitches. "Why won't you look at me, Frost?"

The silence between them is enough to expect an avalanche. Tension seizes my brain, my eyes, my gut. I want to grab her face to force her to LOOK AT HIM. But she's just a deer in the headlights and looking at me instead. Like I'm supposed to help her, but last thing I'm going to do is stop my nun of a sister from experiencing real life. If I make her live this moment, things might actually start to *happen* for Frost. It's not every day a girl is trapped, alone in a hotel room with a hot guy who's apparently not a total stranger.

Besides, she seriously needs practice for when she leaves me for college.

The boy suddenly reaches down and grabs the edge of the bed sheet. He promptly tucks in the corner. Uh, are they soulmates or what?

There's no way he's a serial killer or bad guy. The soft lines in his stubble-free cheeks and round, round baby blue eyes? Yeah, he'd be happy with a little hug.

So I put my big girl britches on and look Raylan square in the eye.

"You and me are gonna go have a chat." And then because I don't want him to fight me, I add, "And some food."

<hr>

The hotel door closes behind me with a bang while I follow Raylan down the hall, disinfectant heavy in the air. "Well, that was awkward," I joke, trying to establish some sort of rapport with this hunk I kind of force-made out with not too long ago.

Raylan basically sprints for the elevator.

"And *this* is awkward," I mumble to the chocolate-colored wall. I know he's not happy to leave his task of fortifying the room, but I'm hoping he'll chill out and that he's not actually just a jerk.

He rounds the corner to the elevator and then presses the smudged yellow "down" button. We stand, waiting, not looking at each other, except that I'm stealing peripheral glances at his perfectly sloped jawline, his hands half in his front jean pockets. He's still as a statue, and I cross my arms to keep from fidgeting.

"What do you want to talk about?" His voice is more low and smooth now. Measured.

For a moment, I have crickets for thoughts. How can he play so cool with everything going on? Fine. I'm cool as a cucumber, too. Cool Girl. This ain't no thing. "Mind filling me in on what's going on? Like, for starters, why are y'all here in San Antonio?"

He only shifts his weight a little in his boots, hands still in his pockets, his flannel shirt bunched up around his elbows. The elevator doors ding, and we step inside. My heart beats a little faster at being in this space, enclosed together, just inches away. My handsome captive audience. Handsome still hasn't answered my question, though, so I nudge a bit more.

"Okay, or what happened at the Alamo? Who's the freaky woman ghost in my room? What's going on with your friend and my sister?" I lean back against my hands on the elevator's railing. "Could you start helping me with *one* of these million dollar questions?" I give an angelic smile—face soft, lots of teeth, batting lashes, head cocked to the side—the best way to score free stuff from any man with eyes. Bonus, it down-plays how desperately I want to know.

Raylan finally meets my eyes with his own ocean blue. I clamp my jaw before it can drop.

"I guess it's a bit much, huh?" He reaches up to scratch his head, but then seems to think better of it and puts his hand back down.

I wait, but he doesn't elaborate, so I prod. "Mmhmm." I raise my brows as high as I can in encouragement. Maybe I can even get him to tell me what a Blurred One is. His eyes are still locked on mine, making my chest shrivel with lack of oxygen. But he must make a decision, because he gives a small nod and a quick exhale while rubbing the back of his neck. "All right, let's talk."

We've reached the end of our ride. We step into the 1930s vibe lobby with its dark oak desks, ornate white wainscoting, and plush seating. The nearest swanky round couch holds *mi amor*, Wade, of the barely blond neck curls. He lounges across the bench like he's been here all night. Kicked out of his room, perhaps? Holding back a giggle of excitement, I seize the opportunity and quickly grab Raylan's strong, perfectly calloused hand and sidle up close.

"Funny how we keep meeting like this," I whisper close to his ear. Wade's spread-eagle Wranglers are hard to miss, and, aware of my tactics, Raylan doesn't fight me. Just bows his head a bit and gives it a little shake, so I see he has a cute little cowlick on the back of his head. An endearing imperfection. We walk naturally, locked hands swaying a bit, to the hotel restaurant. I think I even detect a slight smile. Maybe.

I don't know if Wade even saw us, but in this moment, I'm sure pleased with his existence.

In the dimly lit restaurant, we find a booth. Not pushing my luck, I let go of his hand and sit across from him on the squishy maroon leather bench. I clear my throat, ready for answers.

"So. Talk to me." I am oh-so-smooth.

Raylan looks at me like he's one of those old no-nonsense cowboys with few words, and my heart stutters. Just a couple blinks of his long dark lashes. Does he think I'm too immature for this?

A poised, auburn-haired waitress appears. She's the type of waitress you know is working full-time while also majoring in bio-electrical engineering and knows jiu jitsu. Besides her glossy hair, bronzed skin, and perfectly placed freckles, her uniform looks like it's only ever been dry cleaned and hints at an even better rack than mine. Raylan looks at her with all the charm of a GQ cover model.

"Diet Coke, please," he says, and with a swift glance at her nametag, adds, "Mindy."

Mindy holds eye contact with him—hey, he just did that with me—for a full five seconds before replying, "Sure thing, hon," while batting her giant lashes over her giant brown eyes and tucking a perfectly stray lock behind her ear. Because she is a professional, she remembers me.

"And for you?" she asks a little too nicely.

I have to restrain my eye roll. I am a three-day-old plucked dandelion as I reply, "Same, please."

With one last glimpse at Raylan, she winks, smiles, and blessedly walks away. Raylan is looking back at me with that stone-still poker face again. I take a deep breath, trying to relax and not come across as immature, since he is obviously older.

"You were not saying. . . ?" I grin my most charming grin.

"I shot the ghost with rock salt to buy us time till we can get rid of it. The nasty thing in your room was the same ghost. As for Leo, you should probably ask your sister." I blink a few times. That was forthcoming—and *Leo?* "Looks like you're in a full-on haunting. But somehow you knew that already."

Before I can reply, *Mindy* swishes in with our drinks, and I just stare while Raylan, or the Mister Suave that he turns into when *Mindy* is there, orders some nachos for us.

"You bet, sweetie." She touches his shoulder before she walks away, and I try to keep my eyes from sticking to the top of my skull, I roll them so hard. I recover by the time he looks back for my reply.

"We have an overprotective friend. Frost and I aren't hunters, but you really are, right?" I keep my voice nonchalant.

"Yes."

I tie a knot in my hair with one hand, a habit I picked up instead of biting my nails after Dad cut my nails so short they bled. "Did you come here for this case?"

"No, but we thought we'd check out the area since there's so much history. Usually leads to something."

"So we were just in the right place at the right time?" I wink.

"If that's how you want to look at it." He pauses, all business. "Usually ghosts exist because of unfinished business, so Leo and I will find out what that is. Probably something to do with Albert Knox. As soon as Leo's done talking to your sister, we can show y'all how to stay safe till she's gone."

I dodge the opportunity to admit we ditched ninety percent of our "safety" back in Maggie's Buick.

"So have you figured out where she's buried?" Maggie's burned plenty of bones to make lingering vengeful spirits go away.

A small victory, since Raylan freezes with his drink in hand mid-air for just a moment before setting it down.

"You've got a good friend."

"Psh." I scoff. "Obviously. But I just know a few things. My hands are clean."

Raylan humphs, and I realize too late that was probably offensive, him being a hunter and all. My stomach squeezes.

"Okay," he says. Thankfully he doesn't seem hurt,

although trying to read him is about as easy as reading Arabic.

"So, did you figure it out? Or do we need to call in the Calgary?"

Raylan doesn't correct my expression or fall for my slight jab. Instead, he gives a wide, wry smile. "We can handle it without the Calgary."

"Mmm-hmmm, or even the cavalry?" I tease. He doesn't need to think I'm shallow *and* dumb. It's just my little way of messing with people.

He laughs a short, soft burst. "She's got jokes."

I'm pretty sure my cheeks are red as rubies at this smallest approval.

"Well, let me know if y'all change your minds. Don't be gettin' too big for your britches, but I'll follow your orders for now. I'll let the hunter be the hunter."

He raises his eyebrows but lets it slide, sipping his soda. Not one to fill the silence, this guy.

"Well. My first ghost, and I meet a real hunter in the wild. Awesome. Although, that ghost up there was a lot freakier than I'd pictured. It doesn't freak you out?"

The corner of his lips ticks up, but he doesn't answer.

"Right. Silly question. So how did you get into this, then?"

Quickly clearing his throat, he shifts his body weight and starts playing with his glass, tapping his thumb against the condensation.

"Ran into a ghost kind of the same way you did." He speaks casually, but his bunching shoulders betray his discom-fort. "Leo was there to save me."

I lean forward. *Now* we're getting somewhere. "When was that?"

"A while ago. We've been hunting things ever since."

"Well, maybe you'll have to teach me a few tricks." I try to hold back a mischievous grin at my own double entendre, but no, I would never actually hunt. I would love an excuse to hang out with him again, though.

His eyes sparkle a little bit as the corners of his mouth tilt up almost imperceptibly. Just enough to make my cheeks warm right back up. "One thing at a time, Eva."

My name coming from those lips—it soothes the rejection. I can't look directly at him right now, so I settle for scrutinizing the window blinds next to us for dust.

"So, how old are you?" I ask. "Don't your parents care you're a hunter?"

"They're dead." His hint of a smile disappears into that void of emotion, and his eyes darken.

"Oh. I'm really sorry." My cursed human nature is desperate to ask how they died instead of searching for an appropriate thing to say. Sometimes, my thoughts are so big, they leave no room for tact. I've learned to avoid the taste of my foot in my mouth by not saying anything.

By the grace of Mindy, she brings our nachos, and I dig in. He takes a couple of bites, too, and we sit in small comfortable silence over our pile of oozing cheese, thin, crispy chips, and guacamole with the perfect cilantro to avocado ratio and not too much cumin. I wonder if Raylan would think I'm too picky if I give him all the olives. I glance at him to gauge if I should ask and catch him looking at me. For the first time, his shoulders are down, cheeks smooth; he finally looks almost at peace.

"You like?" I ask, only to accidentally have a tiny bit of spit escape my lips. Mortified and silently vowing to never eat in front of this guy again, I quickly wipe my entire face with the cloth napkin. "Sorry, I love nachos," I say once I'm fairly certain I can speak without spraying. My gut squeezes with embarrassment, but I'm rewarded with an even slightly bigger smile this time. *Both* corners of his mouth have officially moved upward.

"Wait, do I sense some *approval?*" I give him a little kick under the table. "Don't you go for the salad-eating twig?"

"I like food," Raylan non-answers. Ah, fella *did* want my cobbler.

I giggle sort of goofy and reach for a strand of my hair to fiddle with again to keep my cool.

"Good." I try not to beam. "And how old did you say you were?"

"Nineteen. You?"

Ee. I always love the older guys. Lie or tell the truth? Three years isn't that bad, right? I decide he's worth the truth.

"Sixteen," I say with as much confidence as I can. No biggie.

Raylan gives a little laugh—just a "ha" and nods. "Gotcha."

"Gotcha? What does that even mean?" But before I can get an answer from him, my phone rings with a text. It's Frost. Opening it, I feel a twinge of guilt for having forgotten even for a second I'd left her in a hotel room with a stranger.

Get up here please.

Shoot. Time to go.

CHAPTER 5 - FROST

I've pretended that looking into Blurred Ones is akin to playing Bloody Mary or with Ouija boards. The fine and rare delicacy of "the forbidden" is a currency my sister gets. Eva would be sick if she knew just how dangerous approaching this topic is, though.

"You're here," I whisper to the boy I haven't seen since I was seven years old.

Stars shine in his pale blue eyes. Emotions I'm not wise or strong enough to handle bubble up. And I can't help it—I'm seeing myself, five or six years old. Coils of sandy blonde hair grazed the tips of my shoulders, and I poured invisible tea for my dear friends huddled about a miniature table.

Panda hunched across from me, her scuffed nose proof of the chaffing she endured as I dragged her along our house's tiled floors; and Barracuda, snapping at me with his faux-sharp rubber-made teeth, balanced treacherously on a stool at my elbow.

Then, Leo.

While I only caught snippets of his form—glimmers as

the sunlight filtered through Mom's lace curtains—it was in his presence that I felt I was in a warm cocoon of quiet and secret. We didn't speak, but it was his attitude I strove to observe, his discomfort I fought valiantly to diminish. And he did the same for me. Only his knowledge and power seemed to stem from a greater understanding, a foreign realm altogether.

My hand tremors as I try to ground myself in the reality that he's reappeared. But he's possessed a vessel. Before, he appeared to me in spirit form. I recognize him, because there's no *unrecognizing* that mischievous yet earnest soul who used to giggle a little when I looked at him. A giggle that was short and sweet. Like he was reading my mind.

I look down at my brittle fingers, wondering how he could ever forgive me for icing him out. But Mom and Dad insisted he wasn't real, dragged me off to hospitals "to make me forget," even though *they* believe the Blurred Ones exist.

Shakily, I stuff my cracked phone back in my pocket, praying my text to Eva will go through. At least the screen came on when I hit the home button this time. Like a wounded deer, I'm trapped by this handsome, old-school boy, and I have to accept that he is very real.

What it does to me, seeing him in the flesh. I don't *want* to be near him. To smell his bitter and sweet scent. I don't want to think on our memories, which are so grounded in adventures, and laughter, and food.

My voice comes out quiet. "Why have you come back?" My bra's still hanging on the corner of the TV, which has me praying that he doesn't turn and look.

I study his wide cheeks and straight nose. The vessel he's chosen is so similar to his Blurred Ones' soul. His demeanor still hasn't changed—he still has that confident, I-laugh-in-the-face-of-danger look about him, with a hint of playful. Only his shoulders slouch.

He never used to slouch like that.

Strong, male fingers reach out to touch my leg, but I flinch. I'm not ready for his touch. This stranger who's supposed to be him. Luckily, he pauses, maybe because he doesn't know where we stand.

The silence between us makes me want to curl into a ball and recite Latin. *Eieci te ad infernum.* I banish you to hell. But I can't do that.

"I'm back." His hopeful voice fringes with sadness.

I want to evaporate like dew. Catch then release these words, because Mom and Dad would be furious if they knew he was here now. Everything is like a black, two-edged sword. Terrifying and hauntingly surreal.

"I told you I would be," he adds.

I stare at the gray patterned carpet, pushing back the very last day we met—at the oak tree newly chopped down. When Dad discovered it was our favorite spot for meeting up, he grabbed the chainsaw. Leo had traced the circles of the stump, never looking more lost in his boyish form.

"You have a vessel," I say, because I'm Captain Obvious. "He has the same widow's peak as yours."

His pointed chin jerks in assent. I want to ask if he possessed this vessel with permission or by force, the latter being the way Maggie says it typically happens. I do know that this vessel won't age while he inhabits it, but it will eventually wear out, since he doesn't feed on people's essences—like other Blurred Ones.

"I knew we'd see each other again," he says.

My chest twinges as I remember lining my doors and windows with salt. Mom kneeling down to help me say my prayers each and every night so I'd forget him. "That's not how I remember it."

I think of the stack of research I'd burned when pushed by my therapist. How I'd cut up the hat and scarf I'd worn when we would ice skate. The expression on his face had been crushing, but I couldn't continue seeing him when it was so painful for my parents. My mom's sister, Aunt Eva, is dead because she ran off with a Blurred One. Not that my sister knows that. All Eva knows is that a Blurred One was involved—not that our aunt is dead because she was thinking of boys first and foremost.

Leo raises a palm, and it's the exact same gesture he did when we were kids. "You need to know just how dangerous this room is."

I flinch, because there's not supposed to be anything special about this room, six-three-six.

Plus, a touch is never just a touch with him. Leo used to place his shadowy skin next to my hand, and I'd see sunlight bursts of marmalade and lemon. Glimpses of people with long hair—rolling hills of wildflowers and sunsets that looked like they belonged in Wonderland.

When Mom suggested that by fraternizing with a Blurred One, I was putting my sister at risk, I couldn't handle that.

Still, my sister and I are sixteen and seventeen years old. It's high time we know the *facts* about the Blurred Ones so she can stand up to them when I'm gone.

This is why I let Leo touch me, for my sister. When we press our palms together, blackness swoops over my head. He's going to show me a vision, just like when I was seven. I want to pull away, but he holds me like a cyclonic magnet.

In my mind's eye, an oversized butterfly manifests. No, not oversized. I'm peering at it as if through a magnifying glass. Its orange, spotted wings flutter, and like we're in a movie, the screen pans out.

Its feelers press into the glass from the outside door of a brown building. We're near vintage cars, women with stacked hair, and horn-rimmed glasses.

Billboards with smoking advertisements.

When someone opens the door, the butterfly hurls inside of the building, pumping its thin, swift wings. The gray, blurred twinge surrounding the butterfly means the butterfly's possessed.

I—I hadn't known an insect could be possessed.

"Leo?"

The butterfly hovers in assent.

He flaps past the concierge, and I'm hovering there, too, but invisible. Only my consciousness. He flutters past a throng of red and black-suited musicians. One's tooting brassy notes on a coronet.

We flutter past gray walls—or maybe that's just the color of smoke from everyone's cigarettes. The guests' clothes are manicured and starched and pressed. Bow-ties and blouses are a sharp contrast to my typical flip-flops, though I know I'm in the Gunter, because it has the same stately pillars and open floor-plan I walked through with my class.

The butterfly's agile wings turn the corner to an elevator. A man in a red hat is taking up a pair of guests. When the elevator dings, it reopens, and we travel down the hall. We hover at a door that smells of lacquer.

The number on the door screams *six-six-six*. Knox's room. It seems to be near the same spot as Eva's and my room is.

The halogen light flickers before going black, and a woman inside the room is screaming like an untuned instrument. Because Leo's small, and the room's door is cracked, he darts in the room as a sound splinters through, like someone's snapping boards in half. As I linger in the hall, the woman's screams morph to the sound of someone dismembering a pipe organ. All keys pressed at once. But that's not a pipe organ. Those moans are coming from her, and those aren't boards breaking but *limbs* being smashed apart by something like a baseball bat.

Springs groan from the bed and there's this loud *thump!* before a gunshot.

Silence clubs my ears. Blood, like warm bathwater, fills my head. Goosebumps tug from my neck, and I need to join this scene—save this woman. But as the door falls open, the pieces of limbs and torso that used to be this girl sit neatly in a pile on a crimson chair, a bullet in her forehead.

A man's voice hums from the direction of the bathroom. A cheerful, bluesy tune. *Knox*. Has to be him.

I can't tear my gaze from her eyes—they're so wide open. And green. Like two dead olives. Her soul floats from her eyes like they're a small gateway to heaven.

This woman's spirit—her white-tinged spirit—is identical to the one Eva and I saw in the courtyard, and something tells me that she isn't ready to leave just yet.

She floats toward Leo and me like—like she sees us. Her head swivels round like a Lazy Susan, revealing high cheekbones and a white, crepe paper dress. I want to ask her, *Knox, he's a Blurred One? What makes him different?*

But the door swings closed, and her spirit bursts through the door before stopping, somehow clogging halfway through, shoulders jutting out. A horizontal bust. She grips the wood, making me think maybe she's feeling the pull to leave this earth, her mortal existence. But she holds steadfast.

I scramble to be near her. *Why did he kill you? I am so sorry he hurt you like that.* But I'm not really there. She can't sense me anymore. This happened decades ago, in the past.

Something inhuman shrieks from the hall. Leo's fringed butterfly wings breeze through the door's impossibly small crack. The maid's pushing her cart, which shrieks like a ghoul, and I don't know why, but I feel like we must leave before she comes.

The ghost woman's still stuck halfway through the door, like an ice cube pushing through mud. Gritting her pearly teeth, she pulls and pulls before squeezing to the hall side with a *pop!*

I don't know what her goal is, where she means to go next. But she spots that yellow uniformed maid, too, and the fear tearing open her eyes tells me she doesn't want the maid to go inside the room. Like she's worried the maid will get hurt, too. Or maybe she is just vain and doesn't want to be seen like that.

She lifts a hand, displaying four skinny fingers instead of five. And as she lifts it higher, another one of her fingers severs before turning to dust.

Eyes darting to the door, the freshly killed woman realizes what I'm putting together, too. That the man's severing her into smaller bits, and with terror splitting open her eyes, she tries floating back through the door to stop him, but it's like something's preventing her. Like she's being cemented inside the door itself. So, lifting her bloody hand with great effort, the woman grabs the middle "6" on the door. As soon as her translucent blood connects with the brass, there's this hissing sound. The bottom of the middle "6" on the right side melts clean off.

She sobs, because this is not how she expected the morning to go. She would go down for coffee. Order breakfast.

But the bronze number's glowing red. Tendrils of blood float from the woman's neck. I want to make her a tourniquet.

She wails but she is dead.

When she pounds the door, the number on the wood clangs, flipping around, and since part of the middle number melted, it now reads six-three-six. And the maid, eyes stretched wide with questions, is only a few doors down.

Leo pulls away from my hands. His eyes look so sad. "You

never should have stayed in this room, Frost. I know it makes me selfish, but I'm glad you did."

My hands feel cold now that our palms no longer connect.

He offers me a final, shy smile that turns my insides into shreds. "We'll be right next door when you need us."

CHAPTER 6 - EVA

The bus reeks of dust, diesel fumes, and body odor. Always the body odor. We careen over a pothole, and Frost's knobby knee knocks painfully into mine. Not enough legroom for my leggy blonde sister and me. I grasp the back of the vinyl seat to steady myself, mindful of my thighs painfully sticking to the seat beneath me. Twenty-five sweaty teenagers are crammed onto this short bus, heading a surprisingly long ten minutes away to float down the Comal River on inner tubes.

Frost wouldn't spill a word after I got back to the room last night. I arrived to Leo and her staring awkwardly at each other. Then Leo abruptly left, and Frost pointedly got in bed and turned out her light.

Mrs. Sanders prattles on about exploring Texan geography, but I have to distract myself from the smell and heat. Time for one of our favorite games. Once we get on the river, I can safely grill Frost about this boy of hers.

"Would you rather," I whip my face purposefully toward Frost, "eat strawberries or hold a rat?" I laugh my best super villain laugh, knowing these are two impossible choices for her. I'm rewarded by her giving a violent shudder.

"That is not even funny."

"You know the rules, honey bunch. Choose."

"How big a rat?" Frost's grimace is definitely social media material. Too bad we had to leave all our phones back in our rooms so they wouldn't get waterlogged.

I scoff and let her off the hook. "A very large," I pause for effect, "hot pink plastic rat."

We hit another bump, but Frost still smiles in relief. "Rat! Would you rather eat a bowl full of weevils—"

"Sick. No way. Pick another one." I purse my lips in my serious "you better" face.

"It's the rules! You have to let me say whatever I want."

I am saved by the horrific screeching of the brakes. We've arrived. One by one, we unstick ourselves from the seats and hobble off the bus. Our robust bus driver hands us our lime green inner tubes as Mrs. Sanders claps her bangled hands for her last educational plug.

"Class!" Her voice is hoarse. Wrangling the bunch of us is taking its toll. At least her yellow foam sun visor will shade her eyes, which are already framed by sunglasses that make her look like she just had laser eye surgery. "I'll make this quick. As we float, watch out for snakes, stick with your Tejas Hombre, and," she lifts her hands in front of her face to pretend she's taking a picture with a camera, "take pictures in your mind of the floral and fauna for your report!"

A collective groan resonates from the group, minus Frost, as she's probably the only one of us who hasn't completely forgotten about the report.

"Come on, *estudiantes,* let's go float!" Mrs. Sanders whips around too fast and stumbles on her own turn, but catches herself before going down and starts doing a little jog-dance, trying to play it off as intentional. Several kids snicker.

"Shut up, *you'ns.*" I mean it, but say it with a smile so I don't turn myself into the target. Two boys, one with a mullet to rival Wade's and one who's Bic'ed his head, stop and look a little offended. Not wanting any enemies, I give them a wink and then nudge Frost's elbow so she'll start walking. We roll our tubes down the steep gravel ramp to the river after Mrs. Sanders, who's now singing mariachi music to herself. The river calls to me with its deep blue and sparkles.

Frost and I are the first to the river after Mrs. Sanders. Frost pulls a bright blue bottle of sunscreen out of a fanny pack to rival Maggie's and passes it to me. I accept it gratefully, and Frost and I start applying it to each other's shoulders. Frost tries to pass it to the next group behind us, but they're applying copious amount of baby oil to their pasty skin instead.

I stage-whisper to Frost, "They haven't learned about skin cancer in Missouri yet."

"Oh!" She puts a hand over her mouth as if to keep them from reading her lips. "They're going to look like that white guy on Lilo and Stitch with the ice cream." She slips the sunscreen back into her fanny pack. Then, tying our cheap black flip-flops to the tubes' handles with some fraying twine on the tube, we're finally ready for the river's refreshment.

Frost launches herself with ease while I'm still figuring out how to place my butt into the thing without beaching myself like a whale. I look to her, shrug, and just jump backward into it, using the momentum to launch my little watercraft over to Frost. Ever helpful, she grabs my foot to help guide my tube, and we're off. The water is cool, just as I'd hoped. Mrs. Sanders is right after us but thankfully seems content to float alone.

"Look at the guys," Frost mutters out of the side of her mouth, then nods toward mullet, Bic, and our friend Wade, who are moving excitedly around a cooler, with nervous glances toward our oblivious teacher.

"Beer." I roll my eyes, and Frost's eyes double in size. Always last to believe the rebellion of others, that girl.

The flow of the Comal is sloth-like here, giving us ample opportunity to watch our peers pick wedgies and vie for spots closest to the cooler. They're a menagerie of safari animals at the watering hole—terribly drawn tattoos, belly button rings on beer bellies, and badly fitting bikinis. Sometimes my classmates do seem a little subhuman, though to be fair, this must be the first time most of them have crossed their home county line.

Wade gives up prime access to the contraband, darting over to Jenny instead. He drapes an arm around her, having to reach up to make up the five-inch height difference. She doesn't run away, but instead keeps glancing over at the senior heart-throb, Jason. Star of the basketball, baseball, and track teams, his nearly straight teeth and pimple-free face puts him three leagues above the other guys at school. I follow her gaze just in time to see him snap another girl's bikini strings.

"Makes me kinda happy Dad makes us wear one pieces." I size up my own body in my new black and white vertical striped suit. I love the style, my boobs look great, and I'm happy to not accentuate any pudge my love of Mexican food may have produced. I don't even have to look at Frost's sleek navy suit. Skinny girl will always look good.

"Mmhmm," she agrees. She's focused on a leafy green plant nearby, and I'm pretty sure she would make a little camera click with her hands like Mrs. Sanders if she didn't think I would make fun of her. I give her tube a little kick, making her spin and lose focus on the plant.

We drift farther from our group, but a loud, "Whoop!" makes us look back one more time. A girl—Chastity?—in a neon green bikini covers her chest with her arms. I guess Jason's snap went a little too far.

"Makes you want to go hang out with some *older* boys, doesn't it?" Frost reads my mind.

"Always." Raylan's perfect scruff flashes behind my eyes. "Only a few years older, but since these guys act like they're still twelve, they seem twenty years older." I breathe deeply, letting the mossy, muddy air relax me in the moment and forget the National Geographic scene on the bank.

Picturing Raylan and all his many qualities is great, but I do get that little knot in my gut. He's so hard to read. I haven't the foggiest idea what he thinks of me. I glance to Frost to see if she's relaxing, studying, or finally ready to talk. Thankfully, she's already looking at me with her eyebrows tensed in concentration. She's ready to talk.

"So?" I encourage her.

"Yeah. Time to fill you in." But then she pauses, eyes searching, not knowing where to begin.

"Who is this Mr. Leo?" I prompt, drawing out his name to make it sound more scandalous. She laughs slightly, but straightens as much as she can in her tube. She's uncomfortable.

"I changed my mind. I can't talk about it yet," she finally says.

I try not to feel hurt by that. She can't tell me what's going on, or I haven't given her enough time? What does she think I've been doing the last four hours?

I twist my hair at the nape of my neck and secure it with an elastic to give her another fifteen seconds before barging on ahead. "He certainly has a retro fashion." Frost has always had a thing for old-school details. Those suspenders probably drive her wild. "And he certainly smiles a lot more than Raylan does." I try not to grumble, but I've never been very good at pretending when I'm with Frost.

But she just busies herself with paddling with her hands toward the speed launch. It shoots us forward water-slide style to spice things up.

The water catches her tube and shoots her off and I'm not far behind. It's bumpy and fast and without a healthy amount of luck, I could easily capsize—just like I did when we went canoeing on the Current River back home. Frost's never let me live that down. I grip my handles harder and grit my teeth as I try to stay balanced. I'm shrieking and she's shrieking and it's a pure reminder of fighting off that ghost woman.

Reaching the bottom, I sigh long and loud, happy I didn't flip.

The water-shoot must have been exactly what my sister needed for a jump start. Her skinny freckled arm grabs my handle so I can't float away, and in one big breath she says, "It's him and I can't believe it and you're not going to want to listen to me, but I *have* to talk about it."

"Of course I want to—"

"You shouldn't."

A couple of our classmates catch up and paddle right next to us. Bic-head offers us booze but I'm irritated at the interruption, so I try to discreetly push his tube away with my foot. The jolt makes him dump half his can in the water, so he curses and thankfully moves along, leaving us alone again.

"Frost. Talk."

My big sister's normally self-assured face melts into a little girl's. Her lower lip puckers, and her eyes well up. "It's *him*," she says, and something wriggles in my mind. Some question long forgotten.

"Who?"

"And it's not like I was looking for him, but it's Leo." She looks haunted. And lost. "He's a Blurred One."

It clicks. I know what, or who, she means. Her "imaginary" friend. I haven't thought of about him directly in years.

I've wondered how we know about Blurred Ones at all, since Mom and Dad always look a little sideways at Frost when the topic comes up. Had some vague impression it had to do with Aunt Eva, not Frost. But then again, my younger brain never put two and two together.

They stuck her in her room for weeks—just her room— no furniture, no toys, no books. I could always hear her crying, but they said she wasn't feeling well. I didn't know what to do. I was only six, so I had pretty much believed he was real when I was with Frost and not real when I was with my parents. Too young to form my own opinion.

Then, they shipped me off to visit our grandparents in Canada. After what seemed an eternity, they let her out and let me come home. I remember they finally called her Frost for the first time. Lenny's her real name, but she said her name was Frost, and I guess that was their compromise. A name for a friend.

So she quit talking about Leo, but she was sad for a long time, crying every night in her room. She seemed to get over it eventually.

I had forgotten his name was Leo. Just like how I forget her name is really Lenny.

So all this is flashing through my mind when I think of Frost's words, *It's him.*

I don't know what to say, so I play with the twine holding our flip-flops. "Positive?"

Frost nods this helpless way, and it's all I can do not to throw my arms around her. But I'm pretty well beached in this inner tube of mine, so I settle with patting her cute, lanky big toe. "I can't believe it." But I have to, because this girl is as honest as they come and my sixteen-year-old brain comprehends a lot more than my six-year-old one. Like how any time I ask my parents about the aunt I'm named after, they give me that same sideways look they used to give Frost.

Or, really, what's so terrible about being hunters? Maggie seems like the brave one, if I'm being honest. And Raylan? Neither of them seem like the type to have invited evil into their lives. More like, evil seemed bound and determined to worm its way in there.

"So—what does he want?"

"You mean besides dredging up the past?"

I eye my sister warily, unsure of what she means. "Sure?"

Frost grabs the handle of my inner tube again as we meander around a drifting log. "You should've been there, Eva. He *showed* me what happened. It actually was our room where Knox murdered the blonde woman. Maggie was right. He really did hack her apart into bits. It isn't just legend."

My stomach rolls, both horrified and excited by the thought. "Get out."

"The room number—changed."

"And we just happened to end up in there?"

"We need to switch rooms."

"Heck, no! We're *this* close to answers. Plus, then some poor innocent stranger might get hacked into bits."

Frost shoots me a cutting look, so I push back. "What does it have to do with Leo?"

Frost looks to the side and spots our cue for getting out— a black and red graffitied sign on a bridge that screams "Last Public Exit." Way too soon. And with it, I see Frost practically sealing herself back up, mad at me for not wanting to switch rooms, but there's no way. For the first time in my life, we're actually living in the moment. We didn't crawl out of our dang hole back home just to put blinders on.

CHAPTER 7 - FROST

My head feels like it's been run over by a freight train by the time we make it back to our air-freshener spritzed hallway. I must be sixty years old, because the bus radio was loud, and every time Wade and his friends cracked a joke, I felt like my head would crack wide open. If only I could convince Eva to switch rooms. In my mind, all I keep seeing is that blonde woman's body parts stacked on that chair next to the floor lamp. Half of me freaks that it'll be Eva. Maggie drilled into us that Knox, as a Blurred One, could return.

Kids flop into their rooms like mostly dead fish—when Mrs. Sanders is watching, anyway—though Eva and I heard a group or two plotting to check out the hotel bar once Mrs. Sanders turns in.

If only I could convince Eva to curl up with me to read the brochure on the Natural Bridge Caverns I snagged at the gas station.

Eva pulls her hotel keycard from the reader. Neither one of us has spoken the whole ride home. I know she thinks I'm being a stick in the mud, but I don't care if she thinks I'm acting like a grandma.

When she tries pushing the door open, it only opens half an inch.

Crap. Something's blocking it.

"What the heck?" Eva presses her shoulder into the door's wooden grain as she wails, "Sunblock didn't work!"

I halfheartedly press my shoulder into the door, too, finding the exact same pain. Guess we didn't lather each other up well enough. "Well. Guess we should go request another room now."

"What the heck is on the other side?" My sister pushes with a little more effort, her burnt toes in her flip-flops slipping, until she cracks the door wide enough for me to peer through.

The end table the ghost woman crawled out of earlier rests innocently on the other side, and now, after what Leo showed me, all I can think of is Eva sitting in a pile of body parts on that chair.

Eva smashes next to me, smelling like the Doritos we grabbed from the vending machine downstairs. "Ghost woman's definitely trying to keep us out."

I know she heard me earlier, but she's not listening, and it angers me that she can be so stubborn about staying here—but she didn't see what I saw with Leo.

I try to sound as diplomatic as possible when I say, "We should go talk to the manager downstairs."

"Are you crazy?" Eva's voice hitches in anger and excitement. "We're *this* close to answers."

"And you're not the one who heard Knox breaking that ghost woman up into parts!"

Eva's eyes are so round that I find myself wondering what to do. I should apologize, but safety is more important than tiptoeing around the truth. We want to learn about the Blurred Ones, true, but not at the peril of *our lives*. Eva's too important to risk that.

The sound of shuffling comes from down the hall. I look up to find Mrs. Sanders, ice pack to her forehead, waddling toward us in her purple crocs, only she's got them on the wrong feet. "Is something wrong, girls?"

She looks so tired, so drained that I don't know if I have the heart to tell her that we really want to change rooms. Chances are the hotel's already full. Eva's grabbing me by the sleeve of my T-shirt and tugging me toward our door.

"Nope," she says. She suddenly shoves the door so hard that the end table scoots over.

Mrs. Sanders raises an eyebrow.

Eva throws out her hands. "Thanks for checking on us, though!" And she shoves me inside before I can say two more words.

The door latches behind us. We may have just disrupted the salt line at the foot of the door, but doesn't matter. If ghost woman moved that end table, there must be some hair or fiber of clothing linking her to our room.

"Can't believe you just did that." I tug my shirt so it's not crooked anymore.

"And *I* can't believe you're so willing to go back on what we planned!"

I grit my teeth. Eva's never going to have the same priority I have for her safety. "Not like Mrs. Sanders will want to bother with us changing rooms."

"Exactly!" Eva slaps my sunburned shoulder.

When did it get so hard to keep my sister in one piece? There's no chance I'll be falling asleep now.

Eva sidesteps the end table and sprints toward the refrigerator.

"Seriously?" She can't honestly want Diet Coke. "You'll never sleep!"

"Never a problem, Frosty."

I consider eating a little more of Maggie's brownies but settle for fixing the salt line and changing into some yoga pants and a T-shirt, since my stomach's a little off-kilter from the bus ride back.

After settling into my cozy cotton clothes, I feel like I can think a little more rationally. "Maybe she's protecting us." I nod to the end table. I grab one of the down pillows and hug it like a blankie. *Please, let that be the answer.*

Eva lies flat on her back, Diet Coke in hand, and stares at the popcorn ceiling. "If this really was her room."

I fight the urge to sit her down and spell out every single element of the horror show I saw. "It was."

"But the salt line's intact. Even if the ghost lady has something tying her here, Knox can't get in. Besides, his M.O. is to woo women into his hotel room before chopping them up."

I shudder, remembering the woman's screams as I listened from the other side of the door.

"Knox can't hurt us," I say, convincing myself. "So why is the ghost woman so obsessed with lingering here?"

"One of the reports had her initials. 'C.A.R.' was on a cigarette case." She yawns despite the caffeine surging through her system. I knew that detail from our pre-trip reading, but had forgotten. "Maybe her initials are carved somewhere."

We should look, but Eva rolls to her side, and the soft lines in my sister's face tell me she's exhausted. But still pleasant—always pleasant. I love that we usually get along. Most sisters can't stand to be near each other at all, least of all on a regular basis.

I lie next to her as the bed's coils creak, because our bond is the only thing that matters. "Thanks for rooming with me."

She nudges my shoulder with hers, not bothering to say that she could have roomed with anyone else, especially Jenny. "'Course, roomie."

Next door—not where Leo and Raylan are staying, but the other side by the TV—someone bounces something against the wall. It doesn't sound like they should be bouncing it, because glass rattles and breaks before someone starts cussing up a storm.

The air conditioner kicks on, my stomach rumbles, and I tap my foot, almost inviting the ghost woman to reappear so we can know whether or not we're stupid for staying in here.

"Need to brush my teeth," Eva says as she pads toward the sink by the bathroom. I realize I forgot, too, so I grab my blue battery-operated toothbrush as she grabs her yellow, and we do this bit we've done since we were practically toddlers.

We're synchronized brushers. Brush, brush, brush—switch to the other cheek—deadpan, no smiles. Brush top, left, right. Bottom, right, left. And then for the grand finale: we gargle for five long seconds—before spitting away our leftovers.

Neither one of us comments. Our argument is over. I catch her eye in the mirror—her chocolate to my blue-green —and *nearly* quirk a smile.

We're just settling into our cozy cream comforter when the end table drawer squeaks open.

I bolt up, whispering in falsetto, "Here goes."

"There's no turning back now!" My sister almost doesn't sound scared.

"That salt is definitely not keeping her out."

Eva flops to her side to stare down the end table with its plugged in phone and folded card that boasts WiFi.

Just when I think maybe the ghost woman's changed her mind and is throwing in the towel, a three-fingered hand crawls out of the drawer.

I coat my voice with the most authentic of sweeteners. "A piece of hair or skin cell ties you to the furniture?"

The hand scurries toward us like it wants to pull out our eyeballs, and Eva lowers herself a bit lower in the bed sheets.

I put a protective arm around her.

A foot waddles out from behind the refrigerator and approaches us, Frankenstein's monster-style. The lady's head and neck slinks across the patterned carpet, and we've created a horror show of our own.

I lower myself next to my little sister and reach for the silver bobby pins in my hair.

"There are so many parts," Eva says as an eye-ball drops, then bounces from an invisible string dangling from the ceiling.

"And all spread out." I clutch the bobby pin, wishing it were coated with salt.

Eva's arm grows rigid beneath mine as her voice softens like she's speaking to a toddler. "Poor thing."

A knee—I'm pretty sure it's a knee—starts jabbing me in the side. I didn't know it even existed, let alone was so near. My voice pitches, "I don't think she's really in the mood for sharing details."

Eva tries to comfort the woman's detached head by patting it with a portion of the bed sheet when the woman's teeth clamp on Eva's pinky.

Eva snarls.

The teeth are just releasing her finger when I grab the comforter and dive bomb the head that's sort of running around like a chicken with its head cut off, only it's the head this time.

I lay atop it like a champion wrestler. "Maybe we intimidate her."

The head slips from an unattended corner of the

comforter, and her ravenous chompers take a giant bite out of my knee like I'm a delicious cadaver.

Eva launches herself across the room and grabs a handful of salt the boys left behind. Flinging it at the lady's face, she hits her eyes, which burn red before turning to dust and disappearing into the comforter.

A shoulder and partial arm squirm toward me from beneath the bed. An ear attached to only a corner of her mouth nibbles my neck, and there's no way in Hades this is the way to protect my sister.

"I'll take the left, you take the right!" Eva says, unzipping her bag and pulling out her flask of holy water. She sprinkles the body parts, which sizzle like they're being doused with acid.

I roll from the bed and climb-slash-crawl across the floor to the window to the other salt line Raylan left for us and grab the powdery substance, flinging it at the eyeball which has reappeared, dangling from the ceiling. The three-fingered hand crawls toward me again and I douse that, too, in case she feels like melting my bones like she did that brass six on the door.

I hadn't really realized before, but the woman is shrieking, and I'm not entirely sure if those shrieks are coming from one spot in the room or three.

I think we might just be winning when an arm or leg snatches me up in the air and tosses me through the air. I slam into the curtained wall, hitting my head so hard I see spots, and the smooth walls spin like propellers. Eva's prancing around and sprinkling salt and lifting her feet sort of like she's dancing an Irish jig, but there's no music. And instead of songs about ale, she's dropping a few of her own Eva-inspired curse words. We could simply leave, but we need answers, and the salt and holy water will slow ghost lady down.

Eva splashes holy water on a tummy with a decidedly "inny" belly button, and the stomach vanishes—only to materialize above the TV. And it's not just the belly button, but the entire torso—a smashed-ribbed bloody torso, a neck and arms. She's sprouting long, slender legs and two dainty feet. And hair. Hair that looks like fettuccini before morphing into the carefully coiffed curls like Jackie Kennedy's. The woman looms above us, white dress flapping like a fan's pointed directly at her body, and a chill splinters from my neck to my hamstrings.

The white skirt of her dress flits around her slender body. Her face is so sickly thin that Eva would normally make some joke about her needing to eat a hamburger.

The woman, C.A.R., stretches her fingerless hand toward me, eyes black, almost vacant.

"What's your name?" I clutch the curtain in case she tries to choke me. What female names were popular in the sixties? Claire? Cindy? "Tell us about the Blurred Ones. What makes them so different from all the others?"

Fury flows from the woman's tissue-thin face. Wind and tremors exude from her body. And I know lingering ghosts tend to focus more on the hurt they endured before dying, but if she could just let that go for a moment, we could maybe stop Knox. Avenge her death and the other girls he's rumored to have killed.

The woman flies so close to me that her hand wraps around my throat and her other closes over my nose. Like an ice sheet. Breathing. Disappears.

Eva wrenches the window up, and as ghosty hair tickles my face, I pull on the lady's arm bone. Eva flings what's left of her holy water at the lady, who shrieks—a colony of bats. She releases me and I sort of fall, sort of push her through the window to the newly poured cement and orange construction tape down, down below.

Eva and I stare for like three seconds. Neither one of us wants her to fly back inside, so we grab the metal lip of the window and slam it shut, praying she won't reappear the minute we lock it in place.

"Sigils," I say, and Eva nods, running for a paperclip on my desk. The triquetra will ward her off when salt isn't enough. She didn't seem too keen on giving us answers. We couldn't bring Maggie's pocket knives, but we practiced drawing the triquetra with paper-clips when she dropped us at an abandoned factory a month before we came out and made us practice drawing them *just in case*.

Eva scratches the curling triquetra for warding off ghosts in the front door while I dig around in my duffel bag for my own box of contraband. I'm glad, so glad we brought these even if we weren't smart enough to use them before. I scratch the same circular shape into the wall by the window. My panting sister sidles up next to me.

She watches my furious artwork, nodding that I'm doing great. At last I finish. She bumps her sweaty fingers into mine. We've officially warded her off.

Even if she was our most promising link for answers regarding what the Blurred Ones really are.

"You've got style, Abram." She claps me on the shoulder.

"You, too, Abram." And I grin, because I'm full of adrenaline and it's witching hour. We slap high fives, all the while giggling. There's no middle ground for us. Either we celebrate or we don't say anything at all.

She stomps the floor like she's bouncing a basketball through her legs, and I pretend that I'm spiking a football.

We must be making a ton of noise, because it's not long before the front door bursts open—did Leo sneak a key card? —and two male figures rush in.

Hair and clothes whipping behind them, the brawny, male

figures pause mid-step, looking to one another like they're not sure of what they've found.

"You took care of her," a low voice says, and a breathless glance tells me Raylan's smiling a little.

I had thought Leo had come through, too, but he's just standing there outside the door—ah, yes. Because of the sigils.

"She was terrified of us!" Eva whoops, her wide, white smile splitting her flawless face in half. She doesn't mention the fact that we didn't agree about staying in here—and the teeny tiny fact that we actually wanted to *talk* with her—but that's because my sister's always been a glass half-full kind of girl.

We beat the ghost lady even though we've barely floated through Maggie's training sessions.

We high-five all over again while the boys just stand there, hands in pockets, like they're observing an exhibit of primates.

"You're good, though?" Raylan asks, his concerned eyes never leaving my sister's face. He glances away like he's trying really hard to appear unworried. "We heard a lot of thumping and yelling. We couldn't get through the door until now." This he tells the retro floor lamp, which has tipped sideways.

Eva looks like she wants to do her best impression of a modern dance, like she does at one of our secret parties—arms open, feet kicking the air to a song only she hears—but Raylan's probably making her rethink her actions. If we were alone, I'd be joining in, too, but always with much less finesse. So we settle with an awkward, much too loud shriek-laugh.

Raylan scratches the stubble of his cheek like we're contagious, and I'm laughing, decidedly *not* looking at Leo.

The door swings closed, and Eva stretches an arm out and cries, "Don't go!" as Raylan's even-keel voice simultaneously murmurs, "I'm glad they're okay."

She drops her arm to her thigh with a *thwap*. Grinning from ear to ear, she beams. "He's glad we're okay."

So am I. At least now I know Eva and I can handle ourselves relatively well.

CHAPTER 8 - EVA

For the next two days, Frost and I resume our more typical high school activities with our group and check out the frying pan that is San Antonio. We sweat enough for life walking around shops with blinged-up Texan clothes and cafes decked out with horseshoes, cowboy boots, and sombreros. I could see myself living in a place like this someday. Still country, but happening. Less bustle, more rumble.

The history from the missions, the Riverwalk, the Italian and Mexican food, and stands for funnel cakes and ice cream cones make me realize just how much we miss out on back home. There, we have one fast food place and one cafe, and if you haven't lived in Bloodcreek for at least three generations, they look at you like you're an alien.

We visit Ripley's Believe it or Not Museum—land of monkey brains and worms with two heads and a toad that looks more like a dragon with baby's feet. We soar up high on the Tower of America, which feels a lot like the Gateway Arch in Saint Louis, only this one towers above the Emily Morgan Hotel—the one with the sick gargoyles. One grabs his stomach, the other his tongue, sick like those entering the hospital. So much death. Painful death that translates to ghosts.

The death subject never stays away long. Plenty of food for thought on our own mysteries and dilemma. When we sit down at a barbecue restaurant on the river, we discuss what could be different about the Blurred Ones.

"Maybe they're part wolf," Frost muses. She stabs at a piece of lettuce four times before she gets it skewered.

"Maybe they died multiple times," I say.

"*Maybe* they were all murderers before they died."

I mix my ketchup and mayo with a french fry as Jenny and her posse plop down with matching sunburns at the table next to us.

"Maybe they only kill women." I lower my voice, eyeing the gorgeous floral wreath on Jenny's head.

"*Who* only kills women?" Jenny's suddenly grabbing our table and pulling it over to theirs. Grimacing at the screech of iron on cobblestone, Frost scrambles to keep her ice water from tipping over, and we both awkwardly hop-drag our chairs over with the table.

Somewhat settled, I rest my head on Jenny's shoulder for a second and finally answer her question.

"Just your mom, Jens."

She throws her head back in a pretty, hearty laugh. Her friends stare at me blankly. Poor Frost already looks uncomfortable, suddenly drinking a ton of water and shaking her glass when it gets low.

Jenny leans in conspiratorially to Frost and me, other friends forgotten. They resume staring at their phones, checking their hair and makeup with the cameras.

"So." Jenny plays with her turquoise ring and waggles her eyebrows. Her giant personality is contagious and I lean in too, looking to Frost pointedly so she'll join in on the fun.

"You have to come to the bar downstairs when Mrs. Sanders goes to bed. There's this guy I know you'd be into, Eves. All older with that James Bond *manly* thing going on." She says manly with a growl. We've spent many hours in Spanish discussing how men are men and boys are boys and not to be confused—that we are women ready for men. But then a thought pops in my head, bringing with it a twinge of jealousy.

"He doesn't wear a leather jacket, does he?" I say, leaning back a bit. I'm not ready to share Raylan with the world.

"No, a suit with a bow-tie. And *actually*," she fiddles with her ring some more, turning it around and around her finger. "This is the best part. He *asked* about you two. Says he's saving a dance for you." She giggles loudly, eyes sparkling with enthusiasm. "So let's meet down there tonight."

I look at Frost, a primitive instinct waking in my gut. She must feel the same thing. She looks at Jenny, paling, and finally speaks.

"Jenny." She smiles a bit, not wanting to frighten Jenny. "Did you get his name?"

"Yeah-huh." Jenny straightens, proud. "Cheesy and glorious—it's Albert Knox."

CHAPTER 9 - FROST

I'm not about to let Eva go anywhere until we've put on Maggie's temporary tattoos. These works of art with the loopy triquetras should prevent Blurred Ones from possessing us. Danger's in check. We can go.

The boys haven't made contact, but maybe they've found a lead somewhere else. Maybe they're working another case? I don't even know if they know the story as well as we do. Knox was one of a string of aliases he used, and Eva and I've just called him that since we couldn't find an older one.

Eva's charcoal hair bleeds into her sequined blouse, and for the first time she's wearing heels as we wordlessly tiptoe down the hall. It's ten-o-five. Five minutes till Jenny's supposed to meet us, and I pray we won't regret coming down.

The elevator dings as I press the plastic button for level one. I toy with the dressy silver watch on my wrist—a birthday present Eva and Maggie jointly got me that I only wear for special occasions. I can't help feeling a little freaked out that we're actually breaking curfew. We never do. But we're already halfway through our trip and it'll be another few months before we can really leave home again, so we might as well follow through with the plan.

The melody of a sorrowful saxophone crawls toward us as we step from the elevator, warning us that we might have wanted to stay in our room. How will Knox even know us, though? Best case scenario, we find Knox talking to Jenny—and stop him before he hurts her or anyone else. Find out what makes him different and lock him up along with other Blurred Ones.

My sister's already tying knots in her hair, so I reach up and rub her soft hair between my thumb and pointer finger. "Ed Sheeran," I mumble, because that's what the band's playing, but with a bluesier feel. Everything feels a little surreal now that we're here in this smoke-filled room. My ripped jeans are just snug enough that I won't be embarrassed if I have to dance in the middle of the room, but it's almost like we've gone back in time, because the same Knox from the sixties has returned here.

The singer sports a bowler hat, looking out at the patrons without seeing anyone. Men and women sit on bar stools and sway and ponder. Wade's friend—I can never remember his name—the one with the shaved head who, knowing our progressive town, may be a Neo-Nazi—is passed out in a corner with a beer bottle dripping onto his combat boot. His gangly arms slump over a plate of half-eaten hush puppies, and a bartender's eyeing him like he'd like to drag him out to the dumpster.

Jenny's nowhere to be found. Ah, there's why. Mrs. Sanders hunches at the bar, eyes clouded over while sipping a margarita. Jenny would know she hasn't returned, because Mrs. Sanders rooms next to her. Either Mrs. Sanders hasn't seen Wade's friend, or she's decided doing something about it isn't worth the effort. Her clouded eyes are pooled onto the guitar player who's got just enough chest hair hanging out of his blouse to cover a coconut.

Mrs. Sanders is single. Has been for a while.

The guitarist sets down his instrument to guzzle a drink when Mrs. Sanders abruptly stands like she's going to introduce herself, only to jump head-first into the barreled chest of a seven-foot tall bouncer.

The bouncer snarls, his short Hitler-motif mustache curling like a caterpillar, and Mrs. Sanders blushes like she's just been spotted in her underwear. She extends her bracelet-bangled hand to apologize, only to knock her margarita glass askew, splashing the bouncer's silky, flawless shirt.

He clasps her wrist, looming over her like a guard protecting the treasures of the Czars, and I have half a mind to tell him to let go of her. I should splash his still pristine leather shoes with water, but instead, Eva and I duck behind a potted plant as the guard escorts her from the bar. Last thing we need is to be sent home early for breaking curfew.

"Harsh," Eva murmurs. Her breath's filled with the minty mouthwash she gargled earlier. Her perfume tickles my nose —but it's a good smell. Sweet and musky, just like her.

All isn't lost for Mrs. Sanders, though, because that guitarist she'd been eyeing earlier is actually galloping after her, his wavy locks bouncing in time with his Hawaiian shirt.

He calls her name and she spins around, light and hope dancing across her migraine-torn face.

The bouncer huffs, stomping his fancy shoes as Mrs. Sanders and the guitarist stroll toward the elevator. Looks like Mrs. Sanders might get her own little serenade tonight after all.

Eva and I try sneaking out from behind our plant and wall, but something's caught one of the strings of my fringed shirt.

"That was close." Eva helps me extricate myself from an

aloe vera plant that's eagerly wound its way through my hair. "You've really found a friend here." Her eyes shine with possibilities as she pulls my hair loose with a swift tug. "There."

"Thanks."

The crown molding and wainscoting covering the walls makes me see why Knox likes to venture down here. *Class.* Knox is a classy breed with expensive taste, though nastier than all.

"Do the two of you plan on spending all night over here?"

My stomach plummets as a voice like ribbons falls over us. I think it might be Knox, but it might just be the guitarist's twin brother.

Some guy in a Hawaiian shirt and long seventies curls holds out drinks for us. "I thought you two could be my girls."

Eva's carefully veiled look of revulsion is enough to almost make me giggle.

"Oh, we're good." I pat my fringes to make sure I didn't leave half my shirt in that potted plant. "Thanks, though."

The man pulls his sunglasses off the top of his curls with a flourish and says, "But then, why would you two be down here?"

"To meet me," says a low, articulate voice.

Both Eva and I, in sync, turn. The careful side part of his oiled hair, the old-school dark suit—it's Knox, *Knox*—has to be. He's taller, even more handsome than I remembered from the pictures on the internet about the infamous Albert Knox ghost haunting and murder.

He's got the exact sheen of intelligence in his eyes to make me think he's a stockbroker. The pleasant lines round his mouth almost make me believe he likes reading poetry in the moonlight.

The edges of his lips are tilted up. Like it's a game. And he's onto us.

Beyond that, there's this *husk* to his voice. Like he's been smoking cigarettes for forever, and he's got that old movie quality where those cigarettes haven't affected any other parts of his body yet. Only that voice, which has grown sexier throughout the years.

The singer's pulling his bowler hat from his head and earnestly singing along with a saxophone, and the Ed Sheeran tune they were playing earlier unwinds into something more improvisational.

"Jenny said you'd like to meet us," Eva says. "Should I be flattered or scared?"

My sister doesn't even pause when it comes time to flirt.

Eyes planted squarely on me, Knox says, "Care to dance?"

Only he's not asking me. He's asking Eva, because at the very last moment his gaze drifts over to her.

Okay. Truth be told, I shouldn't be surprised since my sister is like catnip to males, but I'm the blonde, and both Eva and I know Albert Knox likes blonde girls.

He doesn't miss a thing, though, as his gaze drifts over to me once again as if challenging me to fight for him. My mouth goes dry as he wraps his powerful fingers round Eva's thin ones and leads her out to the dance floor.

I don't know whether to hyperventilate or scream for them to return. It's like he's reached inside my chest and squeezed my heart to pump double time.

No wonder all those girls fell for him. I shouldn't even be entertaining the idea of letting my sister dance with him, but there's not a whole lot I can do now.

The percussionist joins the singer with the saxophone, and the breathless, wandering tune makes me feel like we're sliding into an avalanche.

As I make my way to the bar, Knox guides Eva so close to me that I can hear his polite southern accent.

"You're not bad." He pays Eva a compliment.

She effortlessly follows his lead as he holds her fingers to the side, ballroom style. He clutches her waist, and they scoot along the dance floor.

With the slight lines round his eyes and mature way he holds himself, he's obviously older. That classic sixties suit Eva and I read about has obviously been to the dry cleaner, but he's a little more—I don't know, stiff?—than I expected. Not robotic. Not awkward. But mathematical, like everything he does has been calculated before he does it.

He whispers in my sister's ear and she laughs a little, but her big eyes rove over to me. *Nervous.*

Eva's black skinny jeans hug her swaying hips as they move to the saxophone and guitar. With Knox's strong command of the dance floor and her natural dancing talent, they actually look quite pretty together.

And it takes me a while to realize this, but his eyes are no longer on me. At all.

It's like he knows this is a game of cat and mouse. We lure him out in the open and try to get him to spill his secrets without getting ourselves killed. Because if we know why he does what he does, I'll be one step closer to leaving for college.

A handful of other couples dance waltz-style, but a few others wrap their arms around each other in the undignified bear-hug. If our classmates were down here, they'd be dancing like that.

But our classmates would have little interest in dancing to the refinement of jazz.

Eva and Knox scoot across the checkered tile, their eyes a little too fixed on each other. And my heart hammers in my chest, because he's *not supposed* to like her. Eva had better not forget who she's dancing with and Knox had better forget about the way he takes girls upstairs.

The baby blue ceiling feels a little too close, and the lantern-like chandeliers make me want to duck my head. What are we doing down here?

The bartender sets a club soda in front of me and narrows his beady eyes. He knows Eva and I are too young to be down here. But what he doesn't know is we're dealing with something far beyond his imagination.

I'm just setting down my drink and about to cut in and tell him to get away from my sister when Eva's purple top brushes against my fringe.

"Your turn," she murmurs. "He splits half his time in Boston." Her cheeks are flushed in the excitement. "He's in *advertising*. Wouldn't answer anything else."

When his long fingers take my hand, his eyes never leave Eva. He gives me goosebumps.

A large, onyx stone on his finger grazes the skin between my jeans and shirt, and I'm sucking in a breath. Is this what he does to girls? "Accidentally" touches them before chopping them up?

"You have an unusual name," he murmurs.

I know he's talking to me, but his gaze lingers on Eva as she slurps down her Diet Coke. His voice is both articulate and warm.

As he spins me in a circle, my hair skirts out before falling again. And when he pulls me to his chest, I feel like I'm being held in a vacuum.

"Isn't your beauty classic." His eyes rove over my face and neck. Sweat breaks out on my forehead. It isn't long, though, before his gaze traipses back over to Eva. Like she's filet mignon and he hasn't eaten that well in months.

We never should have come downstairs. "Stop looking at her."

He laughs, barely making a sound. He twirls me like we're

both having the time of our lives in this dance. "Overprotective, aren't you? The older one."

"*I'm* your type," I snarl.

The musky scent of cigars washes over me, reminding me of his maturity and experience traveling the globe.

And that's part of his appeal—that he's both enticing and indecent.

His warm hand presses into the small of my back, and it sears my skin. I hate that I can understand the attraction. What must my sister have felt when they danced? Is this part of his power? That he convinces unsuspecting girls to fall in love with him?

"You live in Boston?" I veer the conversation toward small-talk.

"When the pool wears a little thin."

The song trails to an end, and Knox leads me back toward Eva with his hand on the small of my back, and a cold shower just about now would be good.

Eva slurps up the remainder of her Diet Coke real fast.

"Merlot for the ladies, please." Knox meets eyes with the bartender. There's no questioning his authority.

Instead of shaking his head, the bald bartender immediately marches over to a sea of brown bottles to fill the order.

If my parents didn't know about the Blurred Ones, Knox could charm *them*.

Eva lifts her mouth in that teasing way I've seen her do a million times. "You're trying to liquor us up."

The bartender nudges two glasses of burgundy wine toward us. The stems on the wine glasses give the drinks an air of healthy respectability and I'm tempted to lift it to my lips—just for show—when Eva does one better.

Daintily, she plucks up her glass and swishes the liquid like she does this all the time. She doesn't move her eyes from

Knox's face, not trusting to drink whatever he's ordered for us.

His testy eyes don't leave hers, either. Like he's weighing his options. Deciding whether or not he's ready to pull out the meat grinder?

At long last, he boldly steps between my sister and me. "What do you say, the two of us get out of here?"

A firecracker of warning goes off in my head, and I know my sister's feeling the warning, too, but she's never been known to back down from a classy guy before.

Please, Eva, remember what he is.

The slight smile on her lips tells me she's tempted to pursue this a little farther, but only a beat passes before she gives a curt shake of the head.

Her smooth throat and clean, sensuous lines of her bodice are enough for a guy to shoot his brains out. Knox is noticing, I'm noticing him noticing, and I'm wedging myself between them. If I had known that he'd have a thing for Eva, no way would I have agreed to come.

By the way, why hasn't Jenny shown up?

Leaning into my sister's ear, Knox purrs, "I'm going to *devour* you."

Eva pales.

Knox chuckles so low there isn't a sound and, grabbing a newly appeared drink, he tilts it back before setting it on the counter. Striding toward the elevator, his smooth, confident steps prove he knows our eyes are glued on him.

Revulsion runs all the way from my heart down to my toes. Maggie and our parents would kill us if they found out we came down here. We found Knox, and Jenny was his unsuspecting errand girl.

I tug on my sister's elbow. "We should *go*."

Eva's eyes flash, because she knows we should, but she's

toying with the glass in her hand. She's shaking. Perspiration beads on her chest.

She grabs her Diet Coke, yanks out her straw, and pours it back. She aims to slam her drink back down on the table, but all she can do is shakily set it down. She wets her lips. Takes a deep breath. "Looks like he has a thing for brunettes."

CHAPTER 10 - EVA

The click of the hotel door closing wakes me up way too early. The morning light peeking through the curtains proves it without even taking the energy to look at the clock.

"Frost!" I manage to groan. "Go back to bed!" I flop over, hiding my face half in my pillow, expecting some chirpy reply about early birds and worms, but she doesn't answer. I crack an eye back open. She's leaning against the door, still in her jammies, her brow furrowed. I wait for her to tell me what's up, but she seems to have forgotten I'm there and her mind is far, far away.

"Frosty," I holler. "What's wrong?"

Her hazel eyes snap to me, back to reality.

"You're not the only one who missed check-in this morning. Jenny missed it, too." She spins around and checks the peep hole, like we're suddenly being spied on. "That was Mrs. Sanders. She's really worried."

"I'm sure she just slept in or ran to Starbucks or something." I yawn and stretch my arms and legs fully out, always happy to have the whole bed to myself.

Frost shakes her head slowly, running her tongue along her teeth, looking for phantom braces that have been gone for almost a year now.

"No, Angela said Jenny never came back to their room last night. Everyone's supposed to stay in their rooms until someone finds her."

"Oh. Well, that sucks in a lot of ways." I lay down on a pile of feather pillows, suddenly extra tired. Mornings are the worst. "I'm sure she's fine." But a flashback to last night reminds me trouble is way too easy to find around here, and Jenny's one of the few residents of Bloodcreek who doesn't look like they've stepped out of a swamp. She and I like playing MASH in Spanish. Not exactly close friends, but friendly enough. She might actually give Wade a chance, because she's always lowering her standards—desperately wanting to fit in.

"Right. I hope she comes back soon." Frost bites her lip and moves to the black leather desk chair. She curls her legs underneath her and sits down, her face void of emotion. The void I know means she's actually a whirlwind of thoughts. She's the embodiment of "still waters run deep."

"You don't think..." She lets her voice trail off. Not daring to say her worry aloud. Her worry that Knox and his tailored suit may have found a different sheltered, boy-crazy target last night.

"No. No way. We saw him leave, and she never came down." I flip onto my stomach to soothe the twinge of worry there. "Maybe she hooked up with Jason. Or Wade. Ew." The memory of his sour breath makes me suppress a gag again.

I army crawl to the now infamous end table, half prepared for our ghost friend to appear. Basking in the soft Egyptian cotton sheets and my favorite superhero jammies, I pick up the hotel's folder for nearby attractions. We need a distraction. "So what are we going to do until we're released? Read fine literature?" I wave the folder, trying to grab her attention. No response.

I prop myself up on my elbows. "Should we bang on our wall until the boys think we need to be saved?" I pulse my eyebrows at her. "Then we capture them and force them to feed us grapes and bon-bons?"

Frost barely looks at me, twitching her lips to the side to show she's "listening," and goes back to brooding. Forcing my eyes not to roll, I give up momentarily and look at the brochures for something to pass a little time.

"Natural Bridge Caverns, Tower of America, Ghost Tours," I list quietly to myself. A beat passes, and Frost and I look at each other at precisely the same time.

"Ghost tours?" we exclaim together, eyes giant saucers as we absorb the possibilities.

"Dude. We have to go," I say. "Nobody has to know. The pamphlet even says the tour guide will talk about the Gunter. Maybe he'll know more about our ghost! Or Knox!" I sit up, cross-legged, and Frost unravels her curled up legs, feeling the excitement.

"That would be really good. Except we're on lockdown and we're leaving tomorrow. And Maggie would die." The buzz leaves Frost and she slumps back again into her chair, but I'm not giving up that easy. This would be so *fun*—and educational, of course.

"So we sneak out. We'll tell the guys and they'll cover for us, 'cause we're totally helping them be hunters. They'll love us." Now my heart is pounding like it always does when I have a borderline brilliant or dangerous plan. Kind of like when I talked the kids in geography into putting glue in Mrs. Walters' coffee. Rarely do people realize I'm half convinced my ideas are terrible as I convince them to go along with them.

But now Frost is agreeing, confident in my faux confidence, so I'll push that little sensible angel on my shoulder off for now.

"What do we do, then?" She looks to me like I have this all planned out. Time to run with it.

I pop up off the bed, quickly put on a bra and throw my hair up into a "Look How Cute I Look When I First Wake Up" do and bounce across the room. I carefully open the heavy door as quietly as I can and peek out. The hallway is empty—just plush carpet and those chocolate walls. I wave Frost over and put my finger to my lips to remind her to be quiet. We can't get caught already.

We overkill our tiptoe like cartoon characters the five feet to the boys' door and, crouching on the floor, I wrap three quick, not too loud, knocks. No answer. I try a few more random knocking patterns, pretending they're code, but no one opens the door.

Pressing my face to where the door meets the frame, I stage whisper into the seal. "Raylan! Leo! It's us!" I glance at Frost, who quirks an eyebrow, which makes me giggle way too loudly for the situation. I press my face to the crease one more time, and suddenly the door whisks open. I stagger, barely catching myself on the frame before falling over. Ever graceful, Eves.

Leo opens the door and smiles at us like a funeral director —much less enthusiastic than what I've seen of him so far. The joke that usually twinkles in his eyes is gone.

"Ladies," he says softly, his voice sounding both old and young at the same time. He beckons for us to come in, eyes now locked on their usual position—Frost. They both belong in some retro high fashion magazine with their beautiful lankiness.

We eagerly comply and walk farther into the room. It's identical to ours, though mirrored, and with two doubles instead of one king. My goodness, our heads sleep so close to each other. The thought makes me warm, but Raylan's strong back is to me, hands on his hips as he stares at his bed.

"Frost, Eva, something terrible has happened." Leo looks at Frost with the intensity of a shaman making a death prophecy. Raylan finally turns his head to look at us, and in his clenched jaw, I see an expression I know from my own mirror. A dare.

I step around him to see the object of Leo's dark omen. On the bed next to us, on the beautiful white cotton sheets, a rusty brown stain surrounds a pale object with a smattering of freckles and a beautiful turquoise ring. My throat closes, and hot tears instantly fall from my eyes.

It's a hand. Jenny's hand.

***

*S*he's dead. Jenny is dead. She had so much spunk. The difference of life without her is jolting. And freakingly terrifying. This stuff is for real and I shouldn't have messed with it at all, but this is reality, and now I'm not just wondering what Blurred Ones are and why they freak out my parents so much. Now I *need* to know what they are so I can kick this one's trash for killing my friend.

I think part of me had romanticized Knox into some misunderstood killer who just wasn't loved enough as a child. I consider throttling Leo right—make him tell us what the heck is going on, but I impress myself with my restraint. That's for Frost to do. She just better do it soon, although the poor thing is fighting legit emotional damage.

The worst part of it all, is she'll just be considered "missing" forever. They'll never find the body. Knox has his ways of *disposal* . . . and it's too risky for Raylan and Leo to turn her hand over to the police. Makes me realize I never asked how they got it in the first place. Still, Raylan can't turn it in or he'd *really* get locked up. I fight back a shudder. Oh, Jenny.

So, although it may be a long shot, maybe we can learn something useful. These people who run the ghost tours take their research seriously and are open to old wives' tales and tidbits, so here we are.

Mrs. Sanders brought everyone sandwiches and brownies to their rooms to cheer us up, so thankfully we hadn't left yet. A sweet gesture, but even I couldn't eat. Mrs. Sanders admitted the bus driver got spooked and just up and left, so she was trying to make other arrangements for us to get home. A couple of parents said they'll head down and help but the rest are more concerned that their week's plans not be disturbed. She seemed so sad and overwhelmed, I almost feel bad about sneaking out here for the tour after after she left. Hopefully this isn't a wild goose chase.

Frost hasn't said a word in like a half an hour. I jiggle her toned arm softly, trying to lessen the worry in her eyes. A tiny gnat flies off her arm, and I bat it away as a minivan drives by, blaring Disney music.

The boys didn't want us leaving the hotel but understand it's personal now. Besides, it's the hotel that's haunted. Instead, they've gone all Maggie and turned overprotective— layering us with salt-loaded pepper spray and silver knives. Leo took extra-long loading up Frost, putting tiny hair-pin daggers in her hair and rubbing extra tattoos on her arms. I've never seen Frost turn so red my entire life.

I pat my own stash of salt spray in my distressed jeans front pocket. It won't do much to any ghosts or Blurred Ones we hopefully won't encounter, but slowing them down would help. And knowing it belongs to Raylan puts a pretty little butterfly in my stomach. Who knew salt spray could be sentimental?

We've been scanning the area in front of the Alamo, but multiple signs scream "Ghost Tour!" So many different tours. My lips twitch into a pseudo smile as I spot a dude in a top hat, wearing all black. We'd been instructed to look for the top hat. He's blaring Monster Mash from a little speaker in his hand. A giant white stone statue of Alamo heroes towers over us from one side—a statue I heard was first chiseled when the models were naked.

Oh, the deep dark secrets of San Antonio.

Only a few people, maybe eight, form a semicircle around Top Hat. No one is talking. Awkward. Frost keeps biting her lip and looking around like Mrs. Sanders is going to show up any minute. Or even worse, Maggie. She stares down at the cracked screen of her phone.

"Maggie has called four times today. I bet Dad already told her about Jenny." She flips through her phone's screens, probably seconds away from calling her back. It amuses me slightly that although Mom and Dad are super overprotective, they haven't bothered to call.

I nudge Frost with my shoulder. "We can tell her all about it when we get back. Just text her and tell her we're fine." I sound a little sterner than I intended to but don't take it back. Silence spills between us. Then, although I hate small talk, I hate awkward silence more, so I try to strike up a conversation with Top Hat.

"Where are we going tonight, uh, what's your name?"

"Wolf." He's tall, pale, with three spiky earrings and a three-inch goatee and long hair sprouting from under his hat. He dramatically splays the fingers in fingerless gloves to point to his forearm, where I see a tattoo that says "Wolf." Holy theater geek.

"Of Texas Wolf Ghost tours. I see." Oh, the insults I could hurl.

"We're going to be seeing about ten of the most haunted buildings in San Antonio."

I sort of stop listening, but I behave, because after a few more moments of watching his dark molten eyes and listening to his smooth, quiet and earnest voice, it's hard to feel superior. He loves what he does. I can respect that. I plan on having everyone I know call me "Agent" when I become an FBI agent.

"The history of the area is vast and tormented—"

"Ooooooh, scary!" A jerk with bloodshot eyes yells out the window of a modified Chevy. "He doesn't know jack!" He waves a Corona in the air, cackling and hollering as his hopefully more sober buddy drives away.

Wolf's eyes twinge, and with a tiny smirk, he quickly responds just loud enough for our little group to hear. "Savages."

I grimace inwardly for him. Frost narrows her eyes in disgust at the truck's taillights. I think she's found a kindred spirit in melancholy Wolf.

"Anyway," Wolf says, "we'll have a spooky time. And we are just about to start." He glances at his big obsidian watch and calls to the group, "One minute, thirteen seconds until the spookiest ghost tour in San Antonio begins." Captaining a tight ship, this guy, and at the end of the minute, he dances about like a villain in an old vaudeville play.

"Welcome to Texas Wolf Ghost Tours!" Wolf calls to our hodgepodge group, as if to a massive theater. "The long history of the area brings many stories of unrest and spirits clinging to their past, unwilling to let go, to forgive." His voice is loud and commanding, then smooth and quiet. Again, I want to snicker, but his eyes are so earnest I forgive his over-the-top drama and just roll with it.

"If he takes himself this seriously, hopefully he takes his content seriously too," I whisper to Frost. I think she barely registers me, though. She seems absolutely fixated on Wolf, eyes locked on him with the intensity she usually saves for playing the piano.

"And to help us on our tour of the paranormal this evening," Wolf says as he raises a clenched fist in the air. He suddenly dives his hand into his satchel. "We do have these handy EMF devices!"

He pulls a small hand-held device from the satchel draped over his shoulder and presents it to the group with a flourish. "Standing for 'Electromagnetic field,' EMF is the most common way to detect paranormal activity." He holds it out like a game show host. The EMF has little lights at the top, a needle display in the middle, and a big flat power button on the bottom, pretty much exactly like the ones Maggie has back home. She's gonna be pissed.

"Although many electric cables above and in the ground will set off our EMF detectors, I will tell you when we are near a haunted area without cables. They should not be displaying lights." He freezes, hands up like he's fending off a ghost. "I've only been haunted twice this month!" he yells, then drops his hands and smiles suggestively. "If you are up to it, follow me."

Feeling inspired and encouraged that we may finally be making progress instead of just making things worse, I sing a little intro into Frost's ear, "Another one fights the dust." We got this.

CHAPTER 11 - FROST

The ghost tour may not be the *wisest* idea—we could be expelled for ditching our room when we're on total lockdown—but Jenny's been murdered, and Knox was way too friendly with Eva. I may have resolved last night to not let my fear of the past hinder our search for answers, but Jenny ending up just like that ghost lady has upped the ante. If we're not careful, Eva could be next. But now, with Wolf lifting his purposeful arms and the other tourists about us, I cinch my inner resolve even tighter.

It's not hard, what with the Emily Morgan Hotel we're currently facing.

I don't know what it is about San Antonio and hotels, but this, too, is creepy. The light-gray stone edifice is fourteen stories tall with that too-tall-for-its-skinny-width quality. Red awnings with the DoubleTree emblem mark several doorways, but I've read how this building's not as innocent as it seems.

Wolf raises his arm to point to the top of the building. "It wasn't always a hotel," he says eerily. "But a hospital, and the top floor, the *fourteenth* floor, is where the doctors conducted surgery."

Eva and I crane our necks to take in the fourteenth story. Kind of hard to see, but it's topped by an ornamental tower.

"Long way to take up a gurney," Eva murmurs.

"Not every surgery was successful, though," Wolf says, his dark eyebrows raising meaningfully. "So, when the doctors were finished, they'd simply drop the body down the *body shoot*, down, down, down fourteen stories." He slams one fist into his palm like even now we can hear the impact. "All the way down to the basement. Or morgue. They'd scoop up whatever was left and shovel it into the crematorium."

A mom-and-daughter pair grunt in disgust, and Eva snickers, "Lovely."

Wolf dramatically gestures from the ground-level window of the decadent hotel to it's posh furniture and lighting. "The hotel uses the exact same pilot light that lit that crematorium to light that fireplace."

Eva and I stare at the fireplace. *Eee.*

We tromp past a few more hotels and stone-faced government buildings, learning gruesome details about a lady falling twenty floors to the street and her arm severing from her body. A homeless man missing half his hair and more than half his teeth stares at us, unmoving.

"Freaky." Eva nods at the man with long stringy hair and a beard who's standing so still, he's obviously high on something. I sort of wonder if he's a Blurred One. An artist's paint fumes lead us around the corner. He's sketching trees with hands and teeth.

We tread over a bridge with the Riverwalk trickling below our feet. We see a fig tree growing straight out the side of a building. It seems like every five minutes, we're seeing a new horse and buggy.

"You should ask Raylan to take you on a ride on one of those things," I tease, nodding toward a white horse with glitter sprinkled all over its face.

Eva's eyes go wide at the thought. "That'd be amazing!"

Wolf has us pose in front of a window where ghosts tend to linger, and my sister takes my picture just in case. There's a smudge in the photo, but I think someone's painted the door on the inside of the building to give credence to Wolf's story.

"And now we have The Gunter," Wolf says, pausing outside our square stone hotel, approximately ten stories.

I side-eye Eva. Hopefully he knows something we missed, or we've risked coming out here for nothing.

Pointing a tattooed finger, Wolf says, "*This* is the site of the most gruesome murder in San Antonio." He tells us about Knox, and how he courted blonde girls and how the maid found him running his pretty date through the meat grinder. He could have taken care of the maid, too, but she wasn't his type, so he merely shushed her with his finger.

His date had O negative blood and tiny feet. Left behind a lighter with the initials C.A.R. carved into the plastic casing.

We know all of these things.

"That night, there was a lot of construction going on, and it is believed that Knox returned and buried whatever he couldn't grind up in that meat grinder in that wet cement and smoothed it over."

I remember reading this but hadn't thought about it lately. A construction crew has been digging up cement around the building our whole stay . . . Maggie always says that ghosts can reemerge when bones are disturbed. They tend to come back angrier, too.

"Knox next stayed at the Saint Anthony hotel just down the street. Used a different name. A man fitting his description checked in and for a whole day paid people to buy food and cigarettes for him. The police got his room key, only to find him sitting on the bed with a gun to his head. When they stepped into the room, he pulled the trigger."

I frown at Eva. If only that was the end to Knox's deeds.

"Both Knox and the woman with blonde hair and a long, flowing dress have been seen peacefully haunting the sixth floor to this day."

Eva nudges me with her elbow. "Until now."

Which concludes all that Wolf has to say. He pulls his mic from his ear and collects EMF readers, which only erroneously blinked when we crossed the street.

"What else?" Eva nods at Wolf like he's hiding something.

Her big eyes catch him a little off-guard, and he fumbles with the final EMF reader before slipping it inside his satchel.

He glances from the mom-daughter duo with matching botox features back to Eva. "I don't know what you mean."

"What *kind* of a Blurred w—*ghost* is he?"

Wolf takes a shaky step back—in the direction of the bar across the street. "Those are good questions," he stammers, obviously knowing something. "Maybe you should research it and get back to me."

He straddles the curb, and my sister's patience is running thin. In a gruff move, she grabs the cuff of his shirt, holding salt spray three inches from his face. "There has to be more you're not saying."

Wolf yanks his arm loose, obviously not impressed with my sister's aggression. "Look." He eyes the pins in my hair and the temporary tattoo on the inside of Eva's wrist. "Don't go digging around on this one. These particular spirits—" He coughs onto his fist. Spotting a spray of blood on his knuckles, he pulls out a handkerchief from his back pocket, hand trembling.

Eva lowers her salt spray, glancing at me. *What's with this guy?* But my sister's not in the mood for detours, so she shoots a spray of salt straight at Wolf's face.

He winces, but she didn't shoot him in the eyes, and he's not a ghost, so he should be okay. But the veins popping from his neck tell me he's a little more than freaked out by Eva's assault.

"It's only salt." I raise my hands to reassure the poor guy.

Wolf eyes me, then my sister, but she's not lowering her salt spray, and is it just me, or are Leo and Raylan approaching us from across the street? They must be coming to check on us.

Spotting the approaching figures, Wolf yanks down the front of his shirt, revealing a tattoo like our temporary ones, but far more permanent and cut in by a thin, almost square-ish line. Screwdriver? No, please.

Releasing his shirt, Wolf says, "You think you're the only ones who thought you could get the jump on this guy?" He raises the insides of his wrists, where more sigils mark his skin. More scars cut into each and every perimeter of ink.

Eva cocks her hand again like she's ready to empty the entire can of spray into this guy. He holds out his hand before tipping his head to the side. Gingerly lifting away his beard, he reveals another tattoo on his neck that's so bright red and swollen that it's clear that he just got this one. Possibly a few hours ago.

Leo and Raylan, in their swift gait, have nearly reached us. Wolf explains quickly, "Making me his court jester is the only reason why Knox has kept me alive. The bastard's drunk—" he coughs into his handkerchief, splattering it with blood "—drunk on infamy."

Spitting a wad of thick black sludge, Wolf's eyes widen before slowly accepting that something is definitely wrong with his body. "If Knox didn't kill you right off, it's because he has an even worse plan for you up his sleeve. He *feeds* off people to keep his vessel strong. He'll do it to you. He'll do it to your friends. For the love, girls, get the eff out of this city."

My body is pumping with way too much adrenaline to be cooped up in a hotel room, so the boys agreed to regroup with us up here. Don't hurt that it's hella romantic.

Feels good to be standing among the skyscrapers. The roof of the Gunter, while not the tallest building around, still holds its own with its fourteen stories. Looking out across the horizon of hills covered in lights is exhilarating—an emotion I need to convince the others of my plan. A gust of wind throws me off balance for a second, and I stagger and look down. Those streetlights and bushes are freakishly small. Hair whipping around me, I teeter over to a chaise lounge for safety.

A car honks down below as Leo toys with a cigarette in the front pocket of his pants. No, not pants, *trousers,* along with a shirt that screams STRAIGHT OUTTA SAN ANTONIO.

Frost, standing next to him, bun a little more frayed than usual, stares at the street below. If not for his star-crossed, not-being-a-full-human status, they would be perfect. If he's a

Blurred One, and Knox is a Blurred One, I guess there are different categories? Overlapping factor is super hotness?

The guy's devoted to her. Keeps glancing at her from the corner of his eye like he wants to bring her a piping hot muffin bursting with blueberries. Too bad Frost is constantly switching from acting like he's the center of her universe to deciding he's as dangerous as a black hole.

"Here's how it'll go down," I say, drawing the gaze from everyone. Raylan's standing behind me, and I've successfully not thought about him for a full minute. I'm proud until I remember why we're here. How Jenny would have probably never met Knox if it weren't for us. And then comes the twist of guilt for having been so naive as to think this was going to be some fun adventure.

"Knox seemed pretty into me the other night." I clear my throat, but end up choking a little, so it takes a little long. "So." I pant. "I'm gonna go back to the bar. Let him think I can't resist his charms, that I want to play with a bad boy, and bring him up to our room."

"Absolutely not," Raylan's saying as Leo murmurs, "No." Frost shrieks something between "What?" and "Heck no!"

I expected this, but aw—Raylan's feeling overprotective. "And then, you three spring the trap on him. How do you capture a Blurred One?"

"You want to be bait?" Raylan asks, and it's a little adorable how incredulous he looks. Like a bulldog who didn't get his bone. Instead of his stereotypical look of I'm-going-to-beat-you-down, his eyes are flashing, Let's-duel-right-now.

"I can't even count how many ways that's a terrible idea," Frost says, shaking her head. "No offense."

Raylan plants his chiseled exterior in front of me. "We'll take care of him without getting innocent people involved."

"An innocent person was killed last night," I snap. "And it's partly my fault. So, again, *how do you trap a Blurred One?*"

His eyes instantly narrow, and my mouth sort of dries up. "Do you have any better ideas? This way no one else needs to die. Plus, I have utter faith in your abilities." Maybe flattery will get me somewhere.

"He's too dangerous," Leo agrees. He sticks an unlit cigarette in his mouth.

"Leo is right and *we* will handle this. We'll switch rooms until it's over," Raylan barks, and I think his eyes may have lasers in them, they're so penetrating.

Something splats my cheek. A raindrop. I take a deep breath to center myself. "You can help me or watch me."

Frost looks like she wants to shake me. Force me to see sense. And I want to give her a big ol' hug, but I have to explain. "You know how Dad calls me the childish one? It's not childish to take down a serial killer. I'm gonna prove him wrong. And it's the right thing to do."

Dad's usual advice is, "Marry young and marry rich, before you get fat and try to live off being a professional drop-out." I do have a slightly alarming turnover of interests, wanting to be everything from a graphic designer to a journalist to a chemical engineer. But I've been on the FBI bandwagon now for like a year, so hopefully this one sticks. And I guess I always figured either I hadn't found my thing yet, or I was just meant to be well-rounded. Not lazy or shallow.

Frost throws herself on the chaise lounge, wrapping her skinny arms around me. "You are *nothing* like that. Don't listen to him. We'll find another way."

She's still hugging me when Raylan awkwardly clears his throat. "I have a cage in my car."

Must have his own daddy issues. He shoves one hand in his pocket while leaning against the fire escape door.

"Awesome. That'll do it? Any special weapons?" I try to sound brave, but my heart is slamming even more now. Raylan gives Leo an almost apologetic look.

"Rock salt will slow them down," he says like a commander, prepping for an op. "It won't do as much damage as it will to ghosts. Silver hurts, but mainly, we get him into the cage before he can smoke out."

I ignore the fact that Frost is turning a little green and Leo looks severely uncomfortable. "Smoke out?"

"The spirit leaving the vessel he's possessing," Raylan says.

"I can't let you do this," Frost pleads. "I promised Maggie."

"She'll be pissed, and then she'll calm down and be proud." I wave my hand like I haven't a care in the world.

"I'll call her, then." She pulls her cell phone from her back pocket. Great.

"You'll be armed from head to toe." Raylan blocks her hand, but his now pulsing eyes dig into mine. He's actually backing me up? Loving it!

Frost frantically dials what has to be Maggie's number.

"Frost." I jump to my feet. "Stop!"

"If you won't listen to me, maybe you'll listen to Maggie."

It barely rings once before Maggie's alto voice is hollering, "ARE YOU GIRLS ALL RIGHT?"

Frost must have put her on speaker phone. Maggie sounds like she's shouting into a megaphone. "I HEARD ABOUT YOUR FRIEND. I'M ABOUT SIX HOURS OUT. *DON'T* DO ANYTHING STUPID!"

"I wouldn't dream of it," I yell back. "Curiosity killed the gnat."

"EVA," Maggie booms.

Forgiveness is easier than permission here. I'm not going to end up a five-hundred-pound burger flipper, and if we don't get rid of Knox, surely someone else is going to die. I yell into the phone. "We've got everything under control! Over and out of toilet paper!"

"Mags," Frost yells over me.

"EVA! FROST?" Maggie's voice grows choppy. "I'M LOSING MY—" Wind blasts through the speaker's phone from Maggie's end before going dead and Frost's face . . . it's her finding out she's checking into the psychiatric hospital all over again. It's her finding out our pet boxer, Randy, got hit by a car.

I almost back off. But I have to do this. For her. And Jenny. And all the other women violated before and after death by Knox. And if Maggie's here in six hours, we have our time limit.

"Knox can't suspect we're trapping him." My voice cracks.

A throat clears. I'd almost forgotten Leo was there. In a voice so soft the wind almost blows it away, he speaks up. "Do you want us to stop her, Frost?"

My eyebrows hit my hairline at the same time my jaw hits my chest. "Are you kidding me? Sorry, but this isn't up to you." I look at Frost because this is really between her and me, but her lips are drawn into a grim frown. Surely thinking about me being a bumblebee or something again. Whatever works.

She gives me a look like she's tempted to lock me up, but she wouldn't do that. She knows what being locked up feels like, and she knows I've had enough of being controlled. But she's running her tongue along the front of her teeth again like she's lost in thought. Like she knows more than she's saying. She glances from me to Raylan to Leo before she finally says, "We stick with her *every single step*."

"Woot!" My heart soars. With her on my side, I really do stand a chance. Leo accepts her answer, nodding and fading somewhat again into the background, kind of like a spirit even with a body of flesh and blood.

"Can you get him in the cage, Leo?" Raylan straightens and pushes off the doorway.

"I believe so." Leo fiddles with his suspenders, and I try

not to dwell on the uncertainty of that statement. Frost yelps, but Raylan interrupts her.

"It'll work." He cracks his neck. "Kill the bastard, save the day." He smiles a crooked grin, and I had better not die, because I will kiss that mouth again.

---

*R*ed vinyl squeaks as I straighten in my barstool, fighting its encouragement to slouch. I pray my deodorant holds back my stress sweat. Using the mirror behind the bar to help scan my surroundings, all I see are lonely businessmen and frazzled vacationers. No Knox.

Raylan sits in the corner, black baseball hat low as he plays with his phone to blend in. Every few seconds, I keep telling myself to stop looking at him, to stop checking to see if he's looking at me when he's not. I take that as a sign he really is a good hunter.

Frost and Leo are positioned in the lobby so they can see the moment we get on the elevator. We've got this. And Raylan still isn't looking at me, so I settle for checking myself out in the mirror again.

Dang, I do look good. Hair in loose curls, perfectly winged eyeliner, crimson lips and a black sleeveless midi dress that shows just enough cleavage to make things interesting. It may be naughty, but I love getting to wear it the way it was intended for once, instead of with an undershirt *and* over-shirt. Black six inch wedges I can only wear around men not stunted by hillbilly inbreeding. The perfect finishing touch to the ensemble comes from the emerald necklace with the gorgeous, intricate silver mount I inherited from Aunt Eva. The emerald rests perfectly on my décolletage.

"Beautiful," a deep, Southern voice murmurs behind me.

I don't turn around, and his sudden warmth in his black

wool suit against my bare shoulders makes me shiver. Knox claims the seat next to me. I give him a long look, sizing him up and down. He looks more disheveled today than the night we met. Hair mussed, bow tie untied and top button undone, even a little scruff. Basically, a devastatingly handsome, psycho killer. Same guy we saw on the internet. I suppose hotel employees change often enough they don't realize they've had the same customer for fifty years.

"What's beautiful, the music?" I finally respond, deciding to play coy.

He stares at the emerald on my chest for a long moment.

I pray Raylan can't see me blush from his corner. I take a breath quietly to calm my nerves. I got ready as fast as I could, but it must be past midnight now. Tick tock till Maggie comes and we're back on lockdown.

"I was hoping you might show up here tonight." I look up at him through my lashes, but he chuckles half-heartedly. Not the response I had been looking for. Not to be defeated, I remember he probably likes the chase, so I back off. "You know, to ask you some questions."

He turns his entire body so he is looking at me and only me. Leaning one side against the bar, he is so tall and exudes so much confidence that his presence takes up the entire room. A rock star near mere mortals. Makes it hard to breathe. He reaches up and traces one finger down my arm, softly, leaving goosebumps every inch of the way.

"Eva, you're as beautiful in this body as you were before."

I try not to choke on my own saliva. "Say what now?"

He gives that devilish grin that actually meets his eyes, then slides his strong hand into mine. In one swift move, he's off his stool and twirling me around in mine, making my head spin. Thankfully, I don't topple over.

"Come dance," he commands, gently pulling on my hand like I'm a princess. I hadn't really considered the fact that there would probably need to be some prelude to our tryst trap upstairs, and the request throws off my expectations. It's all I can do to not keep looking at Raylan for security, and I remind myself Frost and Leo are nearby too—somewhere. Nothing is going to get out of hand.

I let him pull me back onto the dance floor. He immediately pulls me close, but not touching like we were the other night. He's keeping literal distance between us, dancing to the piano player's smooth notes. Is he not interested after all? I look up at him, holding eye contact and waiting for him to say something, but I realize he probably knows that game. Then, with a jolt, I realize he probably knows all my games. Dude has been around for ages, plus has who-knows-what super powers. Trying to not let my hands start sweating now—

"I know you, Eva." He interrupts my mental freakout. "You are brilliant, beautiful. Wild. I'm surprised to see you living so puritan. Team God," he says, adding the last part with no small degree of disdain.

"I have no idea what you're talking about," I say with extra eyelash batting, and I hope he explains, because it's true I have no idea. He doesn't know a thing about me.

He waits a few measures, slowly rotating to the music. He starts playing with my hand that he holds to dance, interlacing the fingers, and I don't resist. It's like he wants to feel every inch of my skin. My throat is going dry. Finally, he answers.

"You're fun. Interesting. Not one to be told what to do." Is this something he tells every woman? Probably, and yet— his playful smirk is gone, and his dark eyes look almost earnest. Like embers just barely glowing. Like he really does know me.

He presses his hand on my back, bringing us closer together until my hips are fully against his body, and suddenly the clingy knit of this dress feels very, very thin. I forget to breathe. "So, it's nice to see you here. Glad to see your spark."

He slides his hand all the way down the zipper on my back. Dangerously low. The danger mixed with him actually knowing me gives me a sudden rush of power. His other hand is still playing with mine, running his fingers up and down my arm, then intertwining with my finger. This man, this Blurred One, whatever—it's like he knows parts of me I don't even know myself. It's intoxicating. Needing to clear my head, I look away but remember not to look at Raylan. I settle for the shoulder seam on Knox's black jacket.

"But I am actually a good girl. A prude by your standards, I'm sure," I say. Again, partly to flirt, partly to pry for more. He makes a noncommittal hum and looks at me until I look back. When I do, he slides his hand down my back a little more, until it's most definitely not on my back, and then twirls me once.

I'm completely at a loss for thought, let alone words, when I catch a pair of eyes staring at me. Raylan. His face is unreadable, but noticing him there watching us dissipates the fog rapidly forming in my brain. A thrill runs through me at him seeing me be wanted, but I refocus on my mission. Recommitted, I pull back from Knox a few inches and do my best to look disinterested, hoping that will reel him in. It must work, as he instantly grabs me tighter and pulls me even closer than before. Then, lips against my ear, he says, "Eva, I would love to know this shell of yours."

Heart in my throat, I know I need to seem hesitant to not arouse suspicion. He knows I know how his conquests end up. I shake my head.

"Why, so I can end up in a meat grinder?"

He freezes for just half a breath and then continues moving to the music.

"Bold. I like that. I know you, remember?" His tone is

light but deliberately even. "You are a force to be reckoned with."

Noting that he didn't really say no, I twist my hand in his so he's holding me tighter and press my chest into his. Let him take that as he may. He may be some sort of ancient demon thing, but he's still got testosterone in that body he's in. Maybe he thinks I'm star struck. Maybe he thinks I'm actually so starved for affection that I want to die at his infamous hands. Egotistical maniac.

The song ends, a nudge for action, and I risk one glance to Raylan as Knox leads me out of the bar. I pray nothing can stop Raylan, my sister, and Leo from saving me from this devil.

The elevator doors close, and I gulp. What is it with me and hot guys in elevators these days? Knox pushes my waist until I slam against the wall. I ignore the hand rail digging into my back. He leans down, nuzzling my neck with his scruff and inhaling deeply. My eyes roll back and—oh my gosh he is a serial killer! But I can't rightly make him stop or act like I'm not into it. Oh hell, what a great idea, me. Then his lips ever so slightly start touching my neck. These are not the moves of a Missourian teenage boy. He kisses softly, a trail up to behind my ear, then down, to the nape, to my shoulder, cool air tingling every spot dampened by his lips. Then he kisses further down. With full lips, he kisses the emerald. Sorry, Aunt Eva. I reach behind myself and grasp the railing like I'm grasping my sanity.

Thankfully, the elevator reaches my floor with a ding, and he straightens and looks away, as if suddenly completely bored by me. My stomach drops. These games he plays and he knows I play. I have no idea what's what anymore, just trying whatever instinct pushes me to do to get him to that room. What is this Blurred One?

He strolls out of the elevator and I stand my ground. I clear my throat loudly. When he looks back at me, the doors are starting to close, and I give him an impish grin. He thrusts his hand between the doors to keep them from closing and holds them open for me. I saunter out, making him believe I really do want to put my fate in his hand, and grab his belt loop as I walk past him, pulling him along with me. I keep pulling until I sort of trip into the hallway wall, nearly bumping a framed photograph off its nail. The wall is cold and uncomfortable, but I pull Knox's warmth to me and I'm instantly aflame. Because I am one kiss away from either the looney bin or hell.

When I look at him, he barks out a laugh. Am I funny now? Mortified, I push down the blood that wants to burn on my cheeks. I need to work this more. Finger still in his belt loop, I inch closer and slowly, eyes wide open, kiss him on the mouth.

It's like this is the key to opening the floodgates. There's no holding back now. He shoves his tongue into my mouth, tasting like bourbon and lime. His scruff is painful against my lips. I wince, but kiss through the pain. He puts both hands on my shoulders and pins me to the wall. His hands almost scorch my bare skin. I push him forward. We have to get to the room before my mind shuts off completely. He lets me push but keeps kissing, deep and rough, biting my lips, pulling my hair. Is this what happened with Jenny? Almost hysterical now, I fight back tears. I stumble backward, kissing, pulling him with me, trying to reach my room. Have to get inside so the others can follow. Every sense is screaming— my heart is so loud in my ears. Time and logic are slipping further and further away.

Finally we reach my room, and I pull out my keycard from

my small black sequined clutch and almost drop it. My sweaty hands are shaking so hard. Knox takes it from me and slides it into the silver lock with a deathly calm. Opening the heavy door, he sees the salt line and gives it just a little kick, and the line is broken. The door slams and I jump, as if it just slammed some sense into me. I'm suddenly very aware at what a stupid thing I've done. Panic is a three-ton gorilla dancing on my chest, but I still need to buy just a couple more minutes for the others to arrive. Knowing the cage is but a couple feet away in the boys' room gives me enough courage to not just wet myself and run.

Hoping to play it off as naive nerves, I start to ask Knox for a minute alone in the bathroom, but he looks *ready*. He grabs my elbow and, not gently, steers me to the bed. The bed where his victims are stripped to their underwear and chopped up. I mentally swear to listen to Maggie for the rest of my life—if I make it out of this alive. He pushes me onto the mattress, my hands barely fast enough to brace my fall.

"There's no hurry, right?" I nearly squeak.

"No," he says, but raises one hand and pushes my chest hard enough to make me fall back. "No hurry." His smile is gone, his lips parted slightly, breathing heavily.

With one knee on the bed, he leans over me, just looking. Drinking in my hair, face, arms, all of my dress. I'm suddenly wishing for those extra shirts, but I force a shy smile.

"Yes, you got a good body out of the deal," he says, still staring. He traces the delicate skin near the emerald. "But you would have been *great* on the other side." With the lightest touch, he traces up to my neck, adding fingers until his hand is fully around my throat. He squeezes. Fear grips me as tightly as his vise-like fingers. Oxygen barely eeks into my lungs. Still squeezing, he leans down and kisses me, long, deep, and rough. I push down into the mattress as much as I can, desperate for any space between us.

After a long moment he stops and pulls back, leaving me to gulp down that precious air. Inches from my face, his attraction is gone. His violent eyes no longer glow, but swallow me completely like two deep black holes. Teeth clenched, spittle flies from his lip, hitting mine. "I will enjoy your body." He squeezes my throat harder.

Tears burn my eyes as I start to hyperventilate. My lungs scream for more air.

"Knox," I croak. "Please. I thought—"

He squeezes even harder, and I can't breathe at all. I'm horrified as I listen to myself choke. Where is Frost? Raylan and Leo?

Hurry! I mentally scream at them. I try to kick him, turn to bite, scratch, anything to fight, but he is everywhere and so inhumanly strong.

"Look at me, Eva." He releases just enough so I can get just a taste of air.

I look at him. His face *blurs*. His features sort of melt into each other, like when you look into a mirror in the dark and you know what should be where, but they're missing somehow. And then his skin moves—convulses. The terror that must be so plain on my face, written all over my body, pleases him.

He lets me go completely, and I roll, coughing, gasping for air. A pounding starts at the door. A pounding that scares me more than anything so far. Because my rescuers have a key. They should be in here, guns blazing.

Knox laughs, low, deep, and grabs me by the hair.

"Leonardo won't be ruining our fun," he hisses into my ear, then jerks my head back by my hair. Hot tears come. Then, twisting my hair, he forces me to face the corner of the room by the window.

There, in the corner, are some shadowed, bulky shapes.

People? I blink, tears blurring my vision, and I'm not trusting my own eyes at this point. I peer at the shapes.

A sound like a long exhale comes from the figures, and then they move; I can make out a few features—three small people. They look like girls, from their petite limbs and long curtains of hair covering their faces. Their movements are like twitches, like there's a strobe light in the room, and they start inching toward me, rasping loudly with each second.

They reach a slice of moonlight by the window, revealing their faces. Like watercolor portraits that have been left in the rain, their features are almost completely nonexistent. Similar to Knox's, but worse. A smudge for eyes, a streak for a mouth. Then the streaks for their mouths start to open, and they inhale like they can suck my very life away. And I scream for all I've got.

CHAPTER 13 - FROST

I never should have gone along with this. She's allowing herself to be taken by a Blurred One—just like Aunt Eva.

Tears burn my eyes as I pound my fists on the door, but it won't open.

Maybe Leo's too close to the door? Our sigils could be warding him off. But Eva and I broke the loops of the triquetras we carved into the doors so Knox could get in.

How infuriatingly stupid I am. My sister could die, and I'm just standing on the other side, useless.

So I rattle the cool, brass doorknob, heart tearing open my chest. "Why doesn't my card reader work?" I cry as Raylan tries it for the twentieth time.

"He must have melted the metal." Raylan kicks the door with his hunter's boot. It doesn't budge.

Eva's shrieks curl like flat flute notes through the door, and it's the ghost woman all over again. *He'll be ripping apart her limbs.* "Do something!" I cry.

Raylan turns to Leo, who stares at the door like he has a plan. When Raylan raises his eyebrows and Leo gives a curt nod, I think they might actually have something that will work. I think Leo might pull out some sort of weapon, when his slender frame convulses as his soft lips turn to rubber. His elbows seem to melt as his cheeks tremble like he's being electrocuted.

He slumps to the ground.

I think he might actually be dead when a black, murky smoke bursts through his mouth. He floats to the door and zooms inside the slit of the card reader. The door rattles just once before it bursts open like someone's used a shotgun.

"Leo!" A cheerful, male voice calls from the other side.

Raylan's pistol digs into my hip as we burst into the room. I've a hatchet I grabbed last minute from his truck, but now I feel a little ridiculous. I can't stop Knox. He's holding my sister by the neck three feet above the ground.

It's like I'm in a dream. *Let her go*, I want to cry, but I can't talk. My tongue feels fat. Wrong.

Three dark smudges hover around the pair, too. Smudges like Leo is now. And I *know* them. I remember them from when I was small. They suck the happiness, the life out of every room. But I forbade myself from remembering them because they used to give me the kinds of nightmares where I thought there were a million bugs covering my body and I used to scratch off my own skin.

Their ghoulish mouths stretch open wide like they like to feast on cockroaches. Their eyes are like black eight balls, and they're staring straight at Leo like they know him well.

I hate that he's in this grouping, but he stretches out a smoky tendril. He pops, snaps at the girls, and they hiss.

"Leonardo," Knox croons as the spirits retreat to the air vent like liquid seeping into cotton. "Good to see you. Though, you needn't chase away our friends." Knox releases Eva's throat, and she crashes to the floor like she's not even a person. I tense to help her, but Raylan holds my arm.

"Not yet," he says.

Like a stratus cloud, Leo hovers just over my head. He floats behind me, and I think he might be leaving when he burrows inside his vessel's now immobile body. The boy's eyes are closed, his fingers deathlike, so maybe the real owner of that body is already dead.

Leo hunches once the smoke stops filling his mouth and I think of an ogre come to life, but his beautiful blue eyes flash as he finds his feet again.

Like we're made of paper mache, he shoves Raylan and me to the side. "Leave the girls alone."

Raylan grumbles an assortment of unsavory words. I'd venture a guess that he doesn't like to be shoved around, but *please, God,* don't let anything happen to Eva.

"You're out of control," Leo says, face cast in shadow.

Knox's stubbled cheeks slide into a smile. "I have missed you since you left." He clucks his tongue. "You should return."

A cold shiver runs down my neck as I comprehend what Knox just said. *Return? Are they friends?* "Wait—what?"

Leo's once carefree hands curl into fists. "Choose another playground."

Knox snatches Eva by the skirt of her black dress and drags her like a rag doll to him. She hangs limply, like she's too terrified to look up. "I see you're back to playing the good guy again."

Eva's face is so white I want to curl up with her on the sofa and listen to Depeche Mode like Maggie does when we're feeling off. Bring her ice-cold lemonade and play hangman till she beats me three times.

"I'm bored," Knox says. "Is this the girl you speak so fondly of?" His charcoal eyes drink me in, and it's like beetles consuming my skin. What are they talking about? Leo never could have been as corrupt as Knox. I want to splash cold water on my face. Sit down.

"I prefer the sister," Knox murmurs, sniffing my sister's porcelain skin.

She flinches, and my heart lurches in my mouth.

"I've grown tired of my old habits," Knox adds. "You know how she reminds me of someone else."

"You can rot in hell," I say. He needs to release my sister. How could I go along with this? Raylan has an excuse—he must have seen the desperation my sister has to prove herself —but I knew better. There's no chance in Hades that I'll allow her to do something as stupid as this again.

Knox runs his fingers down the length of her bodice, and I could snap his neck. "You tried to trap me," he purrs. "Do you know what I do to naughty girls?"

Stretching forth a hand and without even touching her, he lifts her with an invisible string from the ground. He's got her like a doll in a giant's fist. Helpless, she hovers in the air. Her eyes are so wide. This can't be happening. We have to wake up.

Eva's terrified gaze meets mine, and an invisible fist tightens around my chest. I want to move to her, help her, but an unseen force is stopping me, holding me back.

Leo? His surprised expression locks on mine.

"How are you so strong?" He asks Knox before realization seems to dawn over his mind. "You gained power from her just now."

I don't care! I want to scream. Must. Save. Eva. I can't breathe—like a plastic bag's over my head.

Lungs scream. Can't find oxygen. Eva's face is so white, and all I can think is Knox will grind up everything but her hand. Just like Jenny.

I'm seeing spots. I'm about to pass out, when Eva flies backward—into the window.

Glass shatters. It's piercing her scalp.

She falls.

And she's falling six stories down to her death.

I leap across the room, stumbling over Eva's strewn-open suitcase with the blonde wig, but Knox looks down at me like I'm just about as threatening as a gnat.

I'LL KILL HIM. Kill those nasty, powerful hands.

Like a second gunshot, the door slams into the wall.

Maggie, in her crumpled paisley shirt, hoists a rust-covered shotgun in her practiced hands. She cocks it as she booms, "GET AWAY FROM HER, YOU PISS ANT."

I reach to get past Knox's leg, but Raylan's there too, and he's firing at Knox with his pistol, but Knox absorbs the bullets like he's made of quicksand.

Knox flicks his wrist, and Raylan's pistol flies through the air. Knox lifts his hand upward, and Maggie's shotgun points to the ceiling as she grunts to regain control of it.

It fires.

The fire alarm shrieks through the door in the long hall. Someone must have heard the commotion and pulled it. Kids will be spilling from rooms any second.

Seeing he will soon have far more witnesses than he planned, Knox smiles wryly. "It was a pleasure seeing you all." Bending his knees, he launches his body through the window after Eva. I scuttle to follow, my Converses squeaking as Maggie runs with me, her hot fingers holding my arm. But Leo's zooming past us, too.

My tongue's trapped. The boy I'd just as soon not remember leaps after my sister and Knox. Knox rolls off a couch lodged in a dumpster. Leo next. And they're running past an idle cement truck and orange cones. Where's Eva? Cotton fills my mouth.

Fragments of ill-constructed curse words bounce through the street as Eva rounds the dumpster a short distance off.

Green stuff mats her hair, and her knees are cut, but other than that, she looks all right.

I all but collapse. *Thank you, God, for keeping her safe. Enough.*

---

*H*ead's in a cloud. We can't be leaving. San Antonio's skyscrapers aren't shrinking from Maggie's back window like forgotten Legos.

Leo's gone. Like smoke to sky, he chased Knox. Who knows where they are or for how long they'll be missing. And Raylan? He disappeared just as fast—didn't even give Eva a goodbye.

My sister's eyes are wet. Her scalp's full of scratches, and her porcelain cheeks are devoid of that dimple I love.

"*What*," Maggie asks for the fourteenth time, "were you girls thinking?" Even her lecturing beats being on the bus Mrs. Sanders found. I don't think I can listen to the other students' theories about what happened to Jenny.

Eva's shoulders match mine. We hunch in the backseat, nunchucks still hidden in the driver's seat's back pockets. The salt grenades are there—in the cupholders—and I almost wish Eva were tying knots in her hair, because then at least she'd be doing something with her limp hands.

How must that have felt, being tossed like a doll out the window by a man she'd kissed? She had wanted so badly to prove her usefulness—to capture Knox. And I am grateful, so grateful that she is brave and that she landed on that couch. But how could Knox even dispose of her like that?

"WHY DO YOU THINK I LECTURED YOU FOR SIX ENTIRE WEEKS ON LEAVING KNOX ALONE?" Maggie asks. "IT'S BEEN DECADES SINCE ANYONE'S BEEN MURDERED. WHY'D YOU HAVE TO GO AND

DIG UP THE PAST AGAIN? WHAT THE 'H' DO I TELL YOUR PARENTS?"

Every single one of us knows she won't tell my parents anything they don't have to know. Maggie's really good at keeping details to a minimal, especially ever since Eva and I got grounded for an entire month for wearing shorts that were shorter than our fingertips.

Where are Eva's cliches now? I want to pull her head to my lap and stroke her hair. Remind her of the time Bobby Warren tried to get her to elope to Arkansas. But she's as stiff as I feel. How *could* we disregard Maggie's order like that?

If none of this happened, I could go back to daydreaming about the three short months until I graduate. How I ultimately accept that Eva will be fine in Maggie's hands, and the truth about the Blurred Ones can be safely hidden under a mat.

As far as Leo, he's gone. He may never come back. Perhaps, when all is said and done, that's for the best.

Maggie snaps the air conditioner on and adjusts the vents to blow straight on her flushed face and the beads of sweat on her neck. The turning signal clicks as she passes several cars, and I don't envy the Beetle currently in her path.

As I watch the brush and weeds tumbling past us, I consider the idea that letting all of this go actually does make sense. We could be the type of girls who would enter barrel racing. Pageanting. In 4-H, I'd enter a fuchsia plant.

But, as we pass a swing set on the opposite side of the road, I'm reminded of the past. Of metal. Rusted. The swing set like the one Eva and I had while growing up.

We used to play on it all the time. Looked forward to it, especially one night.

Dad bought flowers for Mom, and she was sticking them in her blue flowered vase while listening to oldies music, humming, her voice sure and strong.

We had just finished eating dinner, and Eva and I were about to go to play on the swing set.

Eva had to finish cleaning her room before we could go outside, so I waited at the sliding glass window, tracing hearts on the freezing glass.

Sunbeams lit one of my hearts on fire, turning it an orange liquid gray as the sun dipped into the horizon, spraying the landscape just as three dark figures rushed our swings.

The window was closed, so not a sound except a slight squeak of the chains was carried by the wind as I stood, frozen in place.

I knew who they were. Leo had told me his friends were jealous that the two of us played and warned me they were dangerous. They "took great pleasure" in stealing little girls' happiness. I wasn't sure how exactly they did that, but as I watched those figures, palms thick with sweat, they swung back and forth, back and forth. Long, black hair rushed behind them in a stream of black.

Eva clattered out to the kitchen at that moment, having finished tidying her room. Boots clacked the tiled floor as ribbons bounced from two tight ponies. My favorite dimple flashed in her cheek as she beamed up at me. "Ready, Frosty?"

I wrapped my arm around my little sister's scarved shoulder and carefully turned her away before she could spot what was on our swings. "Let's play Candyland."

"But I want to go outside!" She squirmed in my grasp.

"I have *real* Lollipops."

She squealed, and I almost smiled—mission accomplished.

I will protect my sister. No matter what.

We're home. Like an old sweater shrunk in the wash, it's almost comfortable, but it squeezes just enough so you can never entirely relax. It seems weird how everything looks the same here. Like the whole world should look different. We trudge into the house, put our shoes in their cubbies like the perfect little daughters we are, and take our bags upstairs to our rooms. Everything is dark, but we know this doesn't mean everyone is asleep. Lights are a luxury and dark is soothing in this house. My bed looks so inviting, but Dad's already in a bad mood since we've been gone "galavanting across the country," so we don't dare act tired. Or sad.

Our oversized bedrooms and a shared bathroom take up the entire second floor of our house. Thanks to Mom and Dad rarely coming upstairs, we've made it our own. My room's walls are covered in ironic and iconic band posters and abstract art. An expression of me I could never verbalize. I inhale deeply, pleased my over-zealous Febreze spraying is still effective. Frost's room is tidy but welcoming with hung nature prints and soothing lavender linens.

Standing in our doorways across from each other, I let out a quiet sigh and Frost responds with her own. I think we could have a whole conversation in sighs, we're so talented at it.

"We better get down there." I force a grim smile, which, despite my effort, Frost instantly sees through. She comes and hugs me with her bony arms. I don't pull away, but I can't let myself feel it. Can't open my heart even a crack. I don't even know what I'll find in there. Frost lets go and leads the dirge down the stairs to find our parents, because we know they're expecting us.

Dad will want lots of "quality-quantity" time to make up for our week away. He's from old-school farm life, where you only leave home out of necessity, so even though he wants us to have educational experiences, he wants us home more. Maybe the return to normalcy will help me bury the crap that's just happened way down deep. Guilt, failure, loss—no.

We find them talking in the living room in the dark, just loud enough to hear over the roaring cicadas and thrumming toads outside. I can barely see the floral sofas but can make out the dark silhouettes of Mom and Dad in their favorite sage-green recliners. I feel my way to the corner of the soft sofa and curl up in it. My favorite reading spot. Frost sits much more properly on the other side next to me.

"You girls behave?" Dad always starts conversations so subtly.

"Yep," we both reply, as a pit forms in my gut as the image of kissing Knox in the elevator flashes in my brain. Frost braves on.

"The Alamo was amazing. Two hundred people held out for thirteen days against thousands of soldiers. So brave. And it was the first hospital in Spanish Texas." Oh, Frost, always with the valiant effort.

"That's really nice, honey," Mom replies. Dad is silent. We

sit in the bleak quiet for a moment. Two. Three. The silence blares in my ears. I wonder if Raylan's parents were ever this strict? Surely not as creative—who knows what punishments Dad will concoct if we don't cheer him up. Make him feel like our hearts are completely here.

"We made some friends," I venture, trying to not leave Frost out on her own. More silence. I think I see a little nod, though, so I continue. He'll be proud I defended myself. "And one guy thought I was his girlfriend and tried to grab my butt. I was like 'uh-uh!' and set him straight. It was hilarious."

Dad doesn't miss a beat. "He liked my little fatty? Glad you didn't walk around naked like that girl probably did to get herself missing." He speaks with measured coolness. My heart drops, and I am stone.

I could argue. I could defend her and even tell the truth— that she's dead. That it was the Blurred Ones who killed her. That maybe we could have saved her if they would just freaking tell us about them. Admit that I just about got killed too. I can feel the rage building. My throat tightens, hands sweating, teeth clenched. But I can't go there tonight. I'm too tired.

"Jenny was a beautiful person," Frost says softly but firmly. A shouted proclamation under these circumstances. A rebellion she will pay for later, but I promise myself I'll make it up to her.

"Well, I'm glad you two will be staying home for a while." It's a simple statement, but from Dad, it's a decree we know well. We're basically grounded. Probably a couple of weeks. I stay silent, knowing if I utter a peep, the tears will flow. And if I cry now, he'll either get defensive and angry, or try to sweetly psychoanalyze why I'm crying, and I absolutely can't take either.

"What have you been up to?" Frost tries. Ever the peacemaker.

"Oh, I've been replacing the fluorescent light bulbs in the shed. I've got it down to where I can do a couple in just a few minutes. It's really neat. Now we'll have a nice place to work. Gato and I were just sitting and enjoying it earlier."

Sweet Gato. He's got a soft spot for Dad. He's feisty and cute, and helps us see that Dad can be, too. My chest loosens at the change of subject and thought of our kitty. I make a mental note to sneak him a couple extra treats tomorrow.

"Time for bed," Dad proclaims, getting up. We are expected to comply. Never mind it's eight p.m. Oh well, I'm actually tired this time. We sit for a moment longer, our tiny stand for independence. Mom gets up and kisses us both tiredly on the top of the head. She'll probably make our favorite lemon blueberry muffins with fresh orange juice in the morning to welcome us home.

"Glad you're home, sweeties." She shuffles off after Dad.

Frost gives an A-plus sigh and pulls herself off the couch like an overgrown puppet, throwing her arms forward, then dragging her body along. Despite myself, I giggle a little.

A firefly outside catches my eye. I take it as a tiny sign. Tomorrow will be better. And to let Frost know I'm going to be okay, I whisper, "Dismember the Alamo!"

CHAPTER 15 - FROST

*E*va pushes the lawn mower like the bag's filled with body parts, not grass. I trim the edges of the lawn, whacking the feeder every few minutes.

Sweat trickles down my neck, beads across my forehead. No matter how many drink breaks we take, the thirst never leaves us. It might only be eighty-nine degrees outside, but the humidity makes it feel like it's a hundred and five.

Dad, sitting on the porch, watches us work, lemonade in hand. He usually works just as hard as us, but today his feet hurt. He's watching me—it makes me nervous. Like I'm not holding the trimmer right. I'm going to break it. His death stare is worse than any demon's, because I want to please him but know I never will one hundred percent.

Eva hits a rock, and I wince, because Dad's jumping to his feet, arms hanging at his sides like he's readying to hit her. But he's too far away and he almost never actually hits. *Please, don't yell at her, Dad.* But Eva's smart. Immediately, she stops the mower, backs up. She spots the rock—a flat one that I would've mown over—and bends down and plucks it up. Dutifully, she walks to the back of the property to dispose of it. Her stoic face and calculated movements tells me she knows Dad's watching her. Because when he's not around, she more bounce-steps. Adds a dance move. There's so much joy in Eva when she's free to be herself.

When we're done with the lawn, we move on to the car, but Dad surprises us by joining us, sponges in hand. We're so tired, there's not much conversation, but Eva and I slop sponges on the front bumper as Dad sprays water with the hose. He even surprises us by spraying us once.

I'm just scrubbing at a swatch of bird droppings on the driver's door when a carefree voice says, "You girls look like you could use a little love."

I turn to find Maggie, swathed in a new haircut. Her return to her easy walk tells me she's forgiven us for screwing up. Holding out a box of Bavarian Creams, she smiles so large it fills the tree-filled yard.

I drop my sponge.

Eva's ripping open the box and we're both filling our faces with donuts. Dad greets Maggie before picking up his bucket and wordlessly going inside. Even he knows when he's outvoted. And I might be eating my carb allowance for the next three months, but I've more than worked off my breakfast and lunch.

Sugar and bread fill my mouth, and Eva's beaming like she's ridden a unicorn. Maggie offers us Gatorade and surveys the trash we've heaped up on the corner. And the car, which is cleaner than it'd get at any car wash.

She whistles as Dad ascends the front porch stairs and disappears inside the house. "If I'd known you two are offering slave labor, I would've invited you over to my house." She winks. Eva and I both know she would tell my parents she was "putting us to work," before renting more movies than we could ever watch and ordering pizza—with Canadian bacon and pineapple. The best thing about Maggie, like Eva, is she knows how to enjoy the moment.

She—they—almost make me believe nothing's ever gone wrong. That we haven't just colossally failed while trying to determine the identity of the Blurred Ones.

Maggie's got more stories than any other human being I know. "Characters" she's met. Run-ins with the truck drivers on the road. Her foray into religion, and boyfriends. The books on lore and weapons she's accrued ever since she began the hunter lifestyle, over a decade ago. Then, of course, her awkward encounters with ladies her age who simply cannot understand her love for cop shows or the need to keep a tire iron on hand at all times.

"What are you doing here?" Eva asks round her third donut.

"Just checking up on my girls."

The sky's turning pink—just like the permanent pink in Maggie's cheeks. Not that she's nervous or embarrassed. She's pink because she carries so much joy around.

"Look." She pulls a black and blue DVD from her back pocket. "I brought another season to watch."

I smile. Eva and I probably wouldn't ordinarily pick Blue Bloods by ourselves, but with Maggie? Watching that show is an experience all of its own.

"Selleck shave his mustache?" Eva gives her best poker face, which has Maggie shooting her a mock frown.

She waggles her finger. "Don't you go joking about things like that."

Eva deadpans, "All's fair in love and parkour."

It doesn't take us long to clean up our car washing enterprise and for the three of us to huddle around the TV with the donuts and other treats Maggie brought. Luckily for us, it's one of those rare nights when Mom and Dad actually decided to run errands.

By the time we've watched four whole episodes, my feet no longer hurt, and something small rolls over the carpet.

I stare, bewildered, into my old childhood teacup.

Eva and Maggie are laughing about something one of the officers just said, pretzels and Rolo wrappers crackling between the pair of them.

Bending down, I pluck up the broken teacup, one I haven't seen since Leo and I were inseparable.

Hanging out with Maggie and watching movies makes me feel more at home than any family dinner. It's nice to know there's an adult alive who seems to have their act together *and* cares about Frost and me.

"More Beaver Nuggets." I'm sprawled on the floor, so I reach behind me for the tasty morsels we picked up in Texas. Maggie puts the bag in my hand without either of us looking. Efficiency at its best. "Fried sugar, carbs, and salt turned into heaven," I mumble to myself. I love that slight food buzz from eating way too much and washing it down with the giant soda Maggie was so good to smuggle me. Dad doesn't let us drink caffeine. Good thing that what he doesn't know can't hurt him. Plus, if this is the extent of my rebellion, I'm a freaking angel.

A movement in the dark behind the giant sliding glass door snaps me out of my thoughts. Two dark figures stand like specters. Yelping, I leap up and squeeze in between Maggie and Frost on the couch. My mind flashes to Knox's hand around my throat. Not being able to breathe. Has he found us already? I look to Maggie for protection, but she has her gaze leveled sternly on Frost.

"The boys," Frost says, then bites her lip, and now my heart pounds for a whole new reason.

They're here? I scramble, brushing the crumbs off my chest and throwing my hair into a bun. After a quick wipe of my face to make sure it's food free, I jump to the door and throw it open. Raylan's faded green T-shirt finally allows me to ogle his arms, and Leo is rockin' the blue button-up.

"Whaddup, y'all?" I throw my arms around both of them and squeeze their man muscles hard. Raylan's are bigger, of course. They both pat my back with one hand until I let go, but not until after I breathe a giant gulp of Raylan's smell— leather mixed with something like fresh apple cider. They totally love us. "Get in here," I say, bouncing back into the room, where Maggie and Frost are still lodged on the couch. Maggie shoots me some crazy dagger eyes, being all protective.

"Ladies." Leo nods to Maggie and then goes back to fixing his gaze on Frost, his suspenders hanging loosely at his sides.

"Leonardo," Maggie returns, full mama bear, fingers not subtly toying with the zipper of her fanny pack. Thankfully, she doesn't reach for the Reaper she stowed under the couch. It may be movie night, but Maggie is nothing if not vigilant. Leo ignores her, the black circles under his eyes making him look like a weary traveler who just made it to his warm home. It dawns on me he's been here before. Our very own Casper the Friendly Ghost. Raylan cautiously surveys our den, the oversized forest-green sectional, the flimsy white bookshelves brimming with books and white walls. He's always so calm— but calm with a simmering force underneath.

For a moment, there is no sound but the arguing of a couple policemen on the TV.

"What are you doing here?" Frost asks at the same time I blurt, "What happened with Knox?"

"Yes. What *are* you doing here?" Maggie interjects, getting up and angling herself slightly between us and the boys. A reminder of who—what she is. Raylan clears his throat and shoves his hands in his jean's pockets, but Leo looks to her with respect.

"Ma'am, Knox got away, so the girls are still in danger," he says calmly. Props to him for not beating around the bush. Maggie stretches her frame a full three inches so she's almost eye level with Leo.

"They're in danger because *you* didn't stay away." She jabs a stubby finger at him, face getting redder by the second. Does Maggie know about Leo and Frost's past too? "I've kept them safe for years, and one run in with *you,* and I almost lose them both."

I hesitate to bring up the fact we were the ones who tempted fate by searching for Knox. We may need to redistribute the blame, 'cause Maggie's eyeing the Reaper's hiding spot again.

"We're just here to help," Raylan says—probably knows sense would sound better coming from someone other than Leo. "We know your reputation. You're a great hunter, but given Leo's history with Knox," he says, shooting Leo a dirty look, "we thought maybe you could use some help."

I sure hope that's not the only reason he's here.

Maggie puffs, not liking the suggestion she could use help from anyone, especially not a Blurred One, but before she can argue, Frost finally untangles herself off the couch and stands with us.

"Thanks, guys." Her voice comes out pinched, certainly freaking out about being in trouble and/or danger with them being here. "Our parents are going to be home any minute and can't meet you here like this."

"Unless you want them grounded till the cows come home," Maggie grumbles.

"Ma'am." Leo tries one more time, hands up, pleading. "I know how Knox works, and I care about Frost more than anything in this existence. Please let me know how I can be of service." He bows slightly, and my jaw drops to catch flies. Even in this light, I can see Frost's blushing cheeks.

No one speaks for a long moment. Then Maggie blows like a long overdue volcano. "How about I just make a good ol' example of *you* for Mr. Albert Knox?"

Frost looks like I'm pretty sure Juliet did when she found out her lover boy was a Montague.

Raylan, who's been studying Maggie, turns his spectacular gaze on me. "We're not going anywhere."

And my stomach is now an Olympic gymnast. Maggie lets out a terrifying growl and dives for the wicked knife. Frost shrieks, grabbing Maggie by the arm, and I can't tell if she's trying to help Maggie or stop her.

"Y'all, come on," I yell. I don't *think* Maggie would actually hurt Leo, but who knows these days? "Who cares about getting grounded right now? We're all on the same side. Focus on Knox, not Leo." I try to sound authoritative, but talk about too many chefs in the kitchen. I don't think anyone is listening. And why in tarnation is Frost not speaking up for Leo even a little bit?

"I will handle it," Maggie seethes, arms out, blade gleaming from the light of the TV. She escorts the boys out. Raylan does look back at me just as the door closes though, so it's not all bad. My stomach does one last flip.

The second we're alone, Maggie's smirk sets Frost off.

"You act like I'm oblivious that she's—we're in danger," Frost says with a huff.

Maggie snaps something back about San Antonio, but I tune them out. They'll both come around. Then we can all work together to kill the effer Knox, see if Leo is really a good guy for Frost, and Raylan will fall madly in love with me in the process. Perfect.

CHAPTER 17 - FROST

*L*eo's been throwing pebbles at my window for a full minute, and I should tell him to go away. Say it's not safe to have him around, but all I can think about is that time he helped me make a fort with all my covers and we laughed ourselves so silly that Mom thought I'd sipped some of Grandpa's Diet Mountain Dew again.

One of the smaller arms of our sycamore tree is just long enough for me to reach from the roof under my window and shimmy down. So I abandon my covers and tromp past my Aristotle poster. And when I shimmy up the window, I climb out to our sycamore like a decade hasn't passed since the last time I climbed out.

I pat the bark when I reach the grass, grateful, after all these years that it still wants to help. It's a little terrifying, this memory lane, but the stream trickling along the side of the house and trees dotting the property at this late hour is a reminder of happier times. Of when my biggest worry was whether or not Mom found my whereabouts and forced me to set the table.

An occasional car coasts on Bloodcreek Road, but they're

almost inaudible because of the cicadas roaring from the tree-tops. And I breathe in deeply, basking in the pretty scent of honeysuckle.

Leo extends his hand for me, and I feel so shy I can't take it, but I do allow him to lead us round to the back of the house. We tread past the pear trees and over Dad's prized stone path. Crunch broken branches, an acorn the squirrels must have missed. Like two silent wood elves, we trudge to the back of the property, where Leo stops.

Together, we scour the stump of the old oak where we played when we were small. Where we'd hang upside down by our knees by the branches. Once, I convinced Eva to help drag over the trampoline so we could jump from the fattest branches to the tramp. We never would have had the strength to push it without Leo's help, though Eva couldn't see him.

Crouching now, Leo holds his palm on the cool, worn stump. "You have grown," he murmurs before lowering himself to the knobby ground.

I want to say something about how he's obviously matured, too, but would that be weird? I don't even know how old he is. Was he really even a child when I saw him when I was a little girl?

I lower myself to the stump as well, gnarled roots and splinters cutting into my polka dot pajama bottoms. I shift to get comfortable, and when I do, I accidentally brush the side of his leg, and I'm blushing worse than when my skirt flew up while walking past a group of seniors my first day of class.

Smelling that honeysuckle even more now, I look up at the starry sky where the moon's splicing it open like a seeded watermelon. Wind tousles my hair, and I run my tongue along the front of my teeth, wondering what I should say. *I never really forgot you, you know?*

Pulling a cigarette from his front pocket, Leo rolls it on the top of his thigh, deep in thought. How's it possible for someone to look to be in complete control while so adrift in thought? He has one of those faces where his emotions dance below the thinnest layer of surfaces. If I were to lie, tell him that I never wanted to see him again, his eyes would flash, hurt. If I were to tell him I never wanted him to leave, his face would stretch into a smile so wide, my insides would splinter. Oh, Leo, how very good it is to see you. I've missed you more than can be expressed in words.

Somehow, saying it—actually saying it—would make the spell burst.

"The autopsy theater near the city morgue." Leo's gaze matches my eyes and I have no idea what he's talking about. "In New Orleans." He rubs the cigarette between his pointer finger and thumb, a nervous habit. Does he hold these because he believes he's bad? Because he's in the same supernatural category as Knox?

It's like he's reading my mind, because he's saying, "That's when I saw Knox's true colors."

I bite the inside of my cheek, because I don't know if I want to know—his and Knox's past. Did they work together? Hurt people? Is this what became of Leo after I told him I didn't want him around?

Leo stretches out a shaky hand for my own, but I still don't think I can reciprocate. I don't know who he really is. With a soft breath, he drops his hand an inch from my knee and says, "He's still in Texas."

A rabbit hops a few meters off in the grass, finding shelter in a mound of pampas grass. It's like it, too, is spooked by this macabre topic.

"It was something like his twelfth victim," Leo says. "Lying there on that table. Arms purple and bruised. Her arms shackled, throat slit nearly to the bone."

I pull up my knees to eclipse my own throat.

"I had sort of thought it was a game," Leo admits, "following him around, making others miserable. I didn't really think about what we were *doing*. I guess I supposed I had chosen my path. But, looking at that girl—that beautiful girl who had just immigrated to the U.S. from South Africa—and seeing those lacerations all over her torso"—his bangs fall into his eyes—"I finally saw Knox for what he really was."

"You were his friend." Bile roils in my stomach.

Leo sneaks his unlit cigarette back inside his jeans' front pocket and softly says, "I am far more vile than you'll ever know."

But I've the memories of a boy who used to fold my mom's laundry, who used to steal and hide for me the brussels sprouts I couldn't ever manage to gulp down.

"That's when I started visiting you." His somber mouth stretches into a full smile. "Remember how we used to climb these branches until we nearly fell out?"

I smile even though I feel sick now, because he's revealing one of my favorite memories—how bark and leaves scraped my chin as I shimmied as high as the sun.

But that still doesn't explain why, after palling around with Knox, he decided to spend time with *me*, of all persons in the world.

"You're ready for the truth." His hand caresses my knuckles, sending a shimmer of longing at his touch. And that shimmer doesn't ease in the slightest when he murmurs, "You'll want Eva to know."

I can't sleep. Which sucks 'cause that's one of my best talents. But knowing Raylan is around is way too exciting, and when I do finally start to drift off, my subconscious decides to be mean and conjure up images of Knox and his creepy friends. Not Leo—the other ones. The female demon Darth Vaders. I'm gonna need to start joining Frost for therapy. Someday. But for now, I pull my tired butt out of bed and wander to the window. The fireflies and their sporadic glow have always been my favorite nightlight. A reminder good things will come if you just hang in there long enough.

After watching them for a moment, I feel my heart start to slow and shoulders relax when a different movement catches my eye. Someone's down there by the rosebushes. Before I can start to panic, though, the moonlight catches long blonde hair and a taller figure. Frost. Leo is with her? Moving every time she moves, like every breath she takes affects him, she is the world and he's her moon.

And dang, girl, sneaking out now? I beam with pride. He plays with her hair lightly, and I turn away, feeling like I'm intruding. I wonder if Raylan's texted? I plop on the bed again and grab my phone.

Almost immediately, it vibrates with a text message from Frost. Well, that's not the romantic moment I'd pictured for her.

meet us under the house in ten mins

Interesting. Her own little haunt. Our house was built on top of a super old house from like 1910, and you can still go in there. It's kind of creepy, especially at night, with its wicked old pot belly stove that likes to house spiders, but it is a good hideout and the sound doesn't carry into the rest of the house for our parents' supersonic ears to hear. I'm lucky I haven't been yelled at already for being awake. But first, I need to make it out of the house 'cause the old house's only door is outside.

Thanks, nightmares and Raylan, for keeping me awake. I wouldn't miss this clandestine meeting for the world. Great preparation for my future FBI days.

After five minutes that feel like five thousand, I start making my way, stepping around all the well-known loud spots on the floor. I make it downstairs, past Mom's decor of perfectly placed glass figurines and silk flowers, and even out the front door without so much as a creak. I do a victory hop and run around to the back of the house.

The heavy wooden door is already open a smidge, and the smell of ancient stucco and dirt escapes through the crack. They must be inside already. I peek my head through the door, tongue sticking out, which completely freezes when I see who else is inside—Raylan. *Eek!* I quickly switch to my cool demeanor and slink inside, closing the door behind me. The utter Queen of Cool.

Frost, Leo, and Raylan all sit around the ancient, unlit fireplace on big buckets of hard red wheat. Our family's food in case of emergencies. We're not doomsday preppers or anything, but even I can admit it's a good idea to have a little extra food on hand. Hopefully Raylan doesn't think it's too weird.

"What's up, y'all? Should we speak in code for this mysterious meeting?" I wink at Raylan, who twitches his lips in an almost smile.

Frost chuckles softly, then fidgets with her neon green socks. Which are tucked into her Crocs. Oh, Frost.

"I think we're about to get a real explanation," she says, locking eyes with me. Explanation? OH. That. Actual answers! Hoo-freaking-ray! Fashion faux paus forgiven.

"For real?" I yelp and look to the boys for confirmation.

Raylan nods, cheekbones clenched with conviction, and Leo looks like he's just accepted a fate of walking the plank or something. To my surprise, Raylan actually elaborates.

"It won't take Knox long to find us, and Maggie's refusal to work with us, leaving you in the dark, isn't helping. You need to understand what's really going on and how to avoid the Despairity so you can make your own decisions." He pounds his fist on his knee softly. I swear cartoon hearts are floating above his head. He cares. *And* he's not treating me like a little girl. We'll have to work on him liking Maggie later. But wait . . .

"The Despairity what now?" I blab, my mind now having caught up to my heart.

"Knox's posse," Raylan explains. "Those girls."

Leo rolls an unlit cigarette around in his fingers. "It's my fault." He's still looking at Frost's somber face, as always, but finally tears his eyes away and addresses all of us. His boyish face is so open, I simultaneously believe him and reject the fact that he could possibly be involved with something so awful. With a deep breath, he continues.

"Once upon a time, we all lived with God. We were spirits."

"Wait, what?" Some weird religious ghost story is not what I was expecting.

"Think of it kind of like the reverse heaven—you go to heaven after you die, and we all lived in a type of heaven before you were born." Leo rushes on, like he has to get this out before he loses the nerve.

"Then God decided to build the world. He'd make us bodies and we'd be born into them." He pushes himself to his feet and starts pacing in this too-small room. "We would live life on Earth as a kind of test, and if we passed, when we die, we could live with him again, stronger and better from the experience." He glances at Frost, then Raylan and me, whites of his eyes shining. I take it here comes the ugly part.

"But here's the thing. He said life would be really hard. Not impossible, but really hard, and He said He would only help here and there. Basically a gauntlet." He twists his foot on the dusty floor. "And if you fail, you couldn't live with Him anymore." His tone deflates more and more.

"There were a lot of spirits who thought it was unfair. One, you know him as the devil, wanted to control everything on Earth and make all the spirits behave so they could all pass the test."

Raylan grunts. "Maybe that could have been your first clue."

Leo hangs his head a little. "He started a rebellion. It was," he pauses a moment, as if reliving the past, "very ugly. But you have to understand." He drops down next to Frost, grabbing her hand, begging for her to understand. "I liked my life. It was easy. Fun. And I loved God, so I didn't want to risk failing his test." Frost gently pulls her hand away. "I chose the wrong side."

Frost nods vaguely, a sign to go on, but he doesn't continue. Just keeps searching her masked face.

"That's why he's a Blurred One." Raylan straightens on his

bucket. "These spirits who thought they knew better than God are pissed off their devil didn't get his way. They've seen how life is beautiful. How everything's richer with a body. How they chose the wrong side."

He frowns at Leo, eyes so intense I vow never to make an enemy out of him. There's more to his side of this story, and I promise myself I'll get that later. For now, I need to soak in his every word.

"Now the only thing they want is to make the other side miserable," Raylan says. "So they can feel what they feel. They go around feeding on the weak, making them weaker, and trying to make the strong weaker too."

Raylan runs his hand through his hair and leans against the cool stucco wall. "Over these thousands of years, they've lost more and more of their humanity, becoming like those creatures, the Despairity. All they are is their faded desires and despair."

"Knox is obsessed with mortal bodies," Leo says softly, slumping like a popped balloon. He looks so resigned it's hard not to pity him. "He satiates his carnal desires only for a short while by taking everything these women have in life. As if that's not enough, he has to mutilate their bodies—their gift for choosing the right, even past death."

Those women. Almost me. There's not enough air in this little room. It was bad enough thinking about him tearing apart their bodies to dispose of the crime . . . but this . . . he *enjoyed* it. Because he's jealous he doesn't have a body himself?

"I didn't know how far they were taking it," Leo says behind his hands, like they can shield him from our reaction. From the truth. "I didn't know what a monster Knox really was, but with what I am, I thought this was just my life now. Right after what happened at that morgue in New Orleans, I took off on my own." He meets my eyes. "That's when I saw the Despairity feeding on and then possessing a beautiful woman named Eva."

The room spins out of control.

"Knox had been obsessed with her," he says, "but she was smart and got away from him."

I want to puke. She almost dies but gets away from him—and I go running into his arms?

"She was so bright." Leo's soft-spoken words pound in my head. "So full of life. Much like you. So when she ran away from Knox, the Despairity set their sights on her."

I feel all their eyes, full of ridiculous pity, on me now, and he just keeps going.

"I couldn't get them to leave her alone. Withering away her spirit day after day until she couldn't remember anything good anymore. Then she killed herself."

"No!" I whimper, lip quivering. "No. It was them?" Breathe. Think this through. Frost grabs her stomach.

"That's when I first saw Frost," Leo almost whispers to her, but she won't meet his eyes. "You were the most pure creature I had seen in hundreds of years. I watched you, and after just a moment, I realized I *knew* you. We were friends before. You even tried to talk me into coming to Earth."

He's twisted almost to his knees, practically begging. "I don't know why I was so stupid. But I was and I am, and Knox eventually found out I didn't hate mortals and became furious."

Frost won't look at him. Instead she keeps looking at me and then the door, like she's deciding whether or not to bolt.

"I tried to stay away from you," Leo says, "especially after the fallout with your parents. But then I saw you there at the Alamo—" He chokes on his words and falls back down, burying his head into his arms. "He's gotten so strong. I assume it's from feeding on mortals for so long, and now, I'm no match for him. I am so, so sorry for all that I am."

"We're not going to let them hurt you." Raylan reaches for my hand and holds it firmly, and he's about the only thing that feels real right now. I've never been so grateful for anyone's touch.

Frost stands, slowly, tears cascading, and looks down at Leo, her gaze like ice. "You can leave us alone. Eva, let's go." She pulls me up and away from Raylan, and I let her.

CHAPTER 19 - FROST

I'm exhausted and tired and I've—I've had enough. I shove the heavy wooden door open like I'm escaping the jaws of hell itself. I tromp over the stone floor and over the threshold while gripping my sister's smooth elbow, because I have to leave behind the mildew and kerosene lamps. Leo is not my Leo. He made his choice. He shouldn't be here at all.

This is why the topic is forbidden by my parents. Because once you learn the truth, you can't un-know it. It's a truth no one accepts in the Bible Belt. People don't *believe* we lived before. *We're made of the dust of the earth,* Genesis tells us, so why do I feel like there's a layer of truth settling over my stomach?

When we were little, he showed me what life used to be like in heaven. Even the air was so full of light, I burst into tears at the idea of not going back right then. He showed me cherry trees perpetually in blossom. Fruit without bruise or scar. Lions that played like kittens. There, we didn't have a care in the world, but we had no possible way for progression. So, God offered for us to come down.

And Leo? He couldn't handle it all.

The eerie fact squeezes like a pair of pliers in my stomach. He went against *God*. He thought the plan was too risky? What about what Eva risked when she tried to trap Knox? And all along, he *knew* Knox wouldn't be able to help himself.

He should have stayed away. Forgotten our supposed "relationship" where we knew each other in heaven. We had to have known each other, because he used to always tell me that I was only a whisper of what I'd become.

Now, though, looking at my sister's ivory skin and chocolate hair rustling down her shoulders, all I can think of is, *Why, Leo? Why let us attempt to trap Knox when you knew Knox had a relationship with Aunt Eva?*

Eva tugs on my elbow, but all I can see are the lattices and ivy crawling up the side of our wooden house.

"Frost." Her voice is panicked. "Did you know? About Aunt Eva?"

I shake my head.

Relief floods her eyes.

"But I knew she was seduced by a Blurred One."

She bites her lip, apparently unsure of what to say.

What Eva doesn't understand is how *everything* revolving around Leo is dangerous. We shouldn't affiliate ourselves with Raylan, either, but now our lives are inextricably woven.

Knox chops up beautiful girls. For amusement. For the hundredth time, how could I go along with that trip to San Antonio and dig up what should have long stayed buried?

"Don't be mad." Eva brushes the side of my face with the back of her hand, but I'm supposed to be the one comforting *her*. I don't know whether to hug her or panic.

The door creaks open. Raylan saunters out of the storage room in his black hunting vest. He raises his eyebrows at Eva, and I raise my hands to the sky, which is bleak and black. There's no way now I can even conceivably leave this place, not when the supposed Despairity are hovering around.

If I leave, when's the next time Dad slaps her around? What time of day will it be when Knox decides to drag her back to that Bluesy Bar again?

The door creaks open again, and I glance away, because I can't face Leo. And when we lock eyes, I'm reminded of his contagious laughter when we were children. How even his translucent spirit-like hair seemed to raise from static. Last time I saw him, he was just smoke, so was that merely the shape he wanted me to see him in?

But he wasn't even really a kid. "I never want to speak to you again."

I'm not entirely sure if I mean these words, but I honestly don't know how to look at him.

His chest heaves and his face blurs like a melting snow cone. And as my eyes adjust, something that looks like miniature roaches scurries across his skin. Knox's face did that when he had Eva in that hotel room. Now I know it. The "tell" of the Blurred Ones.

Guiltily, Leo takes a step backward, to the base of a miniature redbud. "I'm not denying what I am." Pulling a wisp of white cloth from his pocket, he moves toward me, crunching leaves and grass.

Holding out his handkerchief, he tries to wipe the tears that have apparently fallen, but I can't accept that from him. Everything he does is wrong.

"You were hiding the identity of a killer." I wipe my face with the back of my hands.

"You already knew that's what he was."

"But you knew he was the Blurred One who targeted Aunt Eva!"

"I wanted to tell you, but didn't know if I should."

Dew drips from the redbud to the widow's peak on his

forehead, and the despair shining in his eyes has me wondering how many long years he's endured misery and alone-ness. Did he linger during World War II? The French Revolution? How about the formation of the pyramids?

A tendon quivers in his neck just as Eva's boot crunches grass.

Holding out an apologetic hand, she murmurs to Leo, "Maybe you should leave her alone. For a bit."

Leo takes another hesitant step toward us. "There's something I need to get off my chest."

"What?" Eva bats at a group of gnats. "That you're practically a demon?"

Raylan hovers by a row of bushes and snaps a twig. The sound is so uncomfortable that I sort of wish we were playing Monopoly and sharing sodas instead. What does he, as an experienced hunter, make of all of this? Did he know that Knox would salivate over Eva all along? Or is all of this news to him? And what about the minor detail that his best friend is a Blurred One?

The confident set of Raylan's shoulders contrasts with his somewhat lost voice when he mumbles to Leo, "Maybe you should listen to them."

Leo shakes his head once. "Just for a few moments."

He wipes my face with that handkerchief.

I'm tempted to push him away, but the gesture is sweet if not welcome. How can a boy be kind and sweet and thoughtful and still follow the devil's plan?

"Okay." Eva tromps over the patchy grass to Raylan, who wordlessly takes her hand. "Five minutes. That's it."

I don't know whether to haul my sister's cute bottom into our house or simply listen to her and get this over with. What if I react like her, and think with my hormones?

No, impossible. If history proves anything, I'm practical,

logical. And, since he chose the devil's side, I'm still furious with him.

I stalk past him, narrowly avoiding a hole in the grass, and grip the cool, metal handle of the storage room door. *"Five minutes."* My heart quivers like, from the inside, I might snap in half, but I am Frost Abram, calm and collected. The logical one.

Once inside, instead of perching on one of the wheat buckets across from me where I choose to sit, Leo hovers in the doorway like I've warded him out. Just stands there, leaning against the doorframe, and looking at me like I'm a master painting at the National Museum.

The light of the stars and moon pour in, making him a little bit beautiful and a little bit sad. I think he's about to, I don't know, pay me a compliment, when he says, "I've had four thousand years to make mistakes, Frost."

If I were Eva, I'd make a wisecrack about him being an old man, but even for Leo, who likes to crack jokes, the reply would be wrong. He wants to say something else, but instead of looking at me straight-on, he glances at one of Mom's most visited shelves—the one lined with chicken noodle soup and olives.

I don't know how I should be reacting, so I adjust my position on my wheat bucket.

"Time." Leo pulls out his cigarette. "For pre-mortals is different. We don't sleep. Instead, we hibernate, I guess." He leans against the doorframe like it's propping him up.

This isn't what he really wants to say, but I clutch my hands on my lap. *Wait, Frost.*

Only he doesn't say anything else. Instead, he absently runs his hands over the pockmarked stone walls. I almost want to comfort him the way I comforted the boy who seemed to come from a different land. But it's better—safer—to keep this space between us.

Leo scrapes his shoe, his average, no-name brown shoe over the threshold, and I can't take the awkward silence anymore, so I blabber, "Offer me one?"

Confusion flashes over his eyes until he seems to remember what I remember.

I'd found a package of cigarettes, and Leo had tried to talk me into not playing with them. But I was quickly learning that Eva was the interesting Abram sister—the one boys and adults noticed. Since I'd seen actors in my parents' movies smoking, I thought they might make me look more grown up.

The plastic handle of the bucket creaks as I stand. The floor is uneven, and my own hair tickles my neck.

Leo's eyes flicker like he's an unsure fox. His copper hair hangs over his eyes and he looks sort of angelic which is pretty funny, considering things. He says, "I promised myself that I would help you take down Knox."

Unable to help myself, I run my fingers over the cold, pockmarked stone walls where his hands just touched, knowing I shouldn't stand so close to him.

Mildew and longing toll through me as I stretch out a shaky hand and slip my fingers into the front tip of his pocket. I'm playing with fire. I shouldn't do it. But I want—need—to know how it feels—to be so near—to see, to smell, to touch him.

Pulling out the carton, I tap out one of the paper cylinders and shakily place it between my lips. Not because I wish to smoke, but because it's what we used to do. A dangerous memory with him.

Like a torch, Leo's gaze heats my forehead, and I know he's going to say what he's been struggling to say for ages. With a deep, anguished breath, he murmurs, "You are even more beautiful than I imagined."

I pull that cigarette from my lips and try to say something clever, but my thoughts spill to the floor, like quicksand.

"Like your pre-mortal spirit." He takes my hand, and I don't know what's come over me, but I let him. "Only stronger, wiser." His voice cracks. "Like you've lived through the Renaissance."

The cigarette dangles between our hands.

Maybe he can help me find a way to protect my sister against Knox. Maybe he knows how to exploit a weakness. It makes no rational sense, and I swore I wouldn't prioritize my needs over Eva's, but I want to see and know more than just the look of his expressions. I want to feel his fingers—these strong callouses on his fingers—but I also want to smell his smells. Breathe his breaths.

If it's illogical, I'll take a page from Eva for once.

So I lean in, feeling the heat and hunger of his vision. He searches the lines of my face, and I'm sure he's seeing all the scars I've earned from working outside with Dad. Once, I accidentally grazed a metal rake with my forehead. Another time, I didn't properly prune a honey locust and one of its thorns embedded in the bottom of my chin.

Despite both of these scars, Leo leans his long leg into mine, and all I have time for is a quick a breath.

Lips touch. Three times. And everything feels far more surreal than I could have imagined. Paper and nicotine wash over me in a heady scent, and when his icy eyes lock on mine, every single pin turns in my chest.

Alarm clocks are going off in my mind as he wraps his arms around me like a smooth, woolen blanket. I clutch the front of his polo and dip my fingers into his clammy flesh.

My fingers dig into his scalp. I need to get closer even if this vessel isn't his.

His mouth is smooth and warm and soft, and when we kiss, I know I shouldn't bask in it. But it's sunshine and we're whirling atop our own mountain. It's hot and freezing and it's like we've just been shot with a thousand cc's of happy gas.

I run my hands over his shoulders. Down his masculine chest. I'm about to tell him I always wanted to kiss him like this when—

The storage room door flies open.

We break apart, panting for breath.

White shirt, dark slacks. Dad.

My heart shrivels like torn up tissue paper in my chest.

If there was something I could say. Some way to make him believe we weren't kissing like we were the completeness of two smaller halves. Will he punch Leo in the face? There's no telling when it comes to Dad.

"I beg your pardon, sir," Leo says, lightly placing his hand on the small of my back, and I want him to keep touching me —need for him to keep touching me like that—but Dad's staring at his hand like he would love nothing more than to rip it off.

"You should be asleep." Dad's voice is uber-soft. "I suggest you get to bed."

It would be so much easier if he flew off the handle—if he yelled at us. This quiet talking and refusal to talk about what's really happening freaks me out worse than if he caught me stealing a wad of cash.

He'll ground me for weeks. Maybe until the very day I leave for college. He'll give me so many chores, I'll never even have time to see Leo again. I *knew* getting close to him and kissing him was, quite literally, the kiss of death.

When the wind hits my face as I follow Leo out of the storage room, though, I find that I don't even care. I'm glad it happened. Because every single nerve ending in my body is dancing a jig. And now, when I come to this storage room, I'll remember how Leo kissed me. Like he waited a couple of centuries to do that.

I walk down the long, royal blue-and-white striped high school hallway like I have every business in the world to be here. I learned a long time ago it's easiest to not get in trouble for skipping class if you simply don't act like you're doing anything wrong. Too bad it doesn't work for Dad finding us not in our rooms at 2 a.m. I'm not even going to think about what awaits us when we get home.

As for now, I *cannot* sit in trig anymore. My brain is as loaded as a two-day-old diaper, trying to piece together everything that's happened over the last couple weeks. That, and everyone's clutching onto Jenny's disappearance with greedy little fingers. Every tear is a contest of who loved her most. Who is in the most pain. No one thinks of her pain. How her bright, lovable self has been viciously stolen and snuffed out.

Then there are those who are saying she brought this on herself. Or she ran off to Vegas to be a stripper or something. Those people are lucky I don't bring weapons to school.

I head outside to the library, and the brightness from the sun on my flowy white shirt has me reaching for sunglasses that aren't on my head.

The shabby beige trailer that is our library begs for paint. Blistering, wet summers and the frigid, icy winters of Missouri take their toll on all the buildings around. I pull the metal handle of the door with one finger. It's habit from being burned so many times. Swinging the door open, I fill my lungs with the cool, musty library air. Thankfully, some rich oil dude thought to improve the station of the local Bloodcreek residents and donates constantly to the school library. It's the only source of culture in this tiny town.

I spot Mr. Harris, the librarian, shelving some books close by.

"Hey, Mr. Harris," I say with my best library-whisper speak. He looks at me through his coke-bottle glasses. Beige shirt, gray-blond disheveled hair, it's like his very body is being claimed by the walls.

"Can I help you?" he rasps. I come here pretty often, but he never seems to remember me. I'm lucky enough he never remembers to ask for a library pass. I try to be extra friendly to him—I imagine my fellow students love to pick on the man's hazy appearance.

"Yes, sir. I am doing a research paper on some supernatural stuff. Do we have any books on that?"

He blinks for a moment, presumably accessing his internal catalog. I've looked before, but maybe he'll show me something new.

"We do. We have a few. Over here," he says, and drops the books he was shelving onto a metal cart with a loud clang. He shuffles along, every movement deliberate and slow, and finally stops a couple of aisles over.

I wonder if he's single. Maybe he and widowed Mrs. Sanders could hit it off with a little push? As long as she didn't start anything long-term with that guitar player.

"The parents won't allow anything very in-depth. Don't want the kids messing with any witchcraft. But here's the section." He pats the books like they're little puppies in a pet store, breathing heavily like even the ten steps over here took too much life out of him. Guy has *got* to get out.

But he wasn't kidding. A meager ten, maybe fifteen books grace the section.

"No more? Maybe a secret stash in the back?" I wink at him, exaggerated in case he needs me to be kidding. He just cough-slash-grunts and stares back at the section.

"Thanks, Mr. Harris." I scoop up the books and nudge him playfully with my elbow. He immediately turns beet red, pushes his glasses back up his nose, and stumbles back to his task. Poor guy.

A muffled chuckle resonates from behind the shelf. I duck to see between the books at my audience. Oh holy moly as I live and breathe, sitting at the nearest study table is all six glorious-leather-jacket-clad feet of Raylan Wilks. I immediately straighten and check my clothes, hair, and makeup as best I can with one arm while balancing the books in my other and dart around the end of the aisle.

"What? And what are you doing here?" I run two questions together like it's one sentence.

"Is any man safe around you?" he says with a quirked eyebrow.

"Mr. Harris? Oh please." But it don't hurt for Raylan to see me as desirable, so I won't argue too much. He's got his own couple of books and is working on a scratched up laptop computer. His dark jeans and gray shirt under his jacket are a little rumpled today, and he's got some serious scruff going on. Looks like I'm not the only one feeling a tad overwhelmed, but I doubt it looks as good on me as it does him.

"You'd flirt with the Pope if you met him, wouldn't you?" He leans forward conspiratorially, chair squeaking, and I can see the redness in his eyes.

"Who says I haven't?" I wink, much more flirtatious this time. "But I have no idea what you're talking about."

I slide into the chair diagonal from him. It takes some restraint not to sit right next to him, but I don't want to be presumptuous. This is about as "hard to get" as I can muster with this one. I spread my haul across my side of the big oak table. Now he can see how nonchalantly academic I am. "So. What are you doing?" I ask through raised eyebrows, and he slumps back into his wooden chair and looks back to his computer screen, face flattening to the deadpan expression he wears by default. Like he's terribly bored or about to fall asleep.

"Looking for some objectivity." He pounds a few keys on his keyboard. "And there's nowhere else within fifty miles with Wi-Fi. Your Mr. Harris said the public's welcome as long as he doesn't have a class." The only time he looks at me is when he says "Mr. Harris." Where is a Magic 8 ball for this dude?

"Cool," I answer, ever eloquent. "I wanted to see what else I could learn, since y'all are dropping these truth bombs lately." I grab the book closest to me. *Ghost Chasers Chase Ghosts: An Expert's Guide to Chasing Ghosts.* Has promise." I'm rewarded by a little chuckle, a little bit high pitched for a guy his size, and it is adorable. No way he knows how hot that is.

"You already know about ghosts, though."

"Well, I have a filtered knowledge, apparently. And Frost needs some help being objective." My stomach twinges. She is in such a bad way between not knowing what to do with Leo and being in deep crap with Dad. At least she got some action. Go Frost! "Hopefully there are some good ones in here. How about you? Any luck?"

"Not yet. It's hard when you don't even know what you're looking for. I just want to make sure I'm not missing something important." He looks down at nothing, his dark brows pinching together. Always more on his mind than he says, so I take a guess.

"Yeah, Leo hasn't exactly been Mr. Honesty lately, huh?" I have so many questions for him, but it's so hard to concentrate when my mind is still catching up on the fact that I'm talking to Raylan. Here. At my school. And he hasn't said anything back. Is he offended? Holy crap, stop over-analyzing. Breathe. Focus. Just enjoy having him somewhat captive. I grab a dark blue book from a stack near me. We can be two sexy scholars, falling in love over books.

"Let's give this a try." I skim the first few pages. Raylan's face softens, and he turns his attention back to his computer. The only sounds are the pages of my book and the faint sliding of books from Mr. Harris by the door, which I doubt he will move away from as long as I'm here.

This book is about voodoo and magic around New Orleans, filled with pictures of potions and dolls and haunted houses. Always creepy, but it's really hard to concentrate this close to Raylan. I do my best, and we sit awhile in comfortable silence. I feel at this moment, with Raylan, the quiet, and the smell of musty pages, everything could turn out okay.

The bell rings, but no way am I leaving. Besides, Spanish is next, my class with Jenny and the last period of the day. And I've definitely had enough of Mrs. Sanders to last a lifetime. I also don't need any other girls showing up and trying to get their hooks in Raylan. I turn the page and start "reading" about famous witch doctors. Raylan, whom I have definitely *not* been watching out of the corner of my eye, reaches into his canvas bag beside his chair and pulls out a worn leather book.

"If you want to check this out, here are my notes from different things we've hunted."

My jaw drops in elation.

"Get out. Heck yes, I do." I snatch it, ready to devour the

information he has personally discovered. I gingerly flip through the first few pages, every bit as careful as if this were the Dead Sea Scrolls. Every couple of pages, he's drawn the creature he came across. He's a surprisingly good artist, even with just a pencil in a journal. Our babies would be budding Picassos.

"Dude, that's a vampire, right?" I angle the book down so he can see what I'm looking at. A crazy ugly woman with two giant, razor sharp fangs. Exactly how Maggie described them.

"Yep. My first one." He turns back to his screen. No one could ever call him chatty, but I could swear I feel his eyes on me when I turn back to his journal.

After the vampire is a werewolf, looking super hairy, drooly, and like I would never want to meet one in a dark alley. Those claws. Then a banshee, jinn, shape-shifter, and a bunch I've never heard of. There's space after each monster, which he's filled in with when he met more of that kind. Everything is neat and organized. Like an anthropologist notating people or creatures and their habits.

"You should be an archeologist or something. You're awesome at these notes, and you totally have the Indiana Jones vibe down." I nod toward his leather jacket. "If I were a hunter and had a journal, it would be a hot mess."

Although he doesn't reply, his brows pinch together and his typing stops, like he's actually considering the possibility.

The amount of creatures in the journal is astounding. Each entry is numbered, so I flip to the last one.

"Forty different monsters? I only know like ten. How long have you been doing this?" I try to keep my voice down, remembering the library, but my curiosity is exploding.

Raylan's eyes hold onto his screen, then drift down to his keyboard. He must know I'm not going to let him do any more research. He closes his computer and turns his whole body a little toward me, arms resting on the table.

"Three years. We keep busy," he says with a dip of the head. He doesn't elaborate, but his eyes are still trained on mine. My mouth goes a little dry, but I venture on.

"So, you were sixteen? What got you into this? Where is your family?"

Raylan doesn't respond right away. For a long moment he just looks at me. Then, like in the elevator back in the Gunter, he decides to let me in a little. In his calm, little bit hoarse, quiet voice, he speaks to me like I'm the only person in the universe.

"My parents died. They both used drugs for fun, and then my dad got hooked. He killed my mom because she confronted him about it, and then himself. Leo was there. I think some spirits helped drive my dad to do it, but I'm not sure. Leo tried to keep it from happening, but . . ." He taps one thumb on the table, then rubs the back of his neck and continues. "Maybe it was the Despairity. My sister, Tessa, was already in college in Florida, so Leo knew I was alone, and he decided we should be alone together." He straightens a little in his chair. "If I had stayed, I would have ended up going down the same road as my parents, so we started hunting. It gave me something to focus my anger on and not become a target or a user myself. I left everything behind for a clean start."

His words are measured. Never saying more than he has to, never showing more emotion than his vulnerable eyes or the sudden tightness in his cheeks betray. The way he speaks is like a lullaby, and if his story weren't so sad, I could listen to it night after night. My throat tightens at the thought of the pain he must carry. How many people has he told about his parents?

"I'm so sorry. I'm glad you have Leo, then."

He only nods. I yearn to reach over and grab his hand—

comfort him—but I don't want to take advantage, and it might be awkward on the table. I settle for a question.

"Did you know about Frost?"

"No." His eyes darken a bit, no doubt thinking about what other secrets Leo has kept. Feeling brave at his honesty, I bite my lip and ask the most delicate, troubling question.

"Is he dangerous?"

A flash in his eyes. A moment of doubt.

"No. He really loves her. Like, writing-love-sonnets-in-the-shower loves her."

He bobs a shoulder, and my heart stops for a long second. What on earth has my sister gotten herself into? This is all getting a little bit too real.

"But, like, he doesn't have a body, so he's just possessing someone right now? How is that not dangerous?" I'm trying to grasp this whole concept, but now I'm seeing our past through a different lens. I've only gotten some of the story from Frost, but it's from her perspective as a little girl and she's defensive of him, so it's hard to truly understand.

"He has someone as a vessel, yes. But he wouldn't do it if the guy wasn't half dead already and didn't deserve it. And the vessel looks amazingly like his spirit self. Like it was meant to be." He glances toward Mr. Harris, making sure we're still alone, and leans toward me again.

"Blurred Ones want two things: to have a body, and to make people with bodies miserable. Knox is rotten in the true sense of the word. His soul and vessel are rotting. Vessels only last so long. Maybe he'll become like the Despairity, eventually. They are a whole other league."

I bury my face in my hands for a moment, trying to process, and I can't think clearly while looking at him.

"Well, I want to help figure this out. Seems like we all have something pretty big to lose. You know, love, limbs, *lives.*

How can I make myself useful?" I pretend that Leo's tidbit about Knox's obsession with Aunt Eva doesn't freak me out.

"How about you just stay out of trouble for now?"

Mr. Harris emerges from the book aisles and, avoiding all eye contact, nearly sprints to his desk. School must be almost over.

"I'll try," I say dryly, and I hand him his journal back. "Thanks for letting me read this. Could I look at it more later?" I know better than dare ask to borrow something so valuable. "'Cause like they say, 'just because you're paranoid doesn't mean they're not out to get you.'"

"Right." He carefully puts it back in his bag, then files his computer behind it, but his lips are slightly parted in what I think I'm learning is a smile. "Want to go get a soda? I need some caffeine."

"Heck yes!" Then I remember if I'm more than two minutes late getting home, I'll be grounded for another month. "Um, but we gotta be fast. And drink it in the truck before I get home." He quirks his brow at me again. "Hey, don't hate the playa, hate the game warden."

Knox be darned. This may be the best day of my life.

CHAPTER 21 - FROST

I stare at the college acceptance letter in my hand. I've waited for this day for so long, and now I'm not entirely sure what to do with it. The thin sheet of paper with itty bitty typed letters says I've just been accepted to the University of Texas. But now, all I know is Leo's kiss still blooms across my cheek. My mind's somehow drifted very far away away from college. I want to go, but how am I to face reality when I can't leave Eva and I'm obsessed with a Blurred One?

Leo's kiss—it still singes my tongue. Like hot cocoa laced with something unearthly. He isn't evil. He made a wrong choice, true, but he's trying to make the most of what he chose. He hinted at a past—with Knox. They had enough of a relationship for Leo to find him in that autopsy theater in New Orleans, but now he wants to help us take Knox down.

I didn't want to look earlier, but on the bottom of that teacup he gave me, he'd written his initials and mine. We were little when he first gave it to me, so I didn't think it romantic. Merely knew that he was cementing our friendship. He must have taken it with him when I was a kid, after I was released from the hospital and refused to see him. Now I want to look at that teacup again just to see our initials.

Gravel crunches under my Converses as I make my way from the mailbox and bus stop. A few of my classmates kept pestering me to share my notes with them, but I couldn't pay attention in Calculus. All I could think about over and over was how Leo said I was beautiful, *beautiful,* not to mention the feeling of his fevered skin under my fingers. And now? I've gotten my college acceptance.

Is it weird to think, maybe, Leo could visit me in Austin?

As I ease open the front door, I try to slip inside without anyone hearing me come in. Last thing I need is the third degree about why I checked the mail without handing it over to Dad first, or why Eva isn't with with me now.

She had better get here soon. I'm already starting to feel nervous, though she probably just got a ride home from a friend. I could text her, but she probably has her phone on silent, knowing Eva.

Beyond that, I still haven't seen Dad since he caught me with Leo. Maybe Leo knows how to inflict amnesia.

When I step into the house, I surreptitiously wipe my feet on the entry mat. Mom's Hummel figurines and plastic flowers greet me just as they always have, and I carefully step around the shoe-horn Dad always uses to pull his work shoes on.

A pair of low voices wafts from the kitchen, so I sneak over the newly vacuumed carpet to listen to what's going on.

"I wanted to believe that she gave him up." Pain comes from my dad's fiercely whispered voice as he sets down something heavy, which *clings* on the counter as if it were metal.

"I am sorry he's followed you to your own home," Maggie agrees in her low tone.

The faucet splashes in the sink—probably Dad washing

his hands. A paper towel rips from a seam as he adds, "I need you to take care of it."

Maggie chuckles long. Low. "You know I'll always have yours and the girls' backs."

I hate that they feel the need to conspire like this. Like Leo and I are the enemy, but if they ever knew him, they'd know he doesn't wish us harm. If anything, he wishes to *protect* Eva and me from Knox and everything else.

Scuffing sounds on the tile. It's Dad's slippers approaching where I stand on one of Mom's favorite maroon rugs, and I'm tempted to spring upstairs and look at that teacup before they give me the third degree, just to find a bit of comfort. But that would just be prolonging the inevitable. Plus, I've my college acceptance letter in my hands.

Dad rounds the corner in his white button up shirt and slacks, and, of all things, he's holding a shotgun.

Not that that's a rare sight for Dad, but it's not exactly the mental image a girl hopes to see of her father when she's ready to announce her future and, er, maybe re-introduce her boyfriend.

Of course, typically Dad only ever shoots targets. Once, when I asked him why he never actually hunts, he admitted that he'd killed too many animals when he was young, so he didn't feel good about hunting now. That, and his focus was more on raising me and Eva.

I gaze into his narrowed eyes. *Dangerous.* Usually, he keeps his guns hidden behind doors and couches, but he's holding this long, black barrel like he's waited long enough.

His eyes falter to the paper in my hands. "What is that?"

I hold out the paper. "I've been accepted to the University of Texas, Dad."

In his brown-green eyes, a handful of emotions seem to clash. *She read the mail without giving it to me first? My baby girl was accepted to college. She kissed Leo. We have more important worries now.*

I'm not entirely sure which emotion he'll settle on, so I try to help guide the direction. "Looks like I'll be moving to Austin."

Dad scans the room like he's not entirely sure we're alone right now. Like college is the last thing he can think of at the moment, and I'm not really sure I can accept it, either. Can I really go when nothing's resolved?

"Where's Eva?"

I adjust the paper and envelope in my hands. "She should be home soon." I avoid eye contact. "She missed the bus."

Stepping to the window, Dad peers around Mom's sheer curtain. "Probably getting a ride from one of those filthy boys."

Does he mean Raylan or Leo or the kids from class?

Feeling like my movements are a little too loud, I pull off my shoes while still holding my letter in one hand. So is he not going to comment on my plans? I've worked my entire life to achieve this moment, to progress, and it's like all he has is tunnel vision.

Marching into the living room, Maggie joins us with a pair of forty caliber pistols in her hands. She scans the cuckoo clock, then the doilies decorating the piano like Eva could be hiding under one of those instead. Settling her usually playful gaze on me, she gestures to my backpack. "Still got your salt spray?"

I nod.

"Where's your sister?" she says, her voice dangerously low. "Frost?"

"I'm sure she's coming!" In my hands, the laces of my shoes flop.

Dad paces in front of the window now. But it's not like

this is the first time Eva hasn't ridden home with me. Jenny used to give her a ride home sometimes.

Scuffing comes from the hallway—on the elongated rugs and carpet. I think I might hear a low *buhhrtung*—the Despairity? They've come?—as Dad's knuckles tighten round his shotgun. Mom, her white-blonde hair waffling in a little bob, scoots in.

She's put on a new outfit, black with slimming lines, and her coiffed hair is similar to the ghost woman's.

"Oh, honey. I'm glad you're home." She wraps her arms around me, and I breathe in her scent of rice cakes and sweet pea lotion. How worried has she been? She raised her sister, Aunt Eva, like a daughter and now, I realize with guilt, Eva and I've brought another Blurred One to our home.

Taking in Maggie and Dad all loaded up with weapons, Mom doesn't bat an eye—she's far too familiar with Dad's gun collection to do that—but the tightness around her mouth tells me she'll never be fond of the practice.

Straightening a crinkled doily on the piano, she asks, "Have you set the table?" She's asking me, and she's obviously decided not to join in on Dad's and Maggie's panic.

Relieved for the escape route, I say, "I'll do that now." I shoot Mom a grateful smile, scampering past Maggie and Dad, and I stop just before I can put my shoes in their cubby. "I got accepted to UT!" I hold out my paper, hoping for at least a smile from Mom now.

Mom whoops. "That is wonderful news, Frost!"

Pure joy washes her face, and it's like Dad and Maggie realize how they've butchered their own congratulations. Maggie holsters her pistols and wraps me in her paisley-shirted arms.

"I'm sorry." She holds me so close I can smell the gun oil. "This is cause for celebration."

Dad nods, but it's obvious he's not ready to let go of ruling the roost of his house.

When the front porch creaks outside, Dad's fingers tighten around the barrel of his shotgun.

It's Eva. They have to believe that. And I'm sure they believe she's with Leo and Raylan.

Mom pretends she doesn't see their panic, though, and scoots toward the door like she's merely expecting an ice cream delivery from the Schwann man.

Swinging the door open, she reveals a pair of masculine figures and a dark-eyed beauty—Eva. Dark circles rim Leo's eyes and his blond bangs hang in his eyes, and I try everything in my power not to blush when we make eye contact. He and Raylan are either very brave for showing up like this now, or very stupid. Taking down Knox—forming a plan—must trump any uneasiness or personal embarrassment.

You doing okay? he seems to say, and I hold out my paper.

"I got accepted to college!"

Raylan, standing in the middle of the group, actually cracks open a smile. "That's great, Frost."

I sort of want to hug him for that, and Leo's looking at me with the softest expression. Eva grins like a fool as Dad mutters, "You didn't ride the bus."

Eva's grin stretches fiercer as if she seems to decide it's time to be brave enough for all four of us.

In an uncharacteristically authoritative move, Mom grasps the doorframe, blocking Dad. "Girls, won't you introduce me to your friends?"

Maggie's—or Dad's—breath behind me hitches, but Mom, who typically goes along with whatever Dad says, is being hospitable this time around. Maybe she remembers all too well that a strict approach never worked with Aunt Eva?

Removing her hand from the doorframe, she very carefully folds her hands together like she's the queen of Buckingham Palace.

Sensing the change in mood, Raylan stretches out a hand. "Raylan Wilks, ma'am."

Following Raylan's cue, Leo begins to raise a hand, and I'm reminded of the first time he shook *my* hand, at the foot of the barn, offering to help me pick up nails in a field Dad had wanted cleaned up. But now Dad and Maggie are stepping up on either side of Mom, and it's not a friendly movement.

It's a little surreal how much moods can shift. I still have that thin college acceptance letter in my hands—I'll be living on my own if all goes to plan—but here we are. Standing on my front porch, a hum of crickets in the background, walking on eggshells. Because of Leo. And Knox. And my own selfish plans.

As I wrack my brain for the right words, Eva bounces on the balls of her feet, causing the wooden porch to groan. "I thought Leo and Raylan could eat with us."

Dad and Maggie eye each other warily like they're more likely to open up fire when Mom offers her most hospitable smile. "That's a great idea, sweetheart."

Dad stands there, blocking their path, and I know he's holding that shotgun *because* he loves us. He loves comedies but craves deep discussions. He loves his family—once hid sweet tarts all over the house, claiming the Easter Bunny pooped all over. He's unpredictable. One of the most controlling fathers I know, but I know that, more than anything, he loves us.

Not one to tiptoe around the elephant in the room, Maggie huffs. "What do you boys want?"

Raylan scratches the back of his head, emphasizing his cowlick.

About as formal as if he's actually speaking to the queen

in Buckingham Palace, Leo says, "We'd like to offer our services."

Maggie cocks one of the pistols in her hand as Dad steps up to Mom in mock amusement.

"They mean to offer their services." He whisper-laughs.

Leo's face twinges with embarrassment, but he squares his shoulders again. He looks impossibly old and far too young.

Raylan stretches out a hand. "Sir, we only ask for you to give us a chance."

Maggie growls, "You can go back to where you came from!"

But Raylan faces Maggie like he knows he won't back down. "Leo only wants the best for Frost."

Dad's lips curl into a smile as he talk-whispers, "Is that what he told you before he possessed that boy he's in?" Maggie must have confirmed what he really is.

All eyes find Leo now, and a muscle's working in his jaw. His jaw that brushed against mine when we were in that storage room.

"Put those away." Mom nods at Maggie's pistols and Dad's shotgun. "Invite the boys inside—unless you want a repeat of last time."

Dad grits his teeth, and Maggie plops one of her pistols into my hands with a look like she expects me to use it.

CHAPTER 22 - EVA

This is the most awkward dinner in the history of ever. Mom keeps talking about Raylan's muscles. Frost keeps fidgeting with the pistol on her lap till Dad tells her to stick it on the ground. And, of course, she keeps looking between Dad and Leo like a shootout will come at high noon.

Maggie's unusually quiet, and Raylan continuously stirs his soup and dodges highly personal questions from my mother. Kill. Me. Now. Time to change the paradigm.

I slurp my cream of mushroom soup as loudly as I can so Dad instantly shoots me the look of death. But at least his eyes are off Leo, whose shoulders relax just a little.

"Good soup, Mom," I say loudly. Or it just seems loud because it's been so quiet. "And congrats, Frosty. I knew you could do it."

"My wife sure knows how to open a can and put it in the microwave," Dad adds, looking at Raylan with a small smile, as if waiting for him to laugh. My stomach squeezes, but I hold my tongue. Mom explained to me when I was like ten that he lashes out to make himself feel better, so I should just play along and try to make him happy. Easier said than done, but it keeps me from throwing my food in his face.

"It's good," I say, a little quieter. "Could you please pass the toast, Mags?"

Mom, never one to show her hurt in front of others, maintains the poise of a Southern woman, and in a move that makes me want to silently applaud, turns to Leo and asks, "So, Leo, what are you studying? Frost wants to be a doctor. She's got all the brains."

"I'm not currently enrolled in classes, but I do find anatomy fascinating," Leo says, and Raylan chokes on his soup. Dad and Maggie shoot eye daggers at Leo, and I think Leo and Frost realize at the same time what he said, both blushing. Note to self, Blurred Ones can blush!

A single bark of laughter escapes me, so I cough to try to cover it up. Dad, who hates coughing, turns his attention back to me, and everyone resumes eating.

The only sound is spoons scraping bowls and each dinner guest trying to slurp as quietly as possible. I need a chainsaw to cut this tension.

"Well, Raylan and I are thinking about getting married!" I announce, smiling ear to ear, lifting my glass for a toast. Raylan gives up and puts his soup spoon down, while everyone else stares at me. Hopefully he is starting to get used to my methods and doesn't think I'm just delusional.

"You know," I add. "In like thirty years. He just doesn't know it yet." I wink at Raylan. I know Dad will be annoyed, but I've got to buy time for Leo to start making a good impression before he finds himself on the wrong end of a shotgun.

"You gotta get married before you get real fat," Dad says, reaching over and squeezing my arm playfully as if he just made a cute joke.

I can't look at anyone. Especially not Raylan, who may or

may not already think I'm fat. I force myself to stay in my chair and not run out of the room. Instead, I stir the soup with my free hand and stare at the tiny chunks of mushrooms as if they can stop the tears from falling. The little bird in the cuckoo clock screeches to the silent room.

I don't blame them. Mom, Maggie, and Frost all know to fight back only makes it worse, so I don't blame them for keeping quiet. Like the time Mom argued with Dad to let us use his computer for school and we ended up grounded from all electronics for two weeks.

"She certainly is beautiful, isn't she?" Raylan says. Shocked, I risk a glimpse up and am rewarded with his devastating half-smile. Um, was I kidding that we should get married? He could have pulled out a stick of lit dynamite for the reaction in the room. All eyes dart to Dad's, who can't argue with Raylan's look of utter earnestness, so he gives a quick laugh.

Mom sings an "Ooooo!" and I think Maggie and Frost say something nice, but I'm busy peeling my heart off the ceiling.

Dad lets go of my arm, and I feel a tiny twist in my chest. He's hurt they didn't join in on his joke. I wrack my brain for something to say to bridge the gap. Something so this exchange doesn't have to tie over to another time. Gato meows at our feet and Dad leans over, stroking him softly. Pushing himself away from the table, Dad gathers Gato in his arms.

"Hey, Mags," he says, giving our kitty a sweet hug, then letting him go. "I got some neat flicks to show you downstairs." He strides the dark green carpet, out of the room. He'll view this as mutiny and I will pay for this later. But, Raylan said I'm beautiful.

"Well." Maggie drums her fingers on the table. "I guess that's me." She pushes off the table and, before leaving, locks eyes with me for just a second. It's enough to know she *sees* me and knows how I feel.

Seizing the opportunity to end dinner, Leo daintily wipes his lips with a paper napkin and stands. He looks at Frost again. Every time he looks at her, it seems like he's trying to memorize her. As if it's for the last time.

"Ma'am," Leo says, giving a tiny bow to Mom. "We appreciate your hospitality, but we must be going. We look forward to seeing you again."

As much as I would love them to stay, we need to do some damage control.

Raylan reaches across the table and takes Mom's hand, and with the impeccable manners of a true Southern gentleman, says, "Mrs. Abram, thank you for dinner."

"You are welcome in my home." There's a firm line I'm not used to seeing on Mom's mouth, and my heart warms toward her even more.

Raylan nods once before letting go, and the boys stride for the door. But before damage-controlling Dad, I need to do a little with Raylan. I look to Mom, silently asking for permission.

She nods, and Frost and I jump up, give her a peck on each cheek, and scramble to follow the boys.

Leo and Raylan are already rushing through the front door and scrambling down the porch's front steps. Leo knows how conversing with Dad takes a little bolstering of one's defenses. Dad's gotten into such a habit of negativity, he spreads it all around. But, no matter how damaging, it's his way of being there in the room with you. His way of being present.

It's as unhealthy as anything I know, but, just as Maggie so aptly points out, at least we *have* a dad. When she was just a toddler, hers took off.

We chase the boys past Dad's minutely stacked firewood, and Leo pauses at our chopped oak—our sad little stump—before trailing after Raylan, who's just reached his truck.

I have this feeling in my stomach like the time I ate a whole pizza just to show Eva I could keep up. There's no way they can understand Dad's behavior. Dad may be difficult, but a dozen or so psychology books later, Mom, Eva, and I understand he's the result of a horrible bringing-up.

"Don't go," I say, not really knowing how to convince them to stop. Maybe Maggie will get Dad talking about the latest *Guns and Ammo* magazine to cheer him up. By the time he comes upstairs, he'll be all pleasant.

Gato leaps from a cusp of trees. Spotting Leo, he stops in his tracks. I expect my orange tabby to get all puffy, arch his back, but instead, he pads his way toward Leo and rubs his head on Leo's leg.

Leo stoops down and scratches behind Gato's ear as my kitty purrs and looks up at this human in the crooked way he always does.

It's as if my cat's saying, *It's you?* People say cats are more sensitive to spirits, that the veil's a little thinner for them, so maybe he remembers Leo. He was only a couple of months old when Leo left.

Smiling at Gato's greeting and tickling my kitty on the stomach, Leo asks, "How long has your dad been acting like this?"

Eva and I glance at each other as she cocks an eyebrow. *His entire life?* she seems to ask. *How should we play this one off?*

Raylan climbs up into his gunmetal-gray truck bed and methodically opens his lockbox. He's obviously up to something, so I expect him to explain what, but the guy's words are far and few between. When he sifts through a pair of swords and a number of guns and potions, a lighter clatters out. I wonder if they've hunted the same monsters Maggie has. The scratches on his truck tells me they've faced a few wars of their own. Have they met any ghouls? I always thought facing off with those corpse-eating creatures would be nuts.

Still, I can't help thinking that they've gone a little too fast into panic-mode. Dad was cruel to Eva, but he hasn't threatened to take me to the mental hospital—probably since Leo is here. In the flesh. Even Gato's still nudging Leo's ankle with the crown of his head. The kitty's in the mood for cuddling. Something we all could use more of.

I glance to Eva to see if she has any ideas for convincing them to slow down, but she's too busy tying knots in her hair and yelping when she pulls a little too hard.

Raylan announces, "Knox is possessing your dad." He grabs a meaty-sized pistol and stuffs it in the back of his pants.

Eva's jaw drops like half her face is a forklift. "Wait—no." She waves her bejeweled hand. "Absolutely not. Dad's just—he's always like that."

Leo tries to meet my gaze a little too eagerly. "He thinks we don't know it's him."

"He just needs more yoga," I try to explain. "You guys don't understand. He's always . . . like that."

Leo and Raylan exchange looks like Eva and I both need to be locked up, and Gato leaps toward a grasshopper bouncing around the holly bushes, allowing Leo to awkwardly step toward me.

"Does he always feel the need to clean so many weapons?" He sounds far too formal. Like I'm the demon now.

"Well." Eva unloops one of her hair's knots. "Sometimes, I guess. It's just 'cause y'all are here."

Leo watches the stump where we used to play, climbing the splintery trunk and stuffing acorns into our pockets. Leaves from the nearby sycamore skitter along the lawn, and a squirrel disappears around our pile of wood. When Leo finally opens his mouth to say something, I think he's going to explain Knox's master plan—why he's so obsessed with both Evas—when, as if in a flash of guilt, he looks down.

I turn from the boy I wish didn't always fall for and find Dad.

Like a specter from the second story window, he's watching us. A black shadow of pain and gloom looking down. And I can't help it—I know he's just being a concerned father, but my arms shiver as the breeze picks up. I tuck a piece of corn-colored hair behind my ear and rub the backs of my arms to flatten the goosebumps. "You don't understand," I muster. "He's just watching out for us."

Pain ebbs in Leo's eyes as he clenches his jaw. "You are being blind, Frost."

Eva mutters something about making him blind in a minute.

Leo doesn't know my father. Dad comes from a different world than him. Dad grew up in an era when children were meant to be seen, not heard. He and Mom, in their late fifties, are older than most parents. Plus, and I know they've never been able to forgive themselves for this, when Aunt Eva died, she was on *their* watch.

Sometimes, I see Mom gazing at a framed picture of her sister she keeps hidden in her trunk. Ebony hair, just like Eva's. A smile to woo any man.

"Listen," Leo eventually says. "Knox and I—" He digs his fingers into his longish hair before admitting, "—we talked." He pulls his cigarette out of his back pocket and toys with it between his fingers.

"What aren't you telling us?" I ask.

But Leo only agitatedly scratches his head while still holding that cigarette. "You still have your vials of holy water?"

Eva and I bobble-head nod.

"If you dump it on him all at once," he explains, "it will exorcise him for a bit."

"Leo-nardo," Raylan growls. "What aren't you telling us?"

Leo grips the back of his head with this pent up frustration, which is so very not like the boy I remember. He was always laughing. Sticking pebbles in my juice that weren't really pebbles, but jewels from some other land.

"I've got to go," he says.

I reach for his hand. Where does he think he needs to go

so fast? But he dodges my eye contact and doesn't so much as say goodbye as he sprints for the forest.

*E*va and I huddle together on her bed amidst a sea of brightly colored throw pillows. Square ones, rectangular ones, smelling not so faintly of Mom's fabric softener. I'm amazed Eva was able to work her hoodoo on Mom and Dad to buy them all.

Her walnut end table's covered with a slew of tattered books I recognize as the entire supernatural collection from our school library. We should be sleeping, but all I can think of is how Leo obviously knows something else about Knox but won't tell us. It still makes me feel like roaches are crawling all over my skin—the idea that Knox has set his sights on Eva all because she's just like our aunt. What else is Leo not saying? Does he know Knox's plan?

If he knew something and believed we needed to know it, he would tell us. Or does he think we need to learn it for ourselves?

I lift the top musty volume to read one of the titles. *Ghost Chasers Chase Ghosts: An Expert's Guide to Chasing Ghosts.* "Nice."

There's a green one and a yellow one with faded lettering, and I'm about to check them out when Eva murmurs, "You won't find anything." She lets out a dramatic yawn. "And what is that humming sound?"

I listen for a moment and let *Ghost Chasers* fall back on the others on the stack. "Uh, water heater?" I say, while simultaneously hoping it's not the Despairity hovering somewhere outside the house. Good thing all doors have sigils. There's no way they can get in.

I fall back onto my pillow, wishing for the millionth time

that I'd fallen for a boy who could go with me to college. This whole Blurred Ones thing can really put a damper on a relationship.

But Leo isn't evil or corrupt. Not like Knox. He tried helping me cheer up Dad *all the time* when we were small. Once, Leo swept out the barn for me when my seven-year-old arms couldn't sweep well enough.

Another time, Leo helped me paint the garden vegetables sign Dad told me to write. He started to tell me that all of the words were misspelled—Peeches, Q-cumbers, Zookeene, and Sqwash—but he stopped himself because he didn't want me to feel bad.

The fact is, Leo will share what we need to know, and he knows Dad has mood swings, that he's cutting and stern, so why's he so convinced that Knox has taken over Dad? I want to protect Eva more than even him, more than anybody else. But last thing we need to do is bring a full assault on Dad, who could forbid our contact with the boys at any time.

I grab a particularly squishy purple throw pillow and hug it to my chest. "They're overreacting, right?" Whatever Leo's deep dark secret, it's not worth fretting over, right?

Eva grabs her own throw pillow—an orange one with neon pink sequins. "Of course they are." But her voice is still louder than normal, telling me she's also freaked out.

"If the Despairity tried to get to Dad, he would have filled them with rock salt. Besides, Knox wouldn't possess Dad's body. He's far too outdated for him."

"Knox does like to control," Eva muses, staring where the ceiling comes to a point. But she doesn't add what I'm secretly thinking.

Why did Leo run off?

Maybe he has contacts who can help us take down Knox?

I imagine what must be going round and round in Eva's mind.

How she and Knox made out in our hotel room. Kissed in the elevator, and then in the hall. Leo just about went through the roof when he saw how good my sister was at luring him. There's some specific reason why Knox likes both Evas. What is it?

"Oh, I never told you." Eva toys with the sequins on her pillow. "The boys took care of C.A.R."

"Claire?"

"Whatever. She was buried in that cement outside our building. They got a jackhammer, dug up the cement, and burned the bones. Ghost lady will just have to find peace when we vanquish Knox."

"When did you learn this?"

"On the way home from school. Raylan explained."

"Maybe we should arm ourselves," I mutter.

"Like overboard," she agrees. "Like Maggie does."

"She was unusually quiet at dinner tonight."

"Maybe worried Knox is in Dad?"

I hug Eva's down comforter closer, glad that I've decided to stay in Eva's room tonight.

"No. If she was, she would have told us." She pauses a beat, oddly unsure of herself. "Why'd you never tell me Aunt Eva died because of a Blurred One?"

My heart plummets. "I was trying to protect you."

"From what?" There's a warning, a danger in her voice, so I do my best to explain as diplomatically as I can.

"I was worried you'd take it as a sign that you were destined to become like Aunt Eva."

"What, because I'm evil? Worthless?"

I try not to be offended that she thinks I could ever believe that. "You know you're not."

"But you kept that from me. How could you not tell me, Frost?"

"Because you are *far* better a person than anyone I know. I didn't need you to question your worth, Eva. I love you too much."

Her voice softens just a smidge as she clutches her comforter to her neck. "You should have told me."

"I know."

CHAPTER 24 - EVA

So yeah, things have been rough since being home. Usually our good days to bad days ratio is a bit better. If I have to pick up any more rocks or old rusty nails, I swear I'm going to start eating them to end my misery. Or roll around in the poison ivy we've been spraying to see if it could kill me.

However. While staining the fence, I had the greatest epiphany of all epiphanies. A way to turn things on their head: prove Dad is not Knox and figure out what Leo's really about. Of course, it'd be a whole lot easier if Dad would just get a nifty "Don't-possess-me!" sigil tattoo, but he'd just remind us how Moses says not to mark our bodies. Guess nobody in the Old Testament knew about possession.

Part one of the plan: have a family movie night. These are Dad's favorite, and as silly as it sounds, no way Knox could make popcorn like Dad, so we would know. Part two: this one took a little convincing to get Frost on board, but while Dad is happy, we ask if we can invite the boys over for a bit. That way I can flirt with Raylan and observe Leo in a less intense situation. Sometimes fun is the best way to see what someone is really like. Jury's still out on him since realizing he's basically on God's bad side.

So here we are, about to gorge on this perfect popcorn, and hip hip hooray for that—Dad is *not* Knox.

I think it's funny when in TV shows, teenagers are always watching old movies. I know it's supposed to make them look cultured, but in reality it's just because they're cheap rights for the movie producers to use. That's pretty much all we watch at home. Sitcoms are considered a waste of time, dramas have too much kissing, those women in that period piece aren't wearing enough clothes, yadda yadda yadda. So I wish *other* teenagers actually did watch them, because then I would have this in common with someone. As it is, I secretly have a crush on Dean Martin and Bing Crosby, since those are the celebrities I've grown up watching. And Raylan, that delicious man, reminds me of those manly actors like John Wayne.

Dad pops amazing popcorn on the stove, slathered with a mountain of butter and salt. Tonight, it's *Rebel Without A Cause,* and I'm ecstatic because James Dean also reminds me of Raylan. Okay, most things remind me of Raylan, but whatever. He's off doing who knows what with Leo. This is why I need a chance to text him and see his royal hotness.

Frost, Mom, Dad, Gato, and I all curl up with individual popcorn bowls, and I sneak Gato a piece of popcorn to get him to cuddle with me.

Dad's in the kind of mood that makes me feel terrible for saying things about him when he's *not* in this kind of mood. I do love seeing him this way. He gives Mom a peck on the lips and thanks her for dinner. He tells Frost her piano playing earlier was beautiful. He asks me how my art class at school is going. I almost use the opportunity to ask if I can take an oil-based painting course out in Rolla but stop myself. Gotta hold out for the party.

"He's so handsome," Mom coos when James Dean comes on the screen.

"Yes, ma'am!" Frost and I agree together.

"Ladies, I'm right here," Dad chuckles. "Your mother could never be attracted to another man since she's married to me, right, monkey?"

"That's right, dear." Mom pats his knee, and they look at each other with soft eyes. I realize this is why I'm drawn to art—to show the depth of the reality. What is beyond black and white. Dad can be a jerk and a half sometimes, but he can also be fun, sweet, and kind.

Instead of losing myself in the movie, I steal glances at my family. Even with the shadows of the show playing across their faces, we could be a modern Norman Rockwell painting. Frost rests her head on Mom's shoulder, who loops her arm through Dad's. I give Gato an extra squeeze.

When the credits start to roll at the end, Dad clicks the TV off, leaving the room pitch black except for a small glowing nightlight, but it's a soft darkness, not a scary one. Dad slides to his knees, a signal for family prayer. We haven't done it enough lately. It's Frost's turn to say it, her voice a little tight, and I know it's because she's happy we had this night, too. Then we finish our night with a big family hug, and it's time for bed.

Heading up the stairs, Dad suddenly grunts loudly from below us. My blood freezes—was I wrong? Or has Knox just shown up? Then, in a low, gravelly voice that is only used for fun and games, he sings, "I smell girly feet!" He lunges toward us and we squeal, racing up the stairs before he can tickle our feet. A game we've played for as long as I can remember. Up one flight, across the second floor, trying not to slip in our socked feet. Then up the second flight of stairs, darting and giggling the entire way. Even Mom joins in on the action.

"Cute little girl feet." She chuckles daintily, fingers snatching at us.

Frost and I split at the top of the stairs to our rooms and slam our doors closed behind us. Heaving, I giggle softly as Dad scratches at Frost's door and Mom at mine. The sound makes me think of the Despairity, here to feed on our fleeting happiness, but I shove the thought down and silently count to ten, the finale to the game. Then, in a move we've synchronized since we were tiny, we throw open our doors and tackle Mom and Dad in tickling hugs.

No way Dad's possessed. We can do this. Our family is worth fighting for. And if we can kill Knox and drive the Despairity away, maybe without their influence, that good-to-bad-day ratio can get way, way better.

Then Frost does something rare—she throws her arms around Dad's middle, who closes his eyes and hugs his baby girl. I know Frost feels the same way.

I almost feel guilty for premeditating using this moment, but it's for the greater good, I remind myself. I wrap my arms around Dad's strong shoulders from the back.

"Daddy?" I say lightly, trying to sound like I just thought of this now. "Can we invite the boys over for just like an hour tomorrow? We'll stay upstairs where it won't be loud, but with the door open? I think they could use some good influences." Sometimes he'll go for a little altruism, but I can feel Frost's hands go rigid with nerves beneath me. Easy, girl, easy.

"What do you think, 'Monk'?" Dad doesn't let go and defers to Mom. He does this every once in awhile. I almost think he knows he's got these demons, and sometimes it's easier to let Mom handle something than risk letting them out.

"I think you two deserve a little fun." She rubs our arms lightly, and we slowly unwind ourselves, greedy for confirmation from Dad.

"Sounds like a plan," he says easily, like he's relieved to get to be nice. I hold in a squeal, not wanting to annoy, instead opting for a peck on the cheek.

"Thanks, Daddy. Nighty night." I whirl and bounce into my room, closing the door so I can flail with nobody watching.

CHAPTER 25 - FROST

Mom's hurriedly scraping butter on Dad's toast while Eva and I sip our orange juice. After our family movie night, things can be good as long as we don't rock the boat.

Dad already read his newspaper in his recliner so he's one hundred percent present. I scoot back my chair and grab a muffin just as Dad takes one more teensy bite of a cherry and oat breakfast dish Mom made. He pushes it away with calloused fingers.

"You can throw away that recipe card," he says.

Mom blinks in disbelief, and Eva and I inconspicuously glance at each other.

I can't let him talk to Mom like that, I want to say out loud.

I'm game if you are. It's like I can hear Eva saying back.

But the party!

He'll probably get mad and make us cancel . . .

Gingerly, Mom takes her seat next to us at the table, and I take another drink, forcing myself not to corner Dad. Eva's usually the quickest to lose these inner battles, and I hate myself for not saying anything, but the strategy now is to have this party. Leo will tell us more about how to take down Knox, and Eva and I will be square again.

"Daddy?" Eva's overly chipper voice breaks across the floral tablecloth. "Is the water heater acting up? I keep hearing a weird hum in my room."

The TV's been muted, but Dad reaches for the remote, I suppose to turn the volume on. I can't tell if he's ignoring Eva or didn't hear.

Regardless, I still need to make amends to Eva for our little rift the other night. It's not that I didn't trust her to know that a Blurred One was responsible for Aunt Eva's death—I simply wanted to protect her from thinking she'd turn out like that. Eva's her own person and can make her own choices, no matter how similar she may be to our aunt. And, maybe Dad will soften when he sees how happy both Eva and I are with our impending plans. "We're pretty excited about our par-tay. Thanks again."

"Don't say par-tay," Eva mumbles under her breath.

I stab one of the cherries with my fork when Dad laughs a low, mechanical laugh that doesn't entirely sound like his. "You all seriously let him bat you around like that?"

I skirt my eye's to Eva's. She's on high-alert, fork in mid-air.

Dad—Knox?—takes in my mom's Hummel figurines and the plastic plants adorning the top of her curio cabinet. But he shouldn't have been able to get in here. We have triquetras on the house! Knox possessed Dad when he went outside, I guess?

With an amused twist of his mouth, he says, "He's in here, you know. Your Father. Quite the psychological conundrum, he is. He loves you girls a great deal, and yet doesn't know how to squash the criticism. Just like he learned from *his* dad." Dad-Knox takes another tentative bite of the oatmeal. "I was lying earlier, Donna. The cherries are delicious."

I reach for the pistol I strapped to my ankle under my pants, but Dad-Knox clucks his tongue.

"Is that any way to treat a guest?"

He sends my Sig Sauer skittering across the tile with the flick of his wrist.

"To think I only arrived before breakfast." Dad-Knox takes another cheerful bite, taking his time chewing before he swallows. "On the lawn. Your father wishes for me to tell you that—" He pauses, listening, tilting his head. "What was that, Jim? You wish for me *not* to know about the rock salt shotgun hidden on top of the curio cabinet?"

Dad-Knox raises an upside down hand, lifting one of my dad's many shotguns like he's raising the dead. Winking at Eva, he brushes his thumb along the knuckle of his pointer finger, snapping the shotgun like a twig.

In half a second, he could kill any of us.

The cool metal handle of my fork digs into my palm. I should stick this in his eye, but that would mostly hurt Dad, and Mom's covering her mouth with a trembling hand. She's trying not to cry, and Eva, on my other side, is trying to pull her vial of holy water out of her jeans pocket, but it keeps getting snagged.

Dad-Knox luxuriously plants his elbows on the table— something Dad would *never* do, as table manners are a must. Cupping his chin, he locks eyes on my sister. "You really are an excellent kisser."

Eva goes as pale as the tablecloth.

"How did you get in here?" Eva yanks the holy water from her pocket. "We have sigils on the house."

"Never underestimate the lure of the morning paper." He *must* have possessed Dad when he went outside to get it.

The fear radiating off of Eva makes me wish we were all cuddled up watching James Dean again.

"I know you have some sick fascination with me," she

says, "and with my Aunt Eva, but you need to leave us alone!" When she attempts to screw off the lid of her holy water, Knox sends the vial to the floral wallpaper behind her.

I reach for my holy water, too, but there's only lint in my pocket.

"Frost, hon," he says, filling his voice with a false sweetness. "Do you not remember? You forgot to put it back when you put on your makeup." Dad-Knox flutters his eyelashes dramatically, mocking my weak attempt to put on mascara. He was watching me? The idea that he saw me dressing makes me blanch.

"Of course," Dad-Knox says, "no matter how much makeup you use, you'll never be as ravishing as your sister."

Mom's chair clatters backward as she cries, "Get out!" She flees toward the refrigerator, her white-blonde hair streaking in a trail behind her. She runs for the shotgun behind the refrigerator, but three dark shapes are rising like black puddles from the tiled floor.

Buhhhr-tung. Buhhhhhhr-tung. A loud purring like Gato, but far more sinister. How did they get past the sigils on the house? Can they slip inside, because they're not possessing someone?

"Leave us alone!" Mom cries. She reaches for the shotgun, but the Despairity's long black silhouettes are surrounding her. Their hair hangs in their faces like heavy, thick yarn. They suck at her spirit the way they did to me before, and Mom drops her hand, shrinking to the floor.

Dad-Knox giggles as his black angels rejoin him, sucking up the joy in the room. Is this how we all die? Where Knox convinces Mom and me to kill ourselves and kidnaps Eva?

Sunlight shoots from the windows, highlighting Mom's old brown salt and pepper shakers at the end of the counter. If I could just get my finger on the salt and douse them with it, maybe that could buy us enough time to grab other weapons. Dad has shotguns behind every door in the house.

A loud rattle at the door tells me someone's coming in. Leo and Raylan? Their frantic voices are shouting Eva's and my names, and Maggie's authoritative voice is shooting over them.

One of the outside sprinklers sprays the window. The room, like rotten eggs, reeks of sulfur. Mom, sobbing on the floor, cries, "What do you want with us?"

Dad-Knox places a tender hand round Eva's cheek and chin. "Isn't it obvious, Donna? I require Eva now."

"Why?" Eva says, looking like she might pass out at any second. She reaches for the tiny daggers in her hair Maggie gave us, but Knox sends them flying with the flick of his wrist.

Like something stronger than gravity is forcing her down, Mom slowly attempts to rise to her feet, grunting from the effort. She lifts her chin. "*Never.*"

The front door bangs open, and as the Despairity and Knox turn to see it, I leap for the salt and pepper shaker. Eva, too, is wrenching away from Knox, who only slaps her body into the front of his chest so painfully that she cries out.

I seize the salt, wrapping my fingers around the wood-grained canister as Leo, Raylan, and Maggie burst into the room.

The boys each harbor a pistol—Raylan with a semi-automatic, and Leo his old revolver.

Maggie, though, hoists a shotgun like a garden hoe. "So, Knox has made it to town." And then, seeing as my sister's glued to Dad-Knox's white shirt and black slacks, her fingers tighten round the long barrel. "Seems you found her faster than I supposed."

I shake the salt canister at the Despairity behind me, and their translucent bodies sizzle. I think I might have a chance

—I'll take Knox down—when the shaker flies from my fingers.

It flings past the Despairity, past a stretch of tiled counters—and imbeds in Mom's throat.

Mom's eyes bulge wide and a cry escapes my mouth. Her hand reaches for the salt shaker as I sprint to help, but that gravity that was holding her down before is now holding me down. I'm an eight-ton truck trying to reach her through ice and snow. Mom's supple body slinks to the floor.

Mom's pink, white, and blue chicken pitcher taunts me from the counter. Mom keeps extra salt packets in there, but as soon as I reach for it, Dad-Knox will embed *those* in her throat.

Gunfire booms. Dust and splinters of wood coat the air, and it doesn't take me long to realize that Maggie's just filled the Despairity with rock-salt. Their ghoul-like mouths shriek as they burst into the faint color of mustard powder.

Maggie and Raylan are leaping toward Mom as Eva and I both shriek, "Is she all right?"

Raylan reaches down to check Mom's neck for her pulse, and Maggie's hand drifts to her sewing shears in her back pocket like she just might stab him now. But when he nods once as if to say, "She's all right," Maggie drops her hand before spinning and setting her sights on Leo.

"HELP ME GET KNOX OUT OF THIS HOUSE."

"Leo doesn't want him here, either," I whimper as my eyes burn from sulfur. The Despairity still haven't returned, but that's not to say that they won't in any second. They shouldn't have even been able to come. Maybe Knox, inside Dad's body, invited them in?

I'm holding onto the backs of my arms. Leo isn't bad. He's not with them. A low *buhhhrtung* flits over the room, and God, please, please let Mom be okay.

As if they've trained for this in basic training, Raylan and

Maggie look to one another before Maggie nods, and then they're sprinting over the tiled floor toward Knox. They both have a target, a mission, and Raylan tenses his fingers like he'll pull the trigger, but the pistol flies out of his hand.

I think Dad-Knox did that, but Leo's hand's raised high above his head. He drops it slowly as Raylan seers him with his vision.

"What are you doing?" Raylan roars.

"You'll kill her dad," Leo says.

Raylan's eyes stretch wide in disbelief. "You're defending him."

Leo shakes his head. "He's an innocent."

I thought it was impossible, but Raylan's eyes stretch wider.

Leo holds his hands out. "Their father is still alive in there."

Dad-Knox's eyes widen with pleasure at the debate going on before him. "See that, love?" He leans in toward Eva. "Your boyfriend will kill your father just to chase me out." He looks from Leo to Raylan as if he's at a horse race now. Getting rid of the competition, he launches a chair into Raylan's chest, which makes him fly half across the room.

I think I might know what to say, how to help them, when three black shadows hover over me, clouding my train of thought. My ears ring like I stood too close to a cannon when it went off.

I—I could have killed my mom. First I put Eva in danger, now her. I should jump through the window and on that sprinkler, impale my head.

I'll never be more beautiful. I should do it now.

Thin, strong fingers dig into my brain, wrapping around my body like I'm creme brulee. I lie into their wrappings, because fighting to understand Leo and Raylan's intentions is exhausting, and instead of Mom dying, it should be me.

Their hold is cool silk. Eucalyptus and mint.

Just because I was accepted to UT doesn't mean I'll escape this stupid town.

If not UT, after all this, Leo and I can still run off into the sunset.

Above me, Leo spits a nasty wad of something from his mouth. A wad of chewed up paper falls to the floor in a lump. His cigarette butt? And Leo's spitting what's left of it straight into Dad-Knox, who roars.

A miniature blade embeds in Dad-Knox's arm. His sleeves are rolled—something both Dad and Knox do—and Dad-Knox tries to pull it out with his fingers, but his fingers sizzle like acid.

"I've got a bunch more." Leo pulls a carton from his back pocket, and this must be where he went after he and Raylan accused Dad of being possessed by Knox. To get a weapon to slow Knox down.

Dad-Knox's eyes narrow.

"Don't you want to know where I got them?"

The insides of the cigarettes must be laced with silver or something similar, but why is this a bartering chip between Leo and Knox?

The light dangling over the breakfast table glistens off Dad-Knox's calculating eyes. "You found someone."

Leo doesn't break eye-contact. "I'll take you now."

Dad-Knox's lips peel back as his body ripples with laughter. "You would do that to her?" He gestures toward me. "After all this time?"

Leo doesn't even bother to glance my way. "She's not as precious as I thought."

Those long bangs are lying. I must still be asleep. He's laughing a little now, and those sunlit laughs were meant for me. Why is he laughing that way with Knox? He has to be playing him.

Dad-Knox's eyes skirt to Eva, his lips practically salivating at what Leo's saying. "You know the ritual to use on her?"

Maggie looks like she's just been kicked in the face as the shotgun in her hands falters.

Leo glances at Eva before admitting, "I know where to find it."

I want to scream. What ritual are they talking about? If Leo knew what Knox was after all along, why wouldn't he just tell us?

Dad-Knox's eyes envelop my sister like he's not yet ready to let her go. He takes in her large, doll-like eyes. Her mascara, smudged. He runs his knuckles along her cheek. When he grazes her throat, she flinches.

At her reaction, he lets out an almost-patient breath. "I suppose the best things are worth waiting for." He tries to capture Eva's eye, but she refuses to offer it to him.

"If I promise to go with you," Leo says as the black fringed orbs of the Despairity hover over me, impatient to suck out my hope again, "you must promise to leave them alone—until we come back."

"I thought you said you didn't care." The side of Dad-Knox's lips perk up.

Leo gives a half shrug. "I prefer to keep my positive memories intact. I've been working on them for a long time. They're mine."

I try pushing through the weight of the invisible force Leo or Knox must be using to hold me back, but it all feels so impossible. Leo can't really mean that.

"Why would you do this?" Dad-Knox asks.

"I'm ready to do the ritual myself," Leo says casually, like he's tired of a game of hide and seek. He traps me in his gaze as my heart launches in my throat.

Automatically, I take a wobbly step back. All of this—it

must be for show. He's trying to get on Knox's good side to take him down.

"What is the ritual for?" I ask.

Leo chuckles as Knox raises his head to the ceiling with a laugh.

"See you again, gorgeous." Knox waggles his fingers at Eva as Raylan launches a chair back at him.

The chair bounces off the front of Knox like he's only been hit with a Kleenex.

Leo gives Raylan a half shake of his head as if to tell him, *Don't try to stop me* before enveloping me with his eyes, which are thorned and blue and wrong.

What is going on? I want to scream.

Dad-Knox's lips curl back as a burst of black shoots through his mouth and trails Leo, still in his vessel, out of the room.

CHAPTER 26 - EVA

*I*n the dark of the hallway, the only light sneaks out from under Frost's door. After Maggie put up fresh triquetras on the house, Mom and Dad barricaded themselves in their room, like if they stay in there, the evil won't come slithering back into our house. We could leave, but it seems they'll find us no matter where we go. Frost's been holed up in her room since this awful, awful morning.

I knock quietly. A few seconds pass before I finally hear her muffled, "Come in."

I open the door just enough to get in, like I can keep the moment contained if I make my entrance subtle and quick.

Frost. She's hunched on the floor next to her bed, which is usually made so nicely that the wad of sheets I see now is actually alarming. Surrounded by books and crumpled tissues, she doesn't look at me. It doesn't look like she's looking at much of anything.

I cross the room and sit gingerly on the bed, folding one leg beneath me.

"Frosty." I reach out and barely touch her shoulder, then let go almost instantly at the rigidness of it, and ask the most obvious of questions to just try and start somewhere. "You okay?"

"No," she croaks. I wait a beat, feeling my way through the moment to see how to help. What could I possibly say that would be appropriate? "How could I be okay? Dad got *possessed* and Leo is gone. *Again.*"

And Raylan, my heart whispers. Once Knox and Leo left, with the hollow eyes of a lone survivor, Raylan made sure everyone was going to be okay, then disappeared. It's been radio silence ever since. So much for falling in love at our little party for four. But as much as it hurts, it's nothing compared to what Frost's going through. What Mom and Dad are going through.

Frost talks like her soul is ripping slowly—under the hands of a torturer with a carving knife, taking his time, letting each tiny space of flesh feel its very own pain.

"How did life get so messed up?" I finally venture. She gives an almost imperceptible shake of her head. "Do you think Dad got possessed because he's been doing something bad?" She just whimpers. I continue, trying to fill in the blanks so she doesn't have to find the words herself. "You love him? Leo, I mean?"

A quiet sob. This is it. A seriously messed up situation which best-case-scenario leaves my sweet sister broken-hearted. Not good enough.

"OK. I'm going to Reader's Digest this to help my own brain. Stop me if I get something wrong." I take her silence as approval. "Trying to start at the beginning so I understand. Leo and Knox and their little friends are spirits who chose not to come to Earth."

I start slowly and gain momentum as the pieces fall into place. Frost burrows a little deeper into herself with every word. "You and Leo were heaven BFFs. We chose to come here, and Leo and Knox didn't. So they decided to, what, mess with people who chose Team Body? And the freaky chicks help them?" She barely nods. I can only tell because her messy hair moves.

"But then Leo eventually ditches Knox and sees you and starts hanging out. Mom and Dad, who may or may not have made the connection of him being more than an imaginary friend, decide to *make* you forget him." I pause, letting the weight of all she went through to "forget" her friend hang in the air for a moment. "Then we kind of stumble headfirst into Knox, who now decides to obsess over me because Aunt Eva was like 'the one who got away'?" Goodness gracious.

Frost finally turns to look at me but still doesn't say anything. Her face is so white, like the despair washed all her color away. And this—this is where I wish I had her skill for wording things instead of my tendency for truth bombs. I try to be as sensitive as possible.

"So, Leo was, um, pretty convincing." I quickly tie a knot in my hair and fiddle with the soft sheet with my other hand. Anything to keep me grounded. I can't look at her right now, so I settle for the prickly aloe vera across from us. Then, realizing she hasn't answered, I blurt, "He is just playing him, right?"

She wilts completely into herself, burying her head into her knees, arms shielding her from any more pain. My heart crawls down to my stomach, doubt settling in like a fifty-pound lead ball. "You don't know."

She shakes her head and burrows, impossibly, even farther into herself. Then doubt turns to the much worse feeling—dread. "They could *all* be trying to kill me?" I whisper, scared to hear the words even from myself.

Frost jerks up, scrambling onto her knees and grabbing my hands.

"No," she says, emphatically, but with her mascara-smeared face, matted hair and red nose, it's hard to take comfort in that. "I don't know! I'm trying to sort it out. I believe he's on our side."

With her eyebrows pointed and jaw set, she's determined. I know she believes what she says.

"But you're more than a little biased. This is what they do, apparently. Mess with people's heads." One thing about being my father's daughter is that I've learned people don't always fit neatly into the "good" or "bad" column. Motivations change. I shake her hands gently, trying to ease the words. Letting go, she bites her lip and looks down at her books in defeat. "You've been doing research just in case?"

"Yeah?" She phrases it like a question, caressing the page nearest her, a depiction of a beautiful angel, perfect skin, surrounded by light. The absolute opposite of the Despairity.

"What do you have so far? Because even if Leo isn't really evil, nothing's working against Knox."

"I started a list years ago about all we know about Blurred Ones. I started with everything I knew about Leo, like what he is capable of, his limitations, stuff like that." She takes one long drink from her water bottle. "Then I was curious if there was any pattern as to *when* he would visit me. Usually during the winter, lots of times after school."

I wave my hand for more.

"Then I remembered how I always wished he would visit after church, because that's when Mom and Dad would go take a long nap and I would have been able to play for hours, but he never came, and I would complain to him the next time I saw him."

It's crazy how she had this whole other life I knew almost nothing about.

"So it dawned on me—what if he *couldn't?* What if something about the Sabbath made him—them—weak?" Encouraged, she grabs a big black leather book from one of her stacks. The Bible.

"I started looking up stuff on the Sabbath and found Mark 2:27, that says 'the Sabbath was made for man,' and I don't know, it's such a simple verse and I kind of feel like maybe there's more to it than that." She looks to me with puppy eyes, hoping I agree.

"Makes sense." I sit up straighter, showing way more confidence than I feel. "He never came on Sunday because he didn't have the juice. So hopefully Knox is weak then, too. He just needs to conveniently show up to attack us on a Sunday." I realize I've said too much because Frost crumples back into herself.

"No, no, it's good. Thank you. We can build on this." I ruffle her already messed up hair, trying to lighten her up. "I'm going to go grab some supplies, come back, and see if we can find more to go on, like what this ritual is and how we can keep Dad from getting possessed again. Plus, then we'll have something to bring Maggie and to convince her we can help."

I launch myself off the bed with gusto, springs squeaking behind me, and head back into the dark hallway. Heading down the stairs to the kitchen, I grab the thick wooden stair rail with both hands and squeeze it so hard my skin screams, willing it to take the tension out of me. Is it too late to just steal the car and drive to Mexico? But then Knox would probably kill my whole family to draw me out.

Good news is, I can't be a five-hundred pound burger-flipper if I'm dead.

CHAPTER 27 - FROST

I shouldn't ditch my sister, but I can't talk to her about why Dad got possessed and the ritual Knox wants to use on my sister. Leo supposedly wants to use it on me, but I don't believe that.

Not really.

The fact is, I was supposed to be the big mighty older sister, and instead of securing her safety before leaving for college, I've offered her up like a virgin goddess on a silver platter.

I've got to talk to Maggie. She'll know why Knox is so obsessed with both Evas. There's a reason why she was so silent at dinner the other night, and how, when Leo mentioned the ritual, she looked like Eva and I were already dying in front of her.

The porch squeaks when I try to scamper past it, but I've got Mom's car keys. For the first time in my life, without permission, I borrow it.

When I get to Maggie's place, I hurry toward the one-story white house that was probably built in the thirties. The peeling paint on the shutters and the loose nuts and bolts lying around prove she's far too busy hunting to make everything all perfect.

Raylan's truck is actually parked right in front, and Maggie's hunched over the lock of her garden shed. In her left hand, she hoists a wrench the size of my femur and behind her ear she's planted a pencil. She's obviously deep into a project, so when she spins around and sets me in her sights, she nearly whacks me for sneaking up on her.

"Just me!" I raise my hands. "Just me."

She nods at Raylan's truck and then the house like she doesn't want to disturb him in there and waves for me to follow her to my car.

Rosy cheeked and holding that wrench like she doesn't know what to do with it now, Maggie murmurs, "I'll drive."

It doesn't take long for Maggie to put the car in reverse and peel out of the driveway like we've got a jinn that needs to be followed.

She glances into the rear view mirror and adjusts the side mirrors, and I have to say I feel a little safer having her drive. We haven't spent nearly enough time together lately.

"Talk," Maggie orders, "and I'll vet this boy your sister's head over heels with."

"Raylan?"

She raises a meaty palm. "He's sleeping in my home, Frost. I like to know what I've allowed to come over the threshold. Plus," her voice softens, "he's been passed out ever since he got injured."

Maggie hasn't let anyone besides Eva or me stay in her house since—well. I'm pretty sure, never.

She pauses briefly. "How's your dad?"

I shrug. "He's been holed up in his room."

Compassion flits over her ruddy face, which looks tired. "That's another matter."

I think she's going to say something else, but instead she pats the ginormous wrench on her lap.

"How are we going to vet Raylan?"

Maggie's keen hunter eyes sparkle. "Mr. Harris." She taps the turn signal.

———

The parking lot's full. I should be in AP English—but Maggie pulls up to the library trailer like we have every bit of business being here.

With her favorite railroad spike jutting out of her back pocket, Maggie leads me through the trailer, and with that wrench in her hands, I have to wonder if she plans to lobotomize poor Mr. Harris now.

The pale, beige man barely blinks when Maggie charges toward him like he's supper.

She slams her wrench on his desk, and he vaguely says, "Ms. Darrow."

"Open it," Maggie says.

A tween-aged girl who was secretly starting to pull a lollipop out of her backpack takes one look at Maggie's railroad spike and massive wrench, and quickly scampers out of the trailer.

"Open it, Rupert!" Maggie shoves the wrench at Mr. Harris, who looks like he's never heaved a tool in his life.

He pushes his glasses up the bridge of his nose. "You don't believe me when I say he's registered?"

Maggie shoves the wrench into his chest so hard that it gets oil on his beige shirt.

Huffing, Mr. Harris lifts a thick volume from the bottom of a stack of papers. "No need to open the lockbox, Maggie. I have it right here."

Gliding his fingers over the black tome, slowly he lifts the cover. He turns page after page like he's pulling off the leaves of a romaine salad, and at long last a vague, almost-smile settles over his lips. "There it is."

The tome's still a good three feet away, but even from here I can see the cursive scrawl with Raylan's name plus a date, 2000-something.

Maggie stares at the page for what feels like forever. "You're sure your friends have it right?"

Mr. Harris nods so slowly, it's like he's moving in reverse. "Never underestimate the power of my coven, Ms. Darrow."

I stare at the man's magnified eyes looking at me from behind those coke-bottle glasses, along with the pool of ink that's stained the front pocket of his shirt. "Coven?"

Maggie slams the book shut, which makes both Mr. Harris and me flinch. Grabbing her wrench, Maggie tosses it to me like she's tossing me a bone.

I grapple for the thirty-pound cold metal anvil.

So." I wish Eva was here. "Mr. Harris is actually a witch, then."

"Warlock," Maggie corrects.

"Of course."

Her knuckles are a little less white than when she picked up Eva and me from San Antonio, but even in the dimming light as the sun goes down, I can see they're white enough to know we're still in danger. I know why I came to find her, but I can't get my tongue to work.

"So what's that book all about?" I ask as we follow a truck bed packed full of antlers.

Maggie checks both of her side mirrors and scans the field on our left and the abandoned café to our right. "Rupert and his friends keep a log of hunters who seem to be on the moral side of things. When one writes in his book, the record shows up in all the volumes."

"How many covens are there?"

Maggie presses the accelerator and clicks on her turn signal like she means to pass the antler truck now, but when our side of the road splits to two lanes, the car slows. Maggie turns to face me before slowing down further.

Easing the car off the road, she turns the key to stop the car, and I can't help feeling a little cornered.

Casually resting her hand on her fanny pack, she settles her trained hunter's gaze on mine.

"You really like him."

It's mortifying that she's bringing up Leo now. I think she might grill me with questions, demand why I have been kissing him, when she slowly says, "I don't know why these Blurred Ones always like you girls."

Reclining her seat, she adds, "That's a lie. I know. You know that story in Matthew about the devils possessing some guys?"

I nod.

"You know how they begged Jesus to not kill them, but put them into the swine instead?"

The wrench's pinching the skin by my knee, so I shift it to my thigh. "Yeah . . ."

"Blurred Ones will do *anything* to keep a body." She grabs the wrench from me and heaves it to the back seat, where she deposits it with a *thwump*. "Why else do you think they possess vessels?"

"Their senses are heightened?"

She claps my shoulder. "It didn't take Blurred Ones long to learn that their existence, without coming to earth to learn and progress, is meaningless. Without bodies, they can't gain experience. That and," she glances down at her fanny pack, "there is nothing like human touch and emotions."

Unzipping her fanny pack, Maggie pulls something small like a piece of paper from the top and gingerly re-zips her fanny pack. Holding the note out to me, which looks a little thicker than paper, she says, "Your Aunt Eva learned this faster than any of us."

Accepting the paper, which is really a card, I open it. Rectangular square, bright colors. No one sends these anymore—a postcard.

A row of cars stick out from the ground—they're actually planted, hood-first in the grass and mud. At the bottom, in cursive red letters, reads, "Cadillac Ranch," and on the reverse, a brief note with a pretty but almost boyish scrawl:

STOP WORRYING. I've found it.

"Found what?" I ask.

Maggie stares up at the ceiling of the car, which is gray and splattered with some kind of blood. "Your aunt and I didn't always get along."

So she *did* know her. Maggie always acted like she showed up on the scene after Aunt Eva had gone.

Sensing my incredulity, she offers, "I do not handle death well."

A little ironic, considering her job.

"Your aunt was even more restless than your sister. She was a lot younger than your mom, and your grandparents didn't exactly pay attention to her. So when your parents lavished her with love, she didn't know how to take it—and ran away from home. A lot."

She sighs, like she's been bottling up this story for so long, it actually feels good to let it out. "Of course, your parents didn't know how to handle that. They tried grounding her, but that only made her worse. So—" She closes her eyes. "I suggested a road trip.

"She had itchy-feet. Always liked new experiences. And nothing was enough for her. Your parents actually used all their savings to take her on a road trip like I suggested—to Disneyland. But when they stopped for gas on the way home, she hitched a ride with a truck driver.

"Your parents went insane with fear. I contacted all the hunters I knew and spent weeks trying to find her. She was only sixteen at the time, and it was three full months until she told me where she was." She taps the postcard in my hand. "Here."

"So you think this is where she found Knox?"

Maggie watches a spotted horse grazing in the field outside my window. "Yes." She glances at me, her eyes pained with tears. "Every time she ran away from home, I'd ask her, 'Do you think that's how you're going to find your happiness?'

"Eva would laugh at me, but agree, too. She was duplicitous. She was so hard to read. Sweeter than apricot preserves, but she had the ability to lie. Broke your mom's heart."

I reach to push the down button to crack the window of my door, but the car's off, so the button doesn't work.

Maggie turns the key enough to turn the battery on and rolls both of our windows all the way down. With cooler evening breeze rustling her short amber curls, she says, "So when I got that postcard, I knew she believed she truly had found her happiness."

"When did you learn she was with Knox?"

Maggie's face sours. "When he left a trail of dead bodies everywhere they went."

I think of the meat grinder and his own methods of disposal and feel the rise of goosebumps on my arms.

"Soon, though, your aunt started callin' me. Scared for her life. I was supposed to pick her up in Kansas City but learned Knox had a plan. There's a way for Blurred Ones to stay in their vessels' bodies forever—without wearing them out. If they bind themselves to another person, they can live forever."

"Bind themselves—how?"

"They use some sort of spell or artifact to tie together the vessels. Then, they're free to feed off both the vessel they're possessing and the victim they've bonded with to live even longer before the vessel wears out."

Tears burn in my eyes. Tears like the ones shining in Maggie's eyes now.

"I had no idea," I murmur. I think of Eva again in that hotel room with Knox kissing her. He was probably sizing her up to see if she had what it took for him to bind her like he wanted to do with Aunt Eva.

I know what happened to Aunt Eva in the end. How she decided sticking her head in a woodchipper was better than staying with him. Was that all of her own volition, or did the Despairity help convince her to do that?

Settling a heavy hand on my shoulder, Maggie says, "Blurred Ones are so desperate for bodies, they'll settle for pig's backsides, Frost."

"But once those pigs were possessed, they ran off a cliff."

"*You* imagine being possessed by something as foul as Knox. I'd want to run off a cliff, too." It's fully nighttime as Maggie leans her head back on her headrest with a colossal sigh. "You Abram girls. You're something special, all right. I know it, and apparently the Blurred Ones know it, too."

CHAPTER 28 - EVA

*I*t's a new day and I'm still alive. Baby steps, hooray! After taking a mental inventory of all the weapons I've got in the car, I slam the door shut of Mom's giant baby blue Dodge. I'm a little surprised Maggie isn't already out her shabby-not-very-chic door to greet me. She seems to always know what's going on in every inch of her four wooded acres. I jingle the warm keys in my balmy hand. We haven't exactly had the best of luck lately, and I shoot a quick prayer upstairs nothing is wrong here.

I had to get out of the house. It's been three days since Raylan and Leo went who knows where, and it's like a mortuary in there. Thankfully, Mom and Dad almost always let me come visit Maggie when my chores are done. All I had today was change the oil on ol' Betsy here, and I don't mind that one bit. It's straightforward, quick, and the perfect kind of dirty. A little oil under my nails always makes me feel confident, and heaven knows I could use some of that right now. Poor Frost was stuck sorting nails and bolts with Dad. She'll be a while.

Tapping my pocket, I make sure my vial of holy water is

with me, although a fat lot of good it's done me. I survey my surroundings as I head to the front door like I'm Agent Abram already. Within a few steps, though, I breathe easy as the muffled but unmistakable distortion of the Smashing Pumpkins escapes the house. This song just so happens to be one of my favorites: "Bodies."

I bang loudly on the door to the beat of the song so Maggie will know it's me. Two heartbeats later, she flings open the door, singing loudly, and I join her, both of us head-banging in greeting. Then she winks.

"What?" I poke her arm as I ask. She cocks her head to her saggy green plaid couch, where oh-my-goodness Raylan is sprawled out on it like he owns the place. And he's *smiling.*

"What the heck?" I blurt to neither of them in particular. Or both of them, I don't know.

"Calm your britches, girl, and come sit down." Maggie pats me with her club of a hand on the back, so I squeeze on the edge of the couch next to Raylan. That's when I see the bandage peeking out from under his shirt. His black eye. A swollen lip.

"Oh my goodness, you're really hurt, aren't you?" Seeing him this way, after everything, here in my safe place but so harmed at the same time—a tsunami of tears are barreling out of my eyes yet again.

"I'm okay, Eva, really." Raylan winces while reaching for my hand. The same way he did that night under the house. Holding it tight like he's holding my world together.

And now the heat rises in my cheeks for crying in front of him, so I cry harder. Maggie turns down the music and plops down in her faded denim easy chair, the corners of her eyes creased as if she's in mother-hen mode.

"I take it you haven't talked to Frost since yesterday?" She hands me a box of tissues, giving me the tiniest bit of cover so

I can keep from getting hysterical. I hate that I have to let go of Raylan's hand though.

"Ugh, I'm so sorry," I blubber. "No, why?" How I *hate* crying in front of people. But Maggie is safe and, well, Raylan is seeing all the warts in my life, right? So if for some magical reason he does like me, at least it will be for real. "Someone want to tell me what the heck is going on?" I ask from behind my tissue.

"When Frost's friend disappeared and you girls were busy taking care of yourselves," Maggie says in a soft reproach, "I saw that Raylan here was pretty much up a creek without a paddle, and we hunters got to stick together, eh, boy?" She rustles his hair, and he laughs a little snort. The shock of it all is enough to stop the tears. "And it turns out, he's got great taste in music. Frost came by last night and saw he was here."

"Well, ain't that just randy," I say, dabbing my face to be sure it's gunk free. "She came home after I was asleep, and she was sorting nuts and bolts with Dad when I left."

Maggie drums her fingers on her legs, opens her mouth to say something, then closes it again.

"Since when do you ever filter what you say, Mags?" I adjust so more of my not-tiny butt is on the couch, careful not to hurt Raylan.

She huffs like a bull annoyed at the matador poking at its rump. "Hang on, I need some caffeine for this conversation." She grabs her phone off the little rickety end table brimming with books next to her and grumbles into her kitchen. Glass clinks as she opens the fridge door, then her phone rings. Her irritated "What?" is thoroughly amusing. And now I'm alone with Raylan.

"Funny how we keep running into each other," I say, tying a knot in my hair. But eyeing his injuries adds to the new resident pit in my stomach. "The chair?" I wince, remembering him getting plowed into a cabinet.

"Yeah," Raylan says, eyes a lighter blue than I've ever seen them. "It seems Knox didn't want me anywhere near you." He pushes himself up so he's sitting. He winces a little from the pain, but he looks like he's pretty much mobile. I can't imagine what he looked like three days ago.

"I'm not sure what Leo is playing at, but I've been around enough bad guys to know Leo isn't one of them." He scratches his head, messing his hair up before continuing. "I'm betting he's buying us time to come up with a plan. No more narrow misses." He waits for me to meet his eyes.

"Yes, please." I mumble softly, the tears threatening to come again, so I study the grease stains on my hands. The pit seems to grow even bigger in my gut, and I'm glad I skipped breakfast for the first time in, well, ever. I have to look away. I want to reach for his hand again but chicken out and play with my rings instead.

"Raylan, I'm so sorry I didn't realize you were hurt. When Leo and Knox just disappeared, I was so focused on my parents and poor Frost—and yeah, picturing myself in some ritual where I'm thrown into a volcano."

Maggie's grandfather clock chimes, ten long times.

"By the time I looked for you, you'd disappeared," I continued. "I tried texting you, but when I didn't hear back, I figured you went back home. Got as far away from here as you could."

I study his face for a moment. It's softer today. Extra scruff, like he hasn't shaved since that morning, but he has an openness to him.

"I don't really have a home anymore." So matter of fact. "And with Leo gone. . . ." He doesn't have to finish. He is alone. "But Maggie is cool."

"Dang straight, she is," I say, heart finally warming, and I embrace the lightening mood like a puppy lounging in the sun. "She's the best. And I'm certainly glad to find out you have good taste in music. You're just full of surprises." I dare squeeze his knee lightly and leave my hand there, playing with the fabric of his jeans. He doesn't move away. Instead, his whole face brightens, completely surprising me.

"Oh, you don't even know." He reaches for my hand and pulls on my fingers until we are holding hands.

"I don't, huh? Do tell." I bat my lashes at him and pray my hands aren't sweating.

"You have to come here," he says, his voice getting lower and huskier.

"Okay," I squeak, and he's pulling me closer until my ear is next to his lips, my breathing becoming ragged.

"I think you are beautiful and amazing."

Before I can say anything really stupid to ruin the moment, Maggie booms from the kitchen doorway.

"Well, I don't know what you two are whisperin' about, but we need to talk."

I sit up quickly, accidentally pushing on Raylan's ribs, making him wince.

"And would ya quit hurtin' the poor guy?"

"Sorry," I mumble, and hold my hands still in my lap.

"Just messin' with ya, Eves, but we do need to talk." She hands Raylan and me both a soda and crashes down into her chair again. "Your dad went and got himself possessed." The sentence feels heavy, like suddenly there's a grim reaper standing in the room.

"It's not like he did it on purpose," I say. I know she knows, but I still feel the need to defend him. Raylan gives a little grunt but doesn't say anything. Maggie levels her eyes at me—her scholarly look.

"Of course not. I've been friends with your dad for a long time and I love him like a brother. But it does not mean I'm okay with the way he treats you girls, or Donna for that matter." I feel myself blush, and set to examining the frayed, braided rug. "It's made his spirit weak. Knox only got in because there was a way in."

Raylan rubs a finger along my arm, warming my skin underneath while she goes on. "I blame myself a little for not saying something sooner. Tried to keep the peace or whatnot, but Raylan here's talked some sense into me, and me and your dad are gonna have a nice long talk."

Raylan finally speaks up. "He's going to have to start respecting you more." He pulls my arm into his hand, softly.

"With the added benefit that Knox won't be able to use him as a puppet," Maggie adds, finally leaning back, getting comfortable in her chair. "I had to explain to Raylan that your dad is a little old school when it comes to sigil tattoos." I ignore Raylan's "some people" expression.

"Just don't ruin your friendship with him," I say. "Okay, Mags?"

She chuckles her beautiful Mrs. Claus laugh. "Oh, I don't think he'd find it too easy to get rid of me."

"Well, thanks for caring," I say, allowing myself a little sigh of relief. "So, two layers of protection—better behavior, and maybe Frost and I can work on a way to sneak some sigils on the guy. Think a post-in note would work?" I wink at Raylan so he'll know I'm kidding.

Maggie stands back up. "We've still got work to do," she says with authority. "So you go ahead and scoot and let me get back to it."

Steeling my nerves, I will myself to meet Raylan's eyes. It takes everything I've got, but when I do, it's like I've found a new home there in his gaze. And I will be darned if some old demon dude is going to mess this up.

CHAPTER 29 - FROST

*E*va's giggling trickles across the yard as Raylan wraps his arms around my sister in the moonlight. I try not to make the porch creak as I lie in wait and watch. I don't mean to be a creeper, but what if Knox or the Despairity are hovering around? Or maybe Leo's convinced them to lay off?

When Eva slips out of Raylan's hands to run to the back door before Mom and Dad come back from running errands, I fight a punch in the gut.

What kind of cruel thing would Dad say to her if he caught Raylan with her like that? Or maybe he wouldn't say anything at all. Like when he found Leo and me but I still felt three inches tall.

I need to talk to Raylan. See what ideas he has about protecting Eva. I've thought about making her stay inside the house, but Eva would never go along with that.

So I scurry down the porch steps, past a few thistles, and plant myself next to Raylan's truck. He's digging around again in his lockbox.

"What are you looking for?"

He cranes his neck to see who's talking.

I nod once.

He offers me a half smile before returning to his spread of weapons. "Just double checking the inventory." He closes the lid, locks it with a key from his front pocket, and turns to face me.

When he jumps from the truck bed to the ground, I say, "She doesn't take Knox's threat seriously," while trying not to freak out.

Raylan bobs his head curtly. "She's good at playing it cool."

Crickets chirp in the background as Raylan leans back on the open tailgate. He assesses my face, as if trying to decide whether or not to broach a new topic. He must decide it's worth the risk, because all too soon he's saying, "At least Maggie is going to quit letting your Dad talk to her like that."

I look to the ground.

"Frost?"

I pick at my shirt, because I'm suddenly feeling kind of nervous. "I don't know why, but he's always picked on her."

"She's not a sheep."

I trace the metal grooves of the tailgate. "I know."

When I'm upset, I simply plug in my headphones and practice Chopin on the piano. When Eva gets mad, she fights the urge to blare Metallica in her room. We have different personalities, so different reactions. Only mine happens to be more "kosher" when Dad's around.

"Has he always treated her like that?"

I wander to the side of the truck and trace the tread of a back tire. It's an awkward conversation to have. I throw caution to the wind. "The first time he hit her, she wasn't picking up nails fast enough in the garage."

"Wait. He HIT HER?"

I pick a rock out the tread. "I think it's happened more than once, but she always skirts the topic."

Raylan sounds like he'd like to skin a bear. "She's stronger than that."

I nod, fast. When I'm able to look up from the pebbles I've successfully vacated from the top of his tire tread, I explain, "She doesn't like her troubles to weigh others down. It usually just makes things worse, anyway."

Raylan scratches the back of his cowlick. "I don't know whether to kiss her for being so selfless or put a bullet in your dad."

"Please don't joke about that."

He pushes a fallen shovel farther into the truck bed. "Now that I know, I can't just stand here and watch it happen. If Maggie doesn't get the job done, then I will. No wonder the bastard got possessed."

I wish we had never brought this up. No, I'm glad. More than anything, I want to protect my sister. Still, I feel like I have to explain Dad to Raylan, wish there was time to tell him of the times he told me I'm truly an incredible musician or when he told Eva that she has a sparkle. His tongue is his greatest tool and his greatest weapon. "He's a good dad."

"Good dads don't hit their daughters."

Eva never talks about it, so it's not like I can speak with any authority on the subject, but I do know Dad doesn't live for anything else but us. Mom, Eva, and I are his life. I don't mention his alcoholic father. "He had a rough childhood."

Raylan's voice comes out bitter. "Didn't we all."

Something rustles in the bushes, and for all I know the Despairity are closing in, so I get to the point.

"Do you know about Knox's ritual?"

A little hesitantly, he nods.

"You've told Eva?"

"Just did."

"She didn't flip out." I recall again the way she embraced him before sneaking back into the house.

"She's a lot less drama than I expected." His eyes grow wide, a little dopey, like he's in shock.

Headlights shoot across the driveway's entrance, and the Chrysler tells me it's Mom and Dad. I wonder if they took Dad to the doctor to see if Knox caused any permanent damage to his body. Seems like Dad would want to do something like that. Maybe they have plans of their own for preventing him from becoming possessed?

Raylan glares at the approaching vehicle, looking a little like he wants to reach for his gun. "We're running out of time. It's time to show Knox who's boss."

We're taking the bull by the freaking horns. Making this situation our bee-otch. Maggie's gonna talk some sense into Dad, and Frost and I are gonna get Mom to help us put a temporary tattoo on him while he sleeps. We just need to stay alive long enough to figure out the rest of our plan.

In order to keep working on said plan, we need some free time, so Frost and I brilliantly decided to chop some stumps that have been bothering Dad for a few weeks now. That way, he'll be in a good mood when Maggie tries to talk to him, and we'll be able to spend more time with Raylan—cough, cough, I mean, Maggie. Just three stumps to go.

Rain drizzles over everything, including Frost and me. I love slowly being soaked to the core, the sensation of every inch becoming saturated like steady accomplishment. I breathe deeply, savoring the smell of wet dirt, moss, grass, and honeysuckle. I may still have a giant crimson target on my back, but *now*, we're painting a big ol' target right back onto Mr. Knoxy.

Frost's taking a turn whacking a particularly stubborn

stump with the ax. It's hard work, heaving the heavy thing over and over, but it will make mowing easier, since the mower will be able to go right over these now, instead of around. Since, yeah, the mower is worth "more than our lives put together." Oh Dad, so sweet. That's okay, Raylan seems to be appreciating my life extra lately, with lots of texts of lyrics, GIFs, or hilarious movie quotes.

Frost's lips are pursed in epic determination. No doubt she's going over the whole "Is Leo good or evil?" debate in her head again. Her light hair, frizzing in the rain, creates a halo around her head, but her face is red with exertion. I'm sure I'm a hot mess too.

I'll give her three more whacks before I take a turn. Until then, she needs to lighten up. I grab a handful of wonderfully gooey mud in my hand and lob it at her back. Only my aim is bad from tired muscles, and I hit her right on the neck.

She jerks around, ax poised to strike, eyes squinting in exaggerated anger. "How daaaaaare you?" she sings.

"Who? Me?" I give her my best angelic puppy face and reach out to wipe my hand on her face. A squirrel darts away from us like it doesn't want to get dirty.

"Playing around again while your sister works, Eva?" Dad's voice crawls toward us as he steps across the yard, crunching leaves.

I swear the woods quiet, but it's okay. Make him laugh, and he'll pull me into a warm bear hug, smelling like sawdust and aftershave.

But one look at his dark, bottomless eyes, and I know that's not happening today.

"No, sir, just about to take my turn." I wipe my hands on my nearly soaked jeans. The only reason I don't grab the ax right now is I think it will make me look guilty. It'd be nice if Maggie would show up right about now . . .

Frost, face stoic, heaves her long, lean, strong body and

plants the ax directly into the stump. Then she shimmies the blade out of the stump again and heaves it even harder this time. I flinch at the sound of impact.

Dad's dusty dark shoes crunch a dead grasshopper shell as he plants himself next to us.

His shoes and dark pants are ever in contrast to his white, buttoned up shirt. He just stands there. Like he expects Frost to swing again and again to impress him.

And she keeps going. Again and again, heaving and pant-ing, while I stand there, not knowing what to do with myself. Two more hits and I'll insist on a turn. I reach up to tighten my messy bun on my head.

Whack. I wince again but ready myself for doing my best job. That's one hit.

But then something like a baseball bat, except skin instead of wood, strikes my face. I stagger, not wanting to fall on the ax or stump. I hit the kitchen table's corner in the gut last time he hit me.

Grabbing my face, I focus every inch of my energy on staring at the stump. Do not provoke the beast. Do *not* look at Dad.

CHAPTER 31 - FROST

Shock like gunpowder explodes in my head.

He just slapped her. Slapped her. *He did not.*

Eva staggers back, her already large eyes enormous.

Dad's long arms hang powerfully at his sides, reminding me of a monster I saw on the cover of some book. But he's not a monster. He's Dad. His arms sway infinitesimally as he breathes like a giant. "You're going to make your sister do all the work?"

I don't know whether I want Dad to be Knox or Dad.

He's tensing his arm to strike her once more, but he *cannot* be allowed to do that again, so I raise my ax.

It's not like I would cut him. Love and anger swell like lava in the confines of my head.

His arm locks with the handle of my ax, and his already volatile eyes narrow to slants. The wind whips at his thin hair, and the wrinkles round his eyes make him look both feeble and omnipotent. Eva's crouched on the ground, holding the side of her face, eyes downcast.

Emotional pain's the worst kind of damage. It's the reason why I can never really leave and go away to college.

Dad's thin lips twist in disgust like when he ate Mom's cherry crisp. "You really and truly thought I was him!"

Fear tears through me as I stare into Dad's eyes, which flick to black. Insects scuttle beneath cheeks, the tell-tale sign that Knox is inside Dad again. Blurred Ones' spirits aren't whole, but corrupted. They think they can possess our bodies, but we'll always know it's them.

For this hot, thick moment, I'm sort of glad to see Knox, because that means Dad didn't just backhand my sister.

And Knox? He can't live.

"The genius of this arrangement," Dad-Knox says, as if we're discussing the specifications of a new shed, "is that I could have gone on for days possessing him. Or—" He creeps closer to my sister, shoulders a little more pointed than usual in the direction he means to advance. "I could keep hitting her until she kisses me again."

I'm closing the distance and planting myself between Eva and Dad-Knox. But with the flick of the wrist, he sends me backward and I slam on my back. Leaves and thorns crunch beneath my shirt and dig into my waist some fifteen paces back.

Somehow, I've dropped the ax, and Eva's studying the weapon like she has a chance of grabbing it.

Knox sneers in amusement. With another flip of his hand, Eva falls backward hard enough that her back audibly cracks from the whiplash.

Better me than her. Better me than her. How to stop him?

"Don't hurt my father." I pull his attention from my sister.

Knox gestures, palm up and fingers folding toward him, for three dark shadows lurking behind our sycamore to come closer. Only instead of three, there's four. *Four.* A long, pointed fingernail is running down my spine, because I can *feel* the eyes of that fourth dark shadow looking at me—

standing both apologetically and unwavering only the way Leo does.

I want to scream. *How could you join them? You pretended to be good when you're not.* It's all a big lie? I was wrong? But he loved me. Tears sting in my eyes, because of course he didn't. I never should have believed that he could love someone as plain and unremarkable as I am.

Knox murmurs with Dad's thin lips. "He is a complicated man." He's speaking of Dad. "Did you know that he gave up all his hobbies—his stamp collecting, his birdwatching, his elk hunts—all to spend more time with you girls?" He scoffs.

More tears of anger cloud my vision. Leo's just hovering there, next to his black-smoke friends, and Dad-Knox is reaching up and cupping his own head with his wrinkled hand, and the other cradles his chin. He's poised—just poised like that. Waiting to snap my father's neck.

"The choices are simple," Dad-Knox says. "Eva comes with me, or," his voice brightens, "I kill your father."

The Despairity and Leo swirl closer, their black forms cobwebs clouding my head. I try to scream, to open my lips, but one wrong word, and Knox will snap my father's neck.

Eva scoots over gravel and crawls toward us. Her bloody knees are gouged from—I don't know what. I try to swallow, to find my voice. Obviously, there's no way I can let him take my sister, but I can't let him kill Dad either, so I manage, "Please. Stop."

Dad-Knox lowers my father's long, freckled fingers from his head and neck. "Give me your sister, then."

The four black forms crumple, folding toward one another like they're conversing about who they'll attack next.

"I'm not your freaking doppelganger," Eva says, but she's barely raising her voice. She's refusing to show us her real emotions.

Knox slices the air with his hand, slamming her head

backward into the sycamore's trunk, and I may have just bitten clean through my tongue. "You certainly have the same way with words." His eyes rove over the front of her blouse, which has fallen a little too far down. "Same spirit of rebellion. It's a wonder you came to earth, that you eventually gave in."

Tears shine in my sister's eyes as he twists the dart in the very core of who she fears she is. *Never good enough.* I play the piano, and Dad tells me I'm a good girl. I have talent. Eva records herself singing, and he tells her when her voice is flat.

"Don't listen to him," I warn her, because Eva's always been prone to believing the worst of herself.

"You nearly weren't Team God." Dad-Knox strolls toward my sister, twigs snapping in his path. Gently, he crouches down and wraps his skinny fingers around Eva's arm. She recoils, but he lifts her to her feet as her legs wobble like a baby giraffe's. Twirling his finger in my sister's messy hair, he murmurs, "People like Frost here had to pull you along."

It's like Knox can read my dad's dismissive opinion of her. Once he pointed out how she preferred to eat the meat on her plate first. He chastised her for laughing and being herself like that was all somehow bad.

Knox believes this is a seductive tactic?

"Your aunt certainly knew how to make a young man interested." He rubs the stubble of his chin as if deep in thought. "She was the first one I ever found worth being bound to, honestly."

"You can rot in hell." Eva shrinks into herself, tucking her trembling chin into her chest.

Knox breathes in deeply, like he's sniffing in the richest aroma of blossoms. "Nothing more intoxicating than a hint of rebellion in one's other half." Lifting his arms widely as if in sudden triumph, he seizes Leo and the other Despairity's heads. Their inky clouds of smoke shrink and uncoil as he loops them round his pasty hands. He's whispering in Latin, feeding the boy I've always loved and his companions an ugly confidence. They're doubling in size. Growing like fire—as tall as a creature with a multitude of heads.

Eva scrambles to hide beneath the tree trunk. Palms crackle leaves as she crab-races to get away from them.

Dad-Knox places one of Dad's scuffed shoes in her path. Stooping down, his features soften as if he means to kiss her.

My mouth is moving. "STOP, KNOX."

As if I've never said a word, he cups Eva's face with the slender hollow of his hand. He purrs, "I've waited so long."

Leo rises from the Despairity, a fifteen foot cloud of smoke about to deliver my sister to Knox, so I do the only thing I can think to do under the circumstances. The only thing I can think to make him stop.

I dive for the ax, sweep it up, and plant it—prime-center in the meat of Dad's back.

CHAPTER 32 - EVA

FROST! NO!" I'm screaming like I never knew I could. This is all wrong. So, so wrong. But before I can say anything else, Dad, no, Knox, reaches behind himself, and with a sickening sucking sound, plucks the ax from his back like it's a stick simply scratching him. There's no blood. Just a black goo covering the blade, dripping to the ground.

Even the Despairity seem shocked, the smoke frozen in place, and one—I'm guessing Leo?—moves toward Frost's pale, shaking body. I don't know whether to try to protect her or myself. The tiny bit of hope left in me screams for Leo to help her. He hovers as a buffer in front of Frost, an inhuman shield.

"*Leonardo,*" Knox seethes. "Just like in New Orleans—back to protecting the helpless. You're so pathetically weak. I was wondering how long it would take you to quit pretending you'd grown a spine." He spits black goo on the wet ground.

Leo's form pulses and crackles, darkening with potential energy. A threat. Behind him, Frost is gasping for air and eyeing the screened back door swaying in the wind like it's trying to help. I'm sure she means to run for more weapons, but it's a longshot at best.

"Okay, then." Knox stretches his neck side to side, farther than any live human could. "I'll be on my way." He drops the ax and lunges for me, but I think angels must be here protecting me, because I'm able to dive and grab the ax before he can get ahold of me. I twist on the ground, trying to face him, but he's falling toward me full force. I thrust the ax between us, trying to shield myself from him. Before either of us knows what is happening, the blade slices right into Knox's arm, severing it completely—skin, muscle and bone. The arm flops onto me. Screaming, I try to crawl back, but he's on top of me and he's too heavy.

Face purple, distorted with rage and with bugs writhing under his skin, Knox finally looks like the nightmare that he is. He grapples for the ax, which I realize in horror I've let go of. Leo shoves a tendril of his spirit between the ax and Knox, making Knox fly back and off of me.

Knox grunts and throws his power at Leo, like an unnatural wind. Leo crackles and wilts an inch, but pulses with his own dark energy and hurls the weapon. Knox tries to dodge it, but Leo's aim is true and now Knox's—my dad's—other arm is on the ground.

Knox screams, an unearthly bellow of centuries of pent up frustration. He wails, vessel shaking until black oozes from his eyes, ears, and nose. He coughs and chokes and can barely breathe. He straightens, heaving for a long moment, and I brace myself for whatever is next.

He turns toward me. His obsidian, oozing eyes meet mine, and in them are promises of torture instruments and meat grinders. I consider doing everyone a favor and giving myself up to end it all right now. Maybe I am meant for this. Meant to have stayed with these things and not come to Earth in the first place. But before I can consider any more,

Knox heaves for air one more time, throws his head back, and shoots out of my daddy's body. His smoke races around Leo's form, now lighter and somewhat diminished. The Despairity join him and plunge head-on into the honey locusts and vines of the woods.

I stare at the freckled arm near me, just lying there, still clothed but discarded like a lost dog bone. My father. His arms hugged me and guided me and were always so strong he could toss an eighty-pound bag of wheat like it was full of marshmallows. His shell lies there beside it. It doesn't seem like him at all, just a shell like the grasshopper he stepped on earlier. My dad is no longer there.

All to save me from a fate that may be inevitable anyway. I led this demon on. I invited the evil into our lives, even though my mom and my *dad* taught me over and over to stay away from it. I even dragged Frost into it. And now, I made her do the unthinkable.

CHAPTER 33 - FROST

There's a Hasidic legend," Leo once told me when we were kids.

Our legs dangled over the side of my bed, and we'd arranged all my stuffed animals on the top of my headboard. Panda and Barracuda kept slipping off, so I wedged them a little deeper down between the wood and wall.

"It *says*," Leo said, trying to catch my eye, "that when a baby is conceived, an angel accompanies the soul into the womb."

I remember thinking that "Hasidic" and "conceived" were rather big words, but I wanted to know what they meant, so I mentally scribbled them down.

From the vantage point of my pink bunny pajamas, I scanned my playmate's profile as I often did—his sad eyes but wistful, playful smile. The almost somber slant of his nose and brow. He knew the smoke made me think he was on fire, so he always appeared to me in the shape of a human.

I wanted to touch Leo then, but every time our beings connected, a tickle like a feather trailed down my arms.

Still, I was sort of transfixed by those eyes, like two endless pools.

Leo's tone took on an almost chiding quality. "Aren't you listening?" Though he smiled, the smile was far too bright. It clashed with the anguish in his eyes.

I tucked my foot behind my ankle and parroted like I often did at school. "Angels accompanied babies into wombs."

Leo reached out like he was going to pat me on the head, but he paused and instead rubbed the straight bridge of his nose. This was something adults did when they were trying to be patient with kids. His hand and face seemed to goop together, though, like silly-putty, and I could feel my eyes growing enormous.

"Do that again!"

Pressing his lips together, Leo dropped his translucent hand. "They *say* that when the angel accompanies the baby to the womb, he uses the time to discuss the purpose of the child's incarnation."

I had no idea what "incarnation" meant, and when my foot slipped out of its safekeeping spot, Leo suggested we move on to playing checkers. His black circle pieces didn't get "kinged" nearly as often as mine did.

Before bed, he tucked my purple cotton comforter round my shoulders, his voice as gentle as the wind as he took up where he left off. "All of the angel's hoping and planning for the infant, though, will come to naught. For as a mother is about to give birth, an angel reaches out his finger." He extended his pale, translucent hand. "And presses it to the baby's skin." He placed the tip of his finger above my lip and beneath my nose, tickling me again. Half my face felt like it had gone to sleep, and the other half felt like miniature fairies were pirouetting across my skin. I giggled, reaching for him to touch me again.

My night light clicked on—a reminder that bedtime was to be strictly enforced in the Abram house.

"The angel says, 'Hush, now forget.'" Almost no sound trailed from Leo's cracked lips. "And so the child loses all traces of memory. Loses everything regarding where she really came from."

Frost? Frost!"

Someone's shaking my shoulder—I must have passed out—but I'm still thinking how, in the morning after Leo had tucked me in, I wrote down everything he said. I wrote the detail about how he had silly-putty skin, and I wrote how, when he touched me, it made me laugh. I drew, too, a picture of that angel touching the baby above the lip, because, despite my limited understanding, I was listening as well as I could. Years later, I burned all my journals—as instructed by my parents and therapists—which pretty well sums up how much I'd forgotten.

Grass like tiny needles tickles my neck. My ears are so stuffed, I can't make out the exact words of nearby murmuring voices. Dew seeps through my jeans, and there's something sticky coating the fingers of my hands.

As I blink to open my eyes, soft rays of light encase me, warming my brow and neck. It encases our sycamore tree where two brown finches hop.

Time was supposed to stop ticking, cease working when I did what I did. Is it a just world if I keep living after I killed my own dad?

Eva sobs into my shirt, her warm tears pooling into the hollow of my neck. Maybe I have a concussion, and she must have been the one shaking me awake just now. I planted an ax in my dad's back, and I'm swallowing a lump in my throat, because there's a pale, bloodied dismembered arm just a few paces off.

Eva shouts at someone behind her, and I think it might be EMTs, but the strong shoulders and military-like movements as he shoves his pistol into the back of his waistband prove that it's Raylan.

I glance around the blood-splattered hollies for Leo, past another severed arm with its fingers still curled, when Eva roars.

"HOW CAN YOU EVEN SAY THAT?"

I've no idea what Raylan just said, though it's impossible to miss the stubborn set of his jaw, the strong shoulders tensing like he's readying for combat.

"Sometimes," his voice comes out measured, "people die."

In a blur of black hair, Eva launches to wobbly feet. She doesn't even look like my sister as she thrusts her arms toward him. "YOU SAID HE DESERVED IT."

"He hit you." He glances away and grips the back of his neck. Shaking his head just once, he says, "Stop putting words in my mouth."

Rolling to sit upright on the leaves and dirt, I try to settle my equilibrium as Eva crosses the yard. Flinging herself at Raylan, she shoves him—hard—in the chest.

"You said he deserved it." Her voice cracks.

Raylan holds my sister's arms and firmly lowers them, easing her back. When he lets go, I think he might defend himself, but instead, all he does is tap his thumb on his jeans —just once. He stares at my sister with a cool, blank glare, and I think of the blank stare of the clay mask of Dante, the ancient poet.

My sister's scratching at her own arms, and I know her. She wants him to weep, to regret the death of my dad. But Raylan's whole body's gone into this frightening statue-like silence.

I'm sure she wants to push him again, but the charged sparks flying between them make me glance away. Offer some privacy to them.

That's when I spot Leo pulling a filthy shovel from Raylan's truck-bed. He's wandering past the stack of firewood a few meters beyond that. Pushing the shovel into the earth, he starts digging a hole, I suppose to spare my mom from seeing my dad dead.

He's not evil. Was on our side the whole time.

A twisted sort of peace-offering flashes into my mind when I bring him both of the severed arms, which only blasts open the black, sickening truth:

I'm a murderer, and I'll never do anything worthwhile again.

Shouldn't we call the police and go through the legal process and all that? But he's missing both his arms. How do we explain that?

Raylan's boots crunch leaves and gravel as he stomps across my path, and there's a loud *bang* as he slams the driver's side door of his truck.

A mockingbird screams. I should have tried to exorcise Knox. Mom's in the house, probably descending the stairs like she always does first thing in the morning, now opening the fridge, trying to decide what to make for breakfast. I wish I could spare her this truth. How could I have murdered him?

Tucking my face into my shoulder, I find the cool spot where Eva's tears soaked my shirt, where the salmon color has turned to a deep red. Pressing my cheek into the wetness, I watch as Leo digs, heaps, and digs the earth's charcoal, meaty flesh.

For once, I understand *his* point of view—why he never wanted to be born with the rest of us.

CHAPTER 34 - EVA

$\mathcal{N}$o. No, no, no.

What is my life? Yesterday, I narrowly escaped being Knox's mortality puppet, but my dad is still dead and Raylan is a cold-hearted tool. Of course I'm heartbroken and it sears like a branding iron to my skin that Dad and I had a complicated relationship, but *of course* I would *never* wish him dead. Raylan can rot in hell.

Frost is taking a shift with Mom, holding her in the dark on the floral living room sofa. I escaped to the porch. I've been stewing here for what seems like hours because I have no one to vent to. They've got their own grief, and Raylan is at Maggie's, so I can't go over there. I'm fixin' to go get some soda and junk food to try to dull this fire in my chest. Just gotta get the courage to leave. Heaven knows when Knox will be back to finish the job.

The thought leaves me paralyzed on the squeaky wooden swing.

"Eva, I'm so relieved you're okay."

The calm, lyrical voice of Leo. Leo, who is back in his vessel, although it looks like it's been through the ringer, his clothes wrinkled and filthy. His suspenders hang like a depressed flower. He puts one foot on the step and hesitates, as if asking permission. I leap up and throw my arms around him, surprising both him and myself.

"I'm so happy to see you." I sniffle, squeezing tight. He gathers me up in his arms like a guardian angel, lifting a slice of the pain away. I bask in the hug for a second but let go before it gets awkward. His bright, open eyes let me know he understands. "You saved us."

His face falls just a fraction of an inch. "I should have done so much more."

I shake my head but don't have the energy to argue, instead settling for a question. "Should we be freaking out that he'll be coming back any second now?"

Leo smiles wryly. "No, that kind of damage will take at least a few days to recuperate from."

That's a fit of a relief, at least. "Good." I move back to my spot on the swing, curling a leg underneath me. "It's nice to see you like this again." I spread my arms toward his vessel like a game show assistant.

Leo gives a deep sigh. Must be a meaty subject for him. "It does feel a bit more like *me* in here." He must finally accept he's welcome. He delicately climbs the stairs and leans against the green wooden porch beam. We listen to the roaring cicadas for a minute, and I fumble for words.

"Well, I'm glad you're not evil."

He gives me a tight-lipped smile. "That's still to be determined." He reaches for his pack of cigarettes.

"You're totally not. I know, because nothing evil could understand or appreciate Frost so well."

This makes him pause for just a beat, then he pulls out a cigarette, rolling it between his finger and thumb, considering.

"And you certainly saved our bacon back there. Our

knight in slimy armor." I quirk a small, crooked smile at him to make sure he knows I'm kidding. He twists his shoe on a nail that's starting to pop out of the wood.

"But your father—" He doesn't finish, and I'm relieved. Not ready to go there.

"You were certainly more helpful than Raylan." I wait before going on, testing the waters. Not sure where the bromance stands. Leo stands a bit straighter.

"Be patient with him. It's hard for him to see people in more than black and white."

"Well, he doesn't need to be a jerk about it," I mumble, but it does calm my nerves just a tad. How can I expect him to understand how I feel about my dad when I'm probably years away from understanding it myself? "But he just takes off? Doesn't check in? And where was he when all this was happening in the first place? He's the hunter, not me. I can only do so much."

My voice is getting higher and tighter, but I don't care. It feels good to be angry. "I've been *alone*. To deal with this. My mother and sister are in ruins and I'm just a freaking teenager with no clue how to help." I rap my rings on the swing's chain. "I don't know how to deal with this crap. Even Maggie hasn't been here. You—you at least did something—you chopped off his arm with a flying ax!" I cough, suddenly stunned at the ridiculousness of it all.

"Only after you did." He smiles a small smile and I sort of blush.

"True, that. We're pretty hard core." I hope for a smile, but he hangs his head as if ashamed.

"It shouldn't have come to that. I'm sorry it had to be so ugly. But I *could not* let him take you."

"And you didn't." I uncurl my leg and stop myself from swinging. "And I would rather you chop *my* head off than let him take me."

"We're not going to let that happen. Also, you're good, Eva. Don't let him make you think otherwise."

"I don't know," I murmur, playing with the swing's cool metal chain, a little embarrassed he knows this is debatable.

"I do. Remember, I knew you before this life. You were a force to be reckoned with. Even persuaded many people to follow you down here."

My heart squeezes, and I grunt to minimize the fact that my eyes are now wet. "So I was fifty-one percent good," I say with a shrug.

Leo puts the cigarette to his lips, then back in the pack. "I remember once when you were very little, probably three or four, you had older cousins visiting, and they were playing by the pond. They were shooting frogs with BB guns. You went over there, and with all your tiny might, grabbed one of the guns and threw it into the pond.

"You knew they could tear you to pieces, so you started running away, but crying and yelling at them the whole way about how frogs are people, too."

I lean back in the swing, not daring to believe I'm not some ticking time bomb of evil. "I think I vaguely remember that. So I'm good because I chucked my sister's gun in a pond?" I glance at Leo and spot Gato slinking across the yard toward us. "We'll see." Then, uncomfortable with this vulnerability, I decide to change the subject. "Frost will be happy to see you. I've kept you long enough. But, tomorrow, let's figure out how to kill the devil, 'kay? And also, kick Raylan in the britches." I pad over to the door to let Gato in the house. Gato brushes against my leg and meows, happy to go back inside where it's cool.

Leo takes a step, but pauses before he goes farther. "They don't strand a France."

"Oooooh, Leo's got jokes!" I throw my arm around his. "Very, berry mice, man."

CHAPTER 35 - FROST

Maggie holds onto Eva and me so tightly it's like she thinks she's made of peanut butter. Her mama bear arms hug our shoulders and our backs, but even for a funeral, I don't want her to hold me like that. I did what I did. I killed my dad. Last semester in World History, I learned that in eighteenth century France, I would have been guillotined. Before that, drawn and quartered. Strung up until dead.

If the police knew what I did, I'd be locked up for good. As is, Maggie helped us spin a story—that Dad died in a freak accident while chopping stumps. She has enough friends on the force who understand the hunter lifestyle that they didn't bat an eye when she said it would need to be a closed casket. Of course, the casket's empty, since Leo already put him in the ground.

Now? I live in this alternate reality where even Eva and Leo have become best friends. They've been whispering in the shadows and suddenly stop talking when I enter a room. The boys are no longer banned from the house, but a lot of good that does. Raylan's disappeared to who knows where, and now that Dad's gone, rules don't exist.

I know what Leo, Eva, and Maggie did. They covered up my crime, but what if I want to be punished for it? What if I need that? I thought learning the truth about the Blurred Ones would somehow pave the way for me to head to college, but instead it's sliced apart my family and made my sister a prime target.

Dad was one of those people who loved fiercely but didn't know how to express it. He'd say *I love you*, but he also felt that teaching hard labor was more important than having fun. I'd weed-eat the whole yard thirteen times in a row just to have him back.

But he hit her. *Hit her.* In the garage. And when he was possessed by Knox. Why did he have to be the sort of person who was prone to possession to begin with? There's a reason Knox was able to get in. Because Dad wasn't willing to do the work to guard himself. If only we'd strapped him to a gurney and *made* him get a real sigil tattoo.

Mom hasn't talked since Maggie went inside and told her what happened, just keeps digging around in Aunt Eva's stuff and muttering to herself. It's like the only way she knows how to heal is to focus on the past.

Still, I did the only thing I could do. I emptied my bank account to cover the funeral costs. Mom and Dad have never really saved for the future, lived paycheck to paycheck on his teacher's salary. UT? The dream is dead.

Someone's officiating—the local minister. Dad was a farm boy at heart, so his will stated he wanted to be buried on our land. Mr. Harris is here and keeps giving me the stink-eye behind those coke-bottle glasses.

He and Dad used to confer on gardening books.

Eva quietly cries, her ponytail tied tightly back. If I had my way, I'd make the whole gravesite disappear and let the grief be left just to us, but people I don't even recognize with bald heads and bad perms are crying for my father.

The only thing I keep thinking is, *I killed him.*

When the minister stops talking, Maggie's hands tighten around my shoulder, and her alto voice sings a song for her best friend. I want to listen to the words, but the melody is the only thing that registers in my head. Descending tones, shaking notes. A wind chime made of reeds struck with an invisible mallet. Her voice reverberates with the loss all the way from her shoulders, down to her arms which are cemented onto Eva's and mine.

When she's done singing, her voice cracks as she mourns in plain-spoken words, "One quarter of my family is dead." She'll hold Eva and me even closer after this. "He understood what it meant to hold your loved ones close. First real family I ever had."

I close my eyes against the drooping trees, the black clothes, against the way one woman keeps hiccuping through her cries even though she barely knew Dad.

Mom still hasn't emerged from the house when everyone lays flowers on his empty casket. But I hear her cry from the porch when someone brings her a rose.

It isn't until I'm staring at the green marshmallow salad on the counter, wishing I wanted the sugary sustenance, that it occurs to me that I could simply turn myself in to the authorities. Make amends. It would make the guilt stop. I'm not really thinking it through, but the only thing I can think to do is toss off my heels, grab my rattiest slippers, and mosey out.

I think I just might be in the clear—Maggie's speaking with the minister in the foyer, and Eva's bringing a glass of orange juice to Mom—so I sneak through the back door. There's not so much as a squeak of hinges when I find Leo leaning against the back of the house.

His long blond bangs hang in his eyes, which are handsome and tired. His crisp black suspenders have never looked more dapper, and there's a twinge in my chest as I realize I'm saying goodbye to this boy with sweat glistening across his skin.

I should stop, feel his forehead. Knox must have really injured him. But I can't let myself be derailed.

I killed him.

Gravel digs into my slippers as I tread past, avoiding eye contact. I tromp past car after crookedly parked car. One navy Impala's so hail-damaged that it looks like Maggie let loose on it with her shotgun.

When I make it to the sycamore, I pause for half a beat, trying to avoid the dark circle on the grass where Dad bled and Knox oozed that black tar. Tears burn in my eyes as I glance at the trunk where Leo defended Eva against Knox when I was too weak to even do that, and I'm holding my side because my breathing's started coming out in short gasps.

My slipper grazes a stump I should have chopped eons ago and the world's awhirl when Leo drifts close to me like a specter. "You really do mean to turn yourself in."

I glance at him, side-eyed, and set my gaze on the squad car at the end of the driveway. There's nothing to say. I can't talk about it.

As if accompanying me to my execution, Leo walks silently beside me. He reaches out and takes my hand. His fingers are strong and sure and tough, and I think he might try to talk me out of giving myself to the authorities, but his words are nonexistent.

The sun's going down—streaks of pink scrape the sky—so I have to lift my other hand to shield my eyes from the sunbursts, but by doing so, my watch grazes my brow, and I pause.

"Give this to my sister?" I let go of his hand and pull at the metal clasp at the back of my hand.

He takes it from me, a question about to spill from his lips when I cry, "Officer?" I call to the tall, thick man fiddling with the radio in his squad car. He must have good hearing, because he turns to where I stand.

Only now while looking into those unibrowed eyes do I consider what I'll say to him. *Sir? I murdered my father.*

Take me away.

Don't read me my rights.

I can't do it, and yet I was so sure that I could. Going away means abandoning Eva, and leaving her exposed like this to Knox would make me the *worst* sister in the world. I thought I could leave for UT, leave this town, but now all I can see is the way Knox loomed over her bed in that hotel room.

I've been making this all about me. I'm selfish. Sure, I'm guilty, but Eva—I swore to myself to protect her. I always have. That's what I did, and I realize I can't stop.

"Thank you for coming today," I tell the police officer, my voice shaking as badly as Maggie's did when she sang her song. I want to open that back slick door of his car, but my body's staggering backward.

I don't know which way to go. What to say now. And my slippers are twisting round my ankles like too-big socks. All I can see is gravel and bumblebees and tree limbs—severed limbs like Dad's and that ghost woman's.

My waist is captured by a strong hand, but all I can picture is how I impaled my father with that ax. His shoulders went rigid the exact same way they did when I hit the mower on a rock I didn't realize was there.

Once, I accidentally walked in the house with mud on my shoes when I had to use the bathroom. His shoulders went rigid, too. But then they softened, relaxed, and he asked me if

I'd like to go for a walk. We wandered around the yard, and he showed me each of the fruit trees he had planted. I didn't even really care, but he'd wrapped plastic around their bases and staked them so they'd grow strong and big.

Leo wraps his warm arms around my back, and my breaths come out fast. Somewhere in the back of my head it registers that the officer's asking Leo if I'm okay, but Leo says something about how I'm missing my dad. A green and white paisley shirt tells me Maggie's walking toward us, but Leo pulls me away and into our storage room beneath the house just as the minister calls her back again.

Despite it being ninety degrees, my whole body shivers from sweat. Leo seats me on a wheat bucket. He wraps me in a blanket—a blanket Dad used once to drive a wounded stray dog to the vet—when something in the back of my mind tells me I'm going into shock. Leo combs my stringy hair with his fingers and tells me it's okay to feel sad.

And I'm crying amidst the cans of creamed corn and pork and beans while the front of my black dress sticks to my bra. I pull it loose, away from my skin, and Leo sucks in a breath. I suppose I shouldn't have done that. My father's dead, and I'm already flouting everything he taught.

Leo digs his fingers into his hair, like he's trying not to think about the last time we kissed. I know he is, because he's looking at the doorway where it happened and Dad walked in and confronted us.

Our bodies were so close we felt like we were the same person. My chest pressed into his, and I felt whole in that moment.

Before I can think about what's happening or overthink the moment, I turn to Leo, and he's moving toward me in those beautiful suspenders and starched suit pants.

He drags a wheat barrel close and perches next to me like a seventeenth-century court gentleman. His blue eyes are on me and I'm thinking he might peck me on the cheek when he leans up close and I taste the piney taste of his nicotine mouth.

The storage room smells of Axe deodorant, and I'm crying as we kiss because Dad unloaded it from the car after being proud that he found a deal at Walgreens on it.

Leo's fingers trace the rippled lines on my back. My dress is polyester with some blend of silk, and it slides like butter beneath his hands.

My ears are ringing. I feel like a bomb may explode in my chest, but he's too far away, so it doesn't take long for me to find my way onto his lap.

His legs are strong and solid. His lips press into mine like there's oxygen in my breath. His mouth grazes my chin, pulling goosebumps from my flesh. When his fingers graze my hairline, I hold him closer, and his fingers wander up and down the skin near my waistband.

My thigh presses into his thigh. My black dress folds over his white buttons.

Somewhere in my mind I know my skirt's rising dangerously high, but I want him to trace that part of my leg. Want him to soothe that part of my flesh.

A woman's voice roughly clears her throat sounding eerily like the rev of a chainsaw. "Excuse me."

Maggie. I'd forgotten she saw us come in.

Seeing as how my skirt's nearly as high as my underwear and my arms are twisted around Leo like an octopus, I extricate myself the best I can. My cheeks glow with embarrassment, but Leo has this serene look in his eyes like he's simply happy to have lived.

Spreading those soft, nice lips that had just covered so many wonderful inches of my skin, Leo says, "Would you like help saying goodbye to all your friends?"

I know Leo means this with complete earnestness, but

Maggie still doesn't know that. Her cheeks are flaring red like she's tempted to pull out one of my dad's shotguns.

"You can get!" She throws a little salt grenade she must have kept in her fanny pack, but it misses Leo by a mile, exploding on another nearby wheat bucket.

I giggle as Maggie pulls me toward the guests at the house, because Maggie never misses, let alone as badly as that. "You *like* him."

There's the soft thud of the door as Leo closes the storage room behind us, and I twist in Maggie's grip as I meet his gaze. His tender smile is enough to burst every single artery in my chest.

I killed my father—that I shall never forget—but kissing Leo, my beautiful, pain-riddled Leo, made me forget.

CHAPTER 36 - EVA

*C*ome *pick me up, ya jerk.*

I hit send and pray Raylan is as ready to make up as I am. Seconds later, my phone dings. It's him.

Give me twenty.

Time to enter my heart into Olympic gymnastics. My stomach too, twisting with guilt for doing something other than mourn. Then it wrenches further at the guilt that at least we got to have a funeral at all, unlike Jenny. I pray Leo was right and I'm not a she-demon after all.

I check myself out—old black Depeche Mode T-shirt, yoga pants, and flip-flops. Eh, he's seen me worse. I throw on some raspberry flavored lip balm, tighten my messy bun, and call it good.

Frost is boarded up in her room again. Feeling a bit selfish, I whisper through the door's crack, lips smudging lip balm all over. "Frost, I'm going out with Raylan. I didn't get kidnapped."

"Have fun," she calls, with the vacant tone she has when she's neck-deep in a book.

"I will, I promise." And with that, I bound down the stairs. No use worrying Mom.

I wait on the porch swing in pulsating heat. Hell has come to Bloodcreek this day. Faster than I could have guessed, a gunmetal-gray truck's headlights appear on the long driveway. I don't miss a beat before I'm up and trotting toward the passenger side. Without a smile or wave, I hop in and slam the door shut.

He sits still, an invisible weight pushing on his shoulders. His hair's damp and he looks *good*—he must have hopped in the shower. His shampoo's clean scent fills the truck cabin, masking the would-be stink of his empty Dorito bags.

"I am so sorry for what I said," he nearly whispers. I swear his voice trembles. "I never—"

I cut him off with a raise of the hand.

"I get it," I say firmly, then look pointedly out the windshield at the neighbor's old windmill you can only see from this spot.

Raylan knows what to do with silence. He turns around and backs out of the driveway with ease, then drives even farther from town. The A/C blows the scent of his jacket my way. What *is* his deal with that jacket, anyway? I breathe deeply, heart pounding but chest loosening. How can he make me so tense and yet so relaxed at the same time?

Five, ten minutes stretch on and we drive, listening to the heaviest metal I've ever heard at levels so loud he wouldn't hear me if I spoke anyway. It's almost painful to my ears, and I welcome it. The battering drums match my pounding heart, but the man's voice is clear, beautiful, and sorrowful, but still angry. It's everything I feel.

I stare out the window, watching tree limbs snatch each other while fireflies dance and tease. I completely lose myself in the sounds and sights, then startle when something touches my hand in my lap.

Raylan scoops up my hand in his, warm and calloused. Fingers gently push into my palm, beckoning my fingers to open. When they do, he straightens his own to maneuver them as deeply in between mine as they can be, and our hands are two halves now made whole. My blood boils in the best possible way in every inch of my body. He has the cluelessness to look at me with a question of approval on his face. As if I'm not like a walking billboard of I LIKE YOU! But still, he has no idea what he does to me.

I use his arm to help slide myself over to sit directly next to him. I smash as close as possible, put my other hand on top of our other two, and speak closely to his ear so he can hear without turning down the music.

"Thanks, Raylan." I lightly brush my lips on his ear when I say it.

He responds by pulling me impossibly closer, wedging my arm between his arm and his chest, and tightening his hand on mine even more. I've got to figure out a way for this to never end. An idea pops into my head, something Jenny told me about one day we were bored in Spanish. Something destructive.

***

I've never seen Raylan so on board with anything before. But once I shouted over the metal, "Let's go blow stuff up!", his eyes glimmered like a little boy on Christmas morning.

After ransacking the necessary supplies from a poor, unsuspecting meth dealer down gravel road H, we drive up to the "Death Mine." An abandoned mine in the middle of nowhere, covered with only an iron grate, holes just barely bigger than my foot. Teenagers come out here for keggers and to throw flaming things down and watch them burn.

"Some people just want to watch the world burn, huh, Eva?" Raylan grins at me. He holds a glass beaker filled with kerosene and hands me another. I hold the lighter proudly in my other hand.

"Sometimes, Raylan, yes, we do." I smile almost as big as I would have had my Dad not just been lowered into the ground. "Jenny told me she came out here with Bic-Head and he accidentally set his pants on fire, so he took them off and threw them down."

"And she found that attractive? Should I catch my shirt on fire?" He grabs the bottom of his shirt, pretending to start taking it off.

"Go right on ahead, cowboy. But first—" I hold my beaker out as if I'm going to give a toast. Raylan puts his up next to mine, and I touch the lighter to the kerosene inside them both until they dance with flames.

"To Dad. He was a jerk, but he was my jerk. And he could also be really, really awesome." Smiles gone, we clink beakers and drop them. We watch them fall, fall, fall and get smaller until they disappear, without ever hearing them hit bottom. We stare a few seconds after they're no longer visible, and with a breath, I turn to Raylan. "Your turn."

Raylan nods and fills up our next object, empty beer bottles. I light them and now let him lead the toast.

"To your dad. He probably hated me, but I would have won him over." His lips quirk up a bit. "May he be free from his demons—inside and out. And to my dad. After I die, may I find his spirit and torture it for a thousand years, and then I can forgive him and we can all have peace as a family."

I'm shocked at his sentiment and how perfectly angry and yet longing it is. We clink beer bottles and let them drop, yelling after them.

"Bye, suckers!"

When they're gone, I look at him and smile wide and glittery, like a showman.

"And now, are you ready for the finale?"

"And what is that?" He reaches for my hand, and my heart soars.

"Pour the kerosene on my hand," I instruct. He looks at me like I'm a little crazy, but so is this night, so he obeys, then his eyes widen as I place the lighter to my own hand. The fire engulfs my hand immediately, but it doesn't hurt. It only burns the kerosene, leaving my hand unscathed. I wiggle my fingers and grin at him.

"Okay, that's awesome. My turn." We take turns lighting various appendages on fire, laughing, daring, and mostly forgetting. I realize I feel almost as at home with him as I do Frost. I revel in the smell of the kerosene fumes and dusty road and find comfort that even Knox probably can't find us out here.

Raylan squeezes my hand. "I like you like this."

"Like what? Destructive?"

"Well, yeah, but I can tell this is the real you." His eyes lock on mine, and if I weren't so excited by his sudden openness, I'd be laying one on him right now.

"As opposed to?" I manage to squeak out.

"Worried about what other people think."

"Psh. I don't—" I stop myself. I don't want to play games, but I also have no idea what to say. "Well, thanks, Raylan. I like you like this too."

"I'm here for you, Eva." He puts his strong arm around me and pulls me so close my cheek brushes his scruffy face. We half stumble back to the truck, walking awkwardly but not wanting to let go. He opens the passenger door, and I climb in and slide back to the middle. He drapes his jacket on me, and I let myself fall asleep on his shoulder.

CHAPTER 37 - FROST

I clutch the glass of ice cold lemonade Maggie made to my chest, grateful that we're all ready to strategize Knox's takedown now that we have a clear head. We actually made it to church—for a bit. Listening to the sermon, I realized we hadn't done what was needed before. With Dad, we were too slow, but all of that's about to change. Knox isn't going to take any more of my family.

And, in our matching layered sheer dresses, we'll look good doing it.

Like Eva says, we'll skin Knox alive and stretch him out on the tile like Maggie's bear rug. A lot of neighbors tend to ask why Maggie hordes so many hunting weapons, so she keeps up the charade that she's really into hunting bears and the like.

Leo's sitting close to me—his thigh's touching my own—and Raylan's affectionately rubbing his thumb on the side of Eva's dress. Despite everything, Eva and I could get used to this. We glance at each other with our veiled giddiness. Thankfully, Maggie pretends to be oblivious.

Taking my lemonade from my hand, Maggie says, "There's something you need to see." She takes Eva's and Raylan's next. I expect her to offer to take Leo's, too, but he sets his down on the coaster on the coffee table before she has the time to reach for it.

The five of us tromp and glide past a pair of mounted deer on the walls and a skunk fur on a desk. I always wondered how someone landed that. I spot a framed photograph of Maggie and Dad holding up matching certificates for when they earned the highest shooting scores at the local shooting club. I don't even think I was born yet.

By the time we're outside with thirty-foot tall evergreens and the neighbor's goats bleating somewhere to the right, Maggie murmurs, "It's nothing special." She fiddles with her shed's metal lock.

Eva and I glance at each other with cocked eyebrows.

We get to go inside?

We get to go inside!

Eva fights back a squee and I smile for the first time since before Dad's death.

When Maggie eases open the door, a plethora of antler chandeliers greet us from the wooden ceiling. Swords and ropes hang like streamers between them.

"Not your typical way of arranging." Maggie pulls a random string dangling near the door to turn on the light, which casts everything in a slightly yellow light. "But each and every weapon in here is carded and catalogued. Everything's warded." Maggie gestures to the red triquetras on the walls spray-painted like graffiti. "Most, on the weapons themselves." She lifts a machete with slow precision and shows us a sigil dug into the butt of the handle. "Prevents bad guys from taking my things." She eyes Leo, but not as long as she would if she believed he was bad.

"Takes time, though." She frowns at an abandoned drawer

strewn with knives, screwdrivers, and other things that make me think of Knox.

"My jacket has sigils on the inside," Raylan pipes up.

Eva shoves him on the shoulder. "That explains why you wear it even when it's boiling out."

"My sister got it for me." He shrugs. "And somehow, it's not even hot."

Eva nods. "Nice. And attractive."

Raylan ducks like, for the first time in his life, he's found his usually dauntless self to be embarrassed.

The shed reeks of the heady scent of mildew and rock salt. I glance around for Maggie's stack of books, but she keeps those in her library, I guess. One shelf's stuffed full of potions like an ancient apothecary, and another's full of funny-shaped, small locked boxes.

"You've organized it so nicely," I say. Eva glances at me, and I skirt my gaze back at her.

Brown noser.

Shut up!

But Maggie's smiling from ear-to-ear, because she's always been soft for compliments. "I got these ones," she grabs a slew of daggers dangling from leather strips in the center of the room, "from a garage sale."

Raylan reaches up to look at the silver better in the faint light. "Not bad."

"And these," she walk-trots to another chest of drawers and pulls out what looks to be something like necklaces, "are laced with garlic *and* rock salt." She holds out one like she means to place it on the nearest person, who just so happens to be Leo, who's now blushing in his ageless way. Awkwardly, he steps to the side and extends a hand toward Eva like he's a British officer.

Maggie slips the necklace round Eva's neck. Eva pats it.

"Wear 'em to ward off vampires and demons," Maggie says. "I patented those."

Eva eyes a corded whip hanging on a wall. "And that?" She nods to the bone fragments embedded in it.

"Never ask." Maggie veers Eva toward the back of the garage.

"What I really wanted to show you girls is back here." Maggie leads us around a collection of shovels to a floor-to-ceiling bookcase.

I knew she had more books hidden away in here.

On the second shelf, though, instead of books are a row of blades with neat little labels wrapped around them like Eva and I saw at the Ripley's Believe it or Not Museum. "Your dad helped me label those." Maggie's voice hitches, and the grief is so raw that the room starts to warble from where I stand.

Leo gently places his palm on the sheer fabric on the small of my back, and I lean into his comfort.

A hand, too, closes around my shoulder, and Eva's blearily smiling at me as she says, "He was great at labeling stuff."

I study what's clearly labeled as an "opal glass" white blade that shimmers blue and pink. I imagine Dad writing those words with a pen before carefully wrapping the label round the handle of the blade.

"He spent hours doing these," Maggie says, reading my mind.

On the far-right is a twisted gray-black knife that resembles a railroad spike. Next to it are brass knuckles with knives poking out from every ridge. There's a curved one—a sword, like a Samurai's—and when Leo catches me looking at it, he squeezes my hand.

He murmurs, "Those ones are nice."

Did he spend time in Japan? It's a little unfathomable, the extensive life he's lived.

"And last but not least, my Blurred One cage." She nods to a six-foot-tall black wall, surrounded by thin metal bars. "Just a bit bigger than yours, Raylan."

"Dang, this thing's huge!" Eva runs a ringed finger along a bar, to which Maggie shrugs.

"Never know how big the vessel's gonna be. Anyway, I show you all of this," Maggie says, gesturing to her lair of oddities, "to give you perspective. You never know what will be your secret weapon." I think she might be about to show us what's on the other side when she reaches down and unzips her fanny-pack, which crinkles from disuse.

Between her thumb and pointer finger, she holds up something small and round. A screw and wing-nut. As I absorb the rust and blood coating the screw's grooves, Leo's arm falls away from me.

"Now, I may only be a hunter," Maggie says, "but I do know a thing or two about this doo-dad." She settles her eyes a little too dangerously on Leo. "Do we have a volunteer?"

CHAPTER 38 - EVA

*W*hy not," says Leo, my new friend, and quite possibly Frost's literal soulmate. He reaches for the etched screw.

"Do *what?*" Frost looks like she's just come face to face with a copperhead.

"Remember the legend, Frost?" Leo's smile is sad, but his eyes are on fire. He reaches one finger to her lips. "The angels visit the womb, the child's last glimpse of the spiritual world they came from, and whisper, 'Hush, now forget.'" He turns to Maggie, who looks uncharacteristically uncomfortable, shoving her hands in her pockets and staring at the screw. "Right on the philtrum. Or so says the legend." He taps his own, finger just above his lip, like he's saying "shh."

Maggie grabs the tiny piece of metal as delicately as she can with her stubby fingers. "I reckon it has something to do with that spot being a tie between body and soul." She sounds halfway between mournful and optimistic. "It's supposed to take away their powers. Drive it in, make them basically mortal."

"Whaa—" I stutter, my heart following suit. Yay, but yikes at the same time. Talk about getting screwed.

"Absolutely *not*," Frost yelps, turning maroon, while Raylan demands, "Have you known about these?"

"Just the legend and whispers of this theory." Leo meets Raylan's eyes bravely. "I haven't seen the practice."

"You should have said something!"

"If I shared every whisper of lore I knew, we would be visiting for a decade."

Raylan and Maggie both don't look very pleased, but I gulp and focus on some gnarly looking ice picks to try to hide my queasiness. When I was seven, Frost and I shared a room and had bunk beds. I think it was an effort to keep us from getting spoiled or finding any more "imaginary friends."

I fell off the top bed one night. I hit our desk on the way down, right on my top gums. I cried and cried till Frost sang me back to sleep, but I remember waking up the next morning completely caked in blood. We had to throw my jammies and sheets away, I bled so much, and I didn't have something drilled in there. This wouldn't be pretty.

Leo runs a finger down Frost's arm, who looks like she's about to grab his hand and run. Leo steps closer to Raylan and Maggie. A hunter's gathering. "You need to try it on me to make sure. Knox isn't going to want to leave empty-handed. And I am *not* letting Knox or the Despairity near either one of them again." The way his eyes burn and his lips are a little pursed, it's the closest I've seen this lovable guy to being angry.

"It'll work," Frost nearly shouts. "I know it will. You don't need to go torturing yourself just because you feel guilty." Frost's lip quivers, making her look ten years old.

Maggie looks at Frost, cheeks flushed, and speaks in measured tones. "He has a point, Frost. I'd feel a heck of a lot safer knowing it really works."

"Well, of course!" Frost throws her arms up wide. "Even if it does work, how would we get it in Knox? Find someone else to be your guinea pig!"

Maggie slams a fist on the worktable next to her, making me jump. "We don't have time for this. You think we can just wait around for another Blurred One to show up? What Knox wants to do to your sister is worse than death. And if you haven't noticed, nothing else we're doing is working."

Frost's face flames with rage, but she lowers her voice. "There has *got* to be another way."

Leo takes Frost's face gently between his hands and speaks quietly, as if calming a spooked horse. "I will do this. They'll put it in, see if I'm powerless, and then they'll take it out." His eyes flicker to Maggie's. "Right?"

"Right," she says, low and steady—a vow.

"And, I heal quickly." He lets go, then, straightening, turns to me. "Eva, please take her outside. I don't want either of you to witness this."

"Wait, you're doing this right *now*?" The words are out before I can filter. The dirty looks I get from Leo and Maggie have me scrambling. "I mean, sure. I guess. If you're sure. Yes." I spare a glance at Raylan for moral support, but he's looking at the ground, a little green.

"Come on, Frost, let's go for a walk." I try to take her rigid arm, but she yanks out of my grasp.

She looks like she's going to yell at me, but instead, she coughs a sob. "I can't take anyone hurting anymore. I just want this to be over."

"I know. And I guess this is how it will be," I try to reassure her. More gently this time, I take her hand like I'm the big sister now and guide her out of the shed.

Before I close the heavy metal door behind us, I tell the others, "Y'all be careful. And good luck." They look from me to each other, faces hardening to the stoic expression of soldiers before battle, completely surrounded by weapons.

Let the hunters do their job. We've been through enough. *She's* been through enough.

Once outside, I blink to adjust to the much lighter daylight. It's probably twenty degrees cooler out here, but still scorching. I try to steer us toward the house, but Frost's knees buckle, so we settle for leaning against Maggie's Buick nearby.

The car's metal is burning hot, especially with these flimsy dresses—but Frost leans against it and huddles into herself like she needs the heat. I settle next to her but am careful not to touch the car. I search for something to distract her from this latest pain. Instead I find myself wondering for the thousandth time how we got here.

The image of a blonde wig and lavender bubble bath flashes through my mind. It was so exciting, started so fun. And now, suddenly, this all seems one hundred percent my fault. The weight of it is crushing.

"Frost, I am so, so sorry." My voice wavers, but I have to go on. "I totally got us into this. I wanted to prove myself with Knox, have an adventure, and I got all obsessed and then distracted by Raylan—" A rogue tear darkens a spot on the dusty gravel.

I probably smeared my mascara. Gah.

"It's not your fault," Frost mutters, but she looks at her hands.

"But I'm the one who chased after Raylan in the first place. Flirted with Knox. I opened us up to all this evil." I pick up a pebble and chuck it as hard as I can down the driveway. My stomach sinks so far I feel like it will pull my whole self into some awful abyss. "Leo must have lied about me being a good spirit just to make me feel better. Knox was right. Dad was right."

She finally looks at me with those innocent eyes, and I'm going to promise her I will do better. For her and for Dad. For Mom and Maggie. Raylan. But before I can tell her, the faint, unmistakeable squeal of a drill escapes the shed, and her eyes shoot open with fear. A window must be open somewhere. She's a deer in the headlights, only I know she's considering bolting inside.

I throw my arms around her and pull her as tight as I can. I consider singing, but that's stupid, right? But Frost's nails are digging into my arm and she's falling onto her knees on the nearby leaves, and so am I, and I don't have words to soothe her.

She's clutching her hands in an earnest prayer.

I hold her close. Pray with her, all the while knowing I've always had nightmares—brutal and disturbing, but when I was little, I couldn't go back to sleep. I was too scared to go get Mom or Dad, so Frost would sing to calm me down. Now, desperate for anything to help, I close my eyes and sing as calmly as I can.

> *You and me,*
> *we've been through it all,*
> *more ups than downs,*
> *though the down feels all 'round.*
> *Hush now, sleep,*
> *hush now, dream,*
> *The up's a comin' down this stream.*

A warm, firm hand grips my shoulder. I open my eyes to see Maggie, whose dusty face has been washed clean in smudges by tears. She pulls us up toward her, but once Frost's on her feet, she tears toward the shed.

"Frost, wait," Maggie calls, but softly, knowing it's a lost cause. I nuzzle under her arms, knowing she needs comfort every bit as much as I do. She squeezes me tight for a breath, lets me go, and looks me in the eye.

"It works."

CHAPTER 39 - FROST

Blood drips down the lower half of Leo's face—like he's got a bloody nose, but that's no bloody nose. I know who did that to him.

Maggie.

At the pain still ebbing around my long-lost imaginary friend's face, I wrench my hair from my scalp with my hands.

Leo may only be a Blurred One, but he's still in a body. A body that helps him feel love and pleasure—and pain. It's why Knox covets having his own body so badly. Must be. Because emotions are heightened when spirits are in vessels. It's why we came to earth—to learn, to experience, to love, to choose —in the first place.

I cover my mouth because I'm breathing too shallowly. Raylan's guiltily slipping a blood-splattered drill onto a nearby workbench but not before we lock eyes.

How could you? I want to say.

I didn't. He glances down to the cement ground. *I didn't want to,* he seems to answer.

Leo pulls a handkerchief from his front pockets and dabs at the blood on the lower half of his face, making a mess more than anything. It's not black, though. Well, not as black as Knox's is, because he's not evil. His eyes match the attempt he's making to smile, though his face is a train wreck.

And this is why he is good. He suffers to protect others. Emphasizes the needs of self last.

I itch to throw my arms around him and take him to the sink, but Maggie brings over a wet rag for him to wash his face. She hesitates to wipe the blood and gunk trickling down his chin, but Eva grabs the rag and dabs at the blood like we didn't just conspire against him.

Light shines in Leo's eyes. "This will make him powerless."

Eva tries to smile a little while her hands shake.

Leo snatches her trembling fingers and says, "He'll stop terrorizing your family."

The two of them lock eyes, and I never knew how much I would love seeing this exchange between the two of them. Like they comprehend each other's greatest fears, and Leo's somehow found a way to tell my sister what she needs to believe in herself.

It's all a little wrong. I'm supposed to be flinging hammers and cussing them out for drilling that screw into his face, but the almost tangible hope and relief floating through the room is a life preserver I won't abandon.

"K." Maggie eyes the top of her book-and-weapon crammed bookshelf. "We need a solid plan."

Leo looks like he wanted to discuss something else, but he blinks once, seeming to change gears in his mind. "We need to summon Knox," he agrees, following Maggie's gaze to a wide leather book with gold embossing and three different bookmarks.

"Cage the bastard," Raylan says, "and use the drill. Stat."

Eva blinks her too-big doll eyes in wonder at the plan. "That sounds easy enough."

Maggie begins pacing, which is somewhat awkward in that we're already jam packed in her little shed. "We need to summon him, trap him, and use the drill, but we *need* to keep these girls out of harm's way."

Eva's head jerks in Maggie's direction like she's just said that she's sworn off TV for the rest of her life. "We don't need to be babysat!"

"We also prefer for you not to be dead," Raylan says.

Silence falls over us like a thick layer of dust. I don't really want to cross Eva, but Maggie is right. I swore I wouldn't put my sister in harm's way, so keeping her away from Knox is the best plan.

"We should stay here," I say.

Maggie heaves the big leather book from off the top of the bookshelf. "He doesn't know about this place. We also need to protect Donna."

"Oh, so we're supposed to sit around and knit booties," Eva trills her bejeweled fingers a little like a madwoman in the air, "while the three of you go off to fight the bad guys?"

Leo rests a comforting hand on Eva's shoulder. "Maggie will stay here." He glances at her a little guiltily to be sure she agrees with him, and when she nods in assent, he quickly adds, "Raylan and I will lure Knox and finish him off."

"Are you ready to take him out for real this time?" Raylan asks.

Leo and Maggie exchange a look.

"The screw will trap him so his powers are useless," Maggie slowly explains, "but no one really knows if it's possible to permanently kill a Blurred One."

"Matter can't be created or destroyed." I shrug. "The Law of Conservation."

Eva looks at me like I am the embodiment of nerdiness.

We have a plan, and Leo seems ready to hit the nail on the

proverbial head when he says, "I am prepared to do to whatever is necessary to end . . . Goldi . . . Knox."

Something drips from the corner of the room. A distant neighbor starts a tractor, and, in the other direction, one of the goats bleats in the distance.

Eva and I manage to lock eyes, and thankfully, Maggie's face is twitching with humor until she lifts her ruddy cheeks to the low ceiling and laughs.

The laugh is loud. It's the sort of laugh that I've always loved coming from my pseudo aunt. It's the kind of noise that tells me that she's temporarily forgotten about silver bullets or devil's traps. Maggie's never lost her humanity despite all the horrible creatures she's decided to hunt and take down.

Batting at her eyes with the backs of her hands, she cries, "We have a plan."

"I get to do the screw." Raylan pulls the drill from the workbench.

Maggie rummages around for a few more books and tools as Eva looks at me.

You good?

Yes.

"We need to start the spell the minute the Sabbath is over," Maggie says. She grabs a can of spray paint from a tray of assorted paints. "At midnight."

"Knox will have his full strength by then." Leo takes my hand. "Until then," he lowers his head as if in subservience to Maggie. "Mind if I take Frost for a little time?"

Unsure, Maggie narrows her keen hunter's eyes.

"We'll be back before eleven." He's tugging on my hand to follow him, but is it terrible of me that I want to come?

Maggie seems to release a decade's worth of all the breathable air she's collected in her lungs. "Eleven." She shakes her head, glancing at the spellbook in her hands. "Ten! Ten. You're familiar with the summoning spell?"

Leo bows his head. "Yes."

My cheeks flush at the sobriety in his tone, and I'm a little too giddy as I accept the warm, calloused fingers of his hand. As we traipse past chainsaw blades and wicked looking clubs fatter than my head, I murmur, "Are you all right?"

He tries to force his voice not to sound weak as he says, "I am strong enough."

You just have a screw drilled into your face on your weakest day of the week, I want to say, but I keep my thoughts to myself.

Catching my gaze, Eva shoots me a devilish grin. I know she's probably thinking something about me not actually being a nun, and I shoot her a smile back, too. Maybe Maggie will also allow a little "Reva" time.

Outside, the just-now setting sun illuminates Maggie's house with sharp hues of pink and orange. A cargo truck kicks up dust while rumbling past, and Leo's grip is far stronger than what it should be after what just happened to him.

"Are you sure we shouldn't try to summon Knox now? While he's weak—" *like you are.* I don't add.

Leo's hand squeezes my fingers tighter as if not wanting to consider that there might be a bit of truth to this observation, but then he says, "Knox is still recovering from his own wounds from the last attack. He will be as unreachable as he can be."

As my skirt rustles against the leaves and grass, we wander between Maggie's Buick and Raylan's gray truck, which are both covered with insects and dust. The neighbor's goat continually bleats in the distance and my heart thrums. We crunch over errant weeds and gravel and I feel a little dizzy. He always makes me feel a little warm blooded.

"There's something I've wanted to do for ages," Leo says. "Just you and me, if we ever got the chance."

My voice pitches the way Eva's does when she can't believe someone would say something so nice. "Really?"

He chuckles as we wind through the far side of Maggie's evergreen trees, their heady scent as sharp as laundry detergent.

"Ever watch the stars, Frost?"

I nod.

"When I was fourteen years old—"

I eye him, because he was never exactly born, so he wouldn't have an age.

"When *you* were fourteen," he corrects himself, "*I* believed I was fourteen. Because when you were born, time started to matter. After I left you, I became quite the gypsy. I bought—er, pillaged—a tent to get away from Knox and the others. Find a little space."

Our shoes crunch twigs and leaves as we wander beneath an oak's low-hanging branches. Ever the gallant gentleman, Leo holds the most intruding part out of the way.

"In that tent," he says, lowering the branch as he follows me, "I used to lie on my back and stare at the ceiling. I swore to myself that I wouldn't allow myself the luxury of looking at the stars again until I made things right."

I wander around a hole to find the blown apart Root Beer bottles of Maggie's shooting range, brown bits of broken glass.

"I *promised* myself I would make things right," he says again, gaze trailing over my eyes.

Heat waves flare inside me, the bodice of this dress suddenly constricting.

"To do that," he pauses beneath a somewhat old oak tree riddled with shotgun blasts, "I need to stop Knox from hurting people. Stop the Despairity from ruining lives. Of course there are more Blurred Ones, but these I can do something about."

Thinking on the three distinct beings, I say, "You seem to know them well. Did you used to be . . . friendly?"

He avoids my gaze. "The eldest and I share some memories. She nearly convinced me to go to God's side."

A hummingbird whirs past his head and perches on an abandoned Root Beer bottle, sucking the leftover sugar with its tiny beak. The idea that Leo still remembers what happened *before* twists knots in my stomach. It's all so unfathomable. An impossible reality. And now, one of *them* has a history with him. She nearly convinced him to come to earth, but instead joined him on the wrong side?

"Do you wish you could go back?" I don't even think before I'm asking.

Leo's fingers tighten around my hand. "Every single moment."

My lip quivers as I wish he could stay, that he could touch me like this all the time. But our time is limited. No one has a future with a Blurred One who doesn't really properly age.

When I glance up at his face, I find tears trapped in his eyes. Instead of looking at me, he's looking at the tree-leaf dappled sky. He's readying himself to look at the stars. Something he's wanted to do for years, but has saved to do with me.

What must it be like to be so trapped in your own life? To know, for thousands of years, that one deviant choice kept you forever on the wrong side?

Studying the oblong leaves of a neighboring ash, Leo says, "I knew I was damning myself when I chose the wrong side. And that can't change."

Pulling my hand with a strong tug, Leo suddenly trots through the hull of the shooting range with its strewn bullets and targets with the Nazi-uniformed zombies. We crunch over more glass and tiny thistles that claw into my bare ankles until Leo pulls me through yet another cusp of thorny bushes.

Dandelions and buttercups meet us on the other side, the heady scent of lavender wafting over us. I think maybe he wants to nestle together on a blanket, perhaps look through a telescope at the starry sky, but he tugs me a little farther, past a squatter evergreen tree.

I want to cut him off and ask if there's any way he can change sides, but before I can, he murmurs, "The nice thing about Maggie's property is the elevation is pretty high." He releases my hand. With a low groan, he seizes one of the low-hanging branches and lifts a foot to the trunk of the tree.

"We're going to climb?" I glance down at my dress, but if we are, I can handle it, because I am a warrior woman.

His body shudders as worms writhe over his brow and beneath his eyes. He glances away, embarrassed.

"But you're afraid of heights."

With a painful grunt, Leo heaves himself up and scrambles up the tree. "It's worth it."

I survey the knobby trunk. It's been eons since we've been able to climb, and I love that Leo knows that a dress wouldn't slow me down. The bark is crude and brittle. I'm a safe person, a cautious person, but when it comes to trees? I want to burrow in them, hug them, climb them. And Leo remembers all of this.

It's just like when we were small—the leaves scrape my chin and there's nothing better than the pure, clean scent of wood and dirt and branches. They offer oxygen, they offer loads of shade. How many trees have seen World War II or waved at the first airplanes?

I don't even realize I've made it to the top until I'm surrounded by the charcoal skyline. It's sinking in color as the moon emerges. An owl hoots, and the cicadas are so loud, it's like someone's cranked them up to full volume on a stereo.

Once again, Leo grunts as he tries to catch up. He's not strong enough. Not for this tonight. I shouldn't have jumped at the opportunity to do this. At long last, though, the branch I'm perching on teeters as Leo breathlessly nestles into my side. His hair smells like Head and Shoulders, and I never thought that scent could be nice.

When the branch bows beneath our collective weight, Leo grabs my hand and holds it tight.

"Better than Mr. Freeze," I say, making things light.

His voice fades the way it always does when he has no idea what someone's talking about. "Right."

I take in his white knuckles as he grips the branch, his smile tight. "You really are afraid of heights."

"I will be all right." He pants a little, like he might pass out.

I scrutinize his eyes, which, even though tense—possibly even terrified—reflect joy and love in the starlight. His face is still full of torn skin and blood and it makes me want to cry. His hands are still wrapped around that branch, too, like he'd rather lose an arm than fall an inch away from me.

"Are there no do-overs?" I ask. His shoulders are pointed in my direction, soaking up my every breath, every single syllable I might say.

He stares at me as a halo of stars surround him in silver and white. Leaning toward me, hands still gripping the branch, he presses his forehead into mine. "I do not deserve that."

I hate it when he talks like that, so I press my lips into his. "You do." Gently, not wanting to hurt him, though his wound is almost completely healed now.

He kisses me back. "I'm sorry."

I think of how he gave me my name. How he said nothing was more beautiful and pure than the delicate lines of frost when we first wake in the morning. *"You are frost,"* he said. *"You are like that."*

I kiss him again, because, despite the metallic taste of

blood, his lips feel right. We kiss, gentle and slow, and the tingles running through my body beg for everything to be all right.

When he runs his hand down my shoulder, the tingles come with such power that I nearly teeter from the tree branch, and he cups my elbow and laughs softly—until his eyes fade to a quiet light.

"You should feed on me," I say. I haven't really thought this through, but I'm appalled I hadn't thought of this until now.

"What?"

"To defeat Knox."

"No." He releases my elbow like he's just been shocked.

"You, yourself, admitted that Knox is more powerful than you because he feeds on humans the way you won't. You should feed on me to grow powerful enough to take him down."

Leo cups the side of my face, and his touch is so feather-light, it's impossible not to lean into his hand. We have a plan for taking down Knox, true, but he has to see it's worth the extra precaution.

"I would never do that to you," he murmurs, and I should be glad, but what if it's not enough? What if Knox finds a flaw in our plan?

CHAPTER 40 - EVA

That stupid humming sound wakes me up, and I stretch long and wide, muscles twitching like a cat, till I bump someone's leg and my eyes fly open. Oh *yeah*, we're at Maggie's. Mother Hen wouldn't let us out of her sight. My heart instantly speeds up——shouldn't we have heard by now if they got Knox?

"Frost." I kick her again to wake her up. "It's getting light out. Why haven't we heard from the boys?"

Without moving or opening her eyes, Frost answers. "Already checked with Maggie. They ran out of volcanic ash. They'll be doing it soon."

Volcanic ash, huh? This is a new life we're living in for sure. At least it's going to be over soon. The thought gives me a permagrin. If last night was any indication of how life can be "sans-Knox," things are looking up for sure.

After Frost and Leo took off for their little tryst, Raylan, Maggie and I prepared by making nachos and watching Blue Bloods. Wouldn't you know, Raylan has gotten hooked on the show since staying with Maggie. And somewhere between episode three, where the detective goes undercover, and episode four, when said detective is made and his family gets taken hostage, Raylan snatched my hand and I swear I caught him staring at my lips. He has *got* to be finally getting ready to make a move. The idea of it is enough to makes me all kinds of giddy. Maybe a victory kiss after we vanquish the devil Knox?

The memory of that kiss back in the alley is so delicious. His scruff, his slightly maple taste—and I didn't even know him then. He was just a hot, dangerous stranger. Now? He could very well be my first love. Or the love of my life. He's smart, funny, loyal, still hot, of course, and steady, but not boring. Pretty much absolutely perfect. Certainly a perfect distraction to the other crap going on.

Mom's safely in the third bedroom, snuggled up with all her favorite blankets and smelly-good things the boys helped her bring over. Frost and I get to share the real guest room, complete with a wall of license plates from all over the country Maggie's acquired. I'm sure they come in handy for hunting too.

I can't believe this might actually be over today. I'm so ready. Although I can't believe I'm going to miss all the action . . . but I get that my being there at my house, waiting to be snatched, is pretty dumb.

Ooh, is that bacon I smell? Time to grab some of that and check on things. I throw on my Hello Kitty shorts, which look perfectly ironic with the Rob Zombie T-shirt I slept in. I pad down the hallway, reveling in the feel of the cool hardwood on my bare feet first thing in the morning.

Entering the little kitchen, I mentally say "good morning" to my favorite cow on the wall. Maggie's bovine art-themed kitchen shows the extent of her whimsy, and I embrace that wholeheartedly.

I find Mom instead of Maggie, elbows deep in sudsy water, wearing her cute calico dress. I'm glad she must be feeling pretty comfortable here, in Frost's and my second home, and I'm sure Maggie doesn't mind having Mom's amazing homemaking skills around.

"Hi, Mommy." I give her a peck on the cheek. She smells like her usual sweet pea lotion. "Where's Mags? Any news?"

"Good morning, honey," she says, her eye liner slightly smudged. She nods toward the living room. Maggie's staring out the window blinds, shotgun in hand. "Nothing yet. How are you?"

The question is simple and possibly just habit, but it still makes me smile. I'll let her a little bit into my thoughts. Then she'll feel included.

"I'm good!" I erase her misplaced makeup with my ring finger and head to the fridge. "I had a blast last night hanging out with Raylan and Maggie." Grabbing a soda, I savor the cold metal in my hand. "I think Raylan is realizing I'm the love of his life . . . even defeating the dragon as we speak, right?"

"That's really nice, honey." Her voice is quieter now as she places a pot on the drying rack. She's done with the conversation. But that's okay. Baby steps. I open the soda and drink its first deliciously cold, ultra-carbonated sip, feeling like things are going to be all right.

Frost strides into the kitchen, looking perky but also like she's ready for a *Lord of the Rings* battle.

"Somebody had a good night," I say, popping eyebrows at her. She turns red before she even finishes a step, so I decide to let her off the hook, just since we're in front of Mom. "Bacon?"

"Yes," she sighs, and grabs one off the plate on the counter before taking off to talk to Maggie.

"Eva, honey." Mom turns toward us, drying her hands with a dishcloth. "Go grab the sheets off your bed. I'll wash them before we leave."

"Yes, ma'am," I say after I inhale another piece of bacon. I holler to Frost, "Then we're all gonna have a chitty-chat."

Practically skipping back to my room, my heart feels lighter than it has in weeks. I'm about to tear the sheets off the bed when a small movement in the corner catches my eye. A figure with handsome features and a swagger I haven't seen since that bar in San Antonio looms beside the window. With a twitch of his hand, the door eases closed behind me. I drop my soda and turn to run, but I can't move an inch.

As the cold, amber liquid spills around my feet, Knox's low, raspy voice croons.

"Eva."

CHAPTER 41 - FROST

Not being with the boys—it feels wrong. Eva and I haven't come this far to learn the truth about the Blurred Ones only to hide like damsels in distress. But, I have to constantly remind myself, I'm doing this for my sister. Knox knows where my house is. She isn't safe there. And I need to stay here to make sure Eva doesn't slip out.

She seems determined to stick with the plan, though, as painful as it is, so I have to trust that all will go well. Still, Maggie's pretty focused on that cedar planked front door and rather off-kilter blinds on the windows. Is she worried that Knox really knows where she lives and her sigils won't hold up?

Salty bacon in hand, I wander past artwork of cows and a wood burning stove to where Maggie's camped out in an easy chair. Though there's nothing "easy" about the way she's sitting now. Her usually relaxed shoulders are tense. And she has something like eleven shotguns leaning against her chair within arm's reach.

A drill, too, sits in the corner of the seat's side and pad—with a screw duct-taped to the drill-bit. Ever vigilant Maggie.

As I approach, my tired friend glances away from the door as if caught deep in thought. A meaty book spills across her lap, dark circles rim her eyes, and her hair's a little matted. It's obvious she didn't sleep a wink all night.

She lifts the book. "There's something I've been wanting to show you girls." She glances around for my sister, so I say, "Mom sent her to pull the sheets from her bed."

Maggie rolls her eyes. Laundry's the last thing she'd do while Knox is still on the warpath, but she keeps her mouth shut. She's always been careful not to countermand Mom —or Dad.

I pull up a rickety chair missing half its spools. "What do you have?" I settle into the uneven seat, though I have to balance a little so I don't fall off.

Maggie's bloodshot eyes tell me she could fall asleep at the drop of a hat under normal circumstances, but she angles the book so I can see the yellowing pages from my perch on the chair.

She taps the page, becoming the scholar version of Mags. "See this one?" She points at a symbol of a diamond with a vertical line running down the center and a little line in the middle jutting to the right. "It's Celtic. Means 'closing the gate.' I added them to the triquetras we already have on our homes."

"Smart." I wonder why she felt the need to add more.

"I know your dad felt it was important to ward off evil with the traditional sign, but when Knox showed up at break-fast in your house, I decided it was time to add a few more sigils and runes."

"You don't think the triquetra is enough to keep him out?"

She shakes her head briskly. "I don't know. Knox may have told the truth, possessed your father when he went outside, but the hair standing on the back of my neck keeps telling me we might need more."

"Do you think Knox can break the lines of the sigils?" I wonder out loud, as suddenly an image of Wolf's arms pops into my mind—the loopy, foreign sigils I'd never seen before. And scars that broke the lines of the sigils. I didn't know what to make of them before, but it makes sense that Knox was wearing them down.

A jolt of fear runs up and down my spine. *Can he really break in? Even now?* We're watching the front door, but shouldn't we also be watching the back door and windows?

But Maggie flips to another page in her book. "I also used one from the Navajos." She points to a horizontal arrow with two tails, pointing to the right. "And your traditional Hebrew pentagram. Though some call that pagan." She forages for another page in the book where she finds a five-pointed star.

I am grateful, truly grateful, that Maggie has been researching this, but the collection feels so unpredictable. So random.

"Your father and I used to visit for hours about this stuff. His mom wrote volumes on your family tree and where all the Abrams come from. Abram, short for Abraham, has a bunch of origins. Jewish, English, French, Irish, German. You even have a little Navajo. Hence, the arrow."

She heaves the pages to the Native American section of the book and taps a dog-eared page with the arrow again. "I thought that if I added a few more runes and sigils that connected to your girls' ancestry, you might be more protected."

Despite my need to run to the back door and check all the windows, I fight the urge to lean in and give her the biggest hug. But with all the shotguns surrounding her chair, and my chair, which is about to tip over, I settle with awkwardly clearing my throat—which has become laden with quicksand. "Thank you for taking this so seriously."

"Have to. After what happened to your dad."

CHAPTER 42 - EVA

Frozen. My body, my lungs, my voice. I can't scream for help, I can barely breathe. Knox raises his hand and I float up, dangling in the air like a freaking exorcism movie. He slams me onto the bed like a toddler throwing her doll in a tantrum, and just like that doll, I can't move.

Knox laughs quietly and rises from his chair. In his hand —*NO!* I scream in my head—he has yellow nylon rope. "I'm back," he says quietly, sauntering over to me. He loops one end of the rope around my right wrist and yanks it toward the bed frame. He slides the other end of the rope between the mattress and metal frame and ties it excruciatingly tight. How did he get in here?

He moves to hover over me. Pins me down with his knee and starts breathing hard. Determined. *Excited.* And suddenly I'm free to move, though my voice is still frozen.

I yank as hard as I can, trying to throw myself to the side, but he digs his knee harder into my chest, pushing the air out. I try kicking him but can't get a good angle. I try to headbutt him, but I can't reach. I gather my strength for a breath. Two.

I twist as hard as I can, trying to get him off of me, but he just pushes his knee down harder. Looking me in the eye, watching, he blinks his soulless black eyes, pinning me again with just his mind.

If I weren't so terrified, I would be livid. I've never been so helpless. Even back in the hotel room with this awful thing, I wasn't freaking tied down.

I try to scream but he's seized my vocal cords somehow. I might as well be a kitten facing a two-ton gorilla.

"You're mine now, darling Eva." His usually perfectly gelled hair falls in his eyes. He finishes cinching my left arm down. Straightening, he smooths his hair back, then runs his eyes and fingers down the entire length of my body, assessing me like a new car. He loops another length of rope around my left foot.

"I'm going to let you talk," he says, straightening, surveying his work, "but if you scream, I'll snap your mother's neck." The pressure on my neck instantly releases, and I slam down the urge to scream. They're so close—

"Just stop," I plead quietly, hot tears falling down into my ears. "You don't have to do this! Please!" An image comes of them finding out what happened right under their noses, and my heart pretty much breaks in half.

He finishes that tie, fast now that I'm still as a statue. He lifts a finger to his lips, his black ring catching the morning light. "Keep it down, Eva. You're right, I don't. But I sure *want* to. And—" he gestures around the room, void of anyone coming to my rescue, "get to." He gives a little chuckle, and I see where the tar is building up on his teeth.

"Now. Feel free to fight, but remember, don't scream," he says, cinching his last knot around my right foot with a tug. With a casual wave of his hand, my body can move again, even if just against the ropes that are chafing so much my skin is bright red. I writhe hard enough to break something, and I hear the muffled sounds of female voices. Was that laughter? I picture Maggie, finally leaving the window for some breakfast, joking with Mom and Frost. I clench my jaw as tight as I can to hold in the cry for help.

"Now. We make this a permanent arrangement," he commands with such a condescending tone. Again, I'm a child to this ancient demon. "We're going to be together for a very long time."

They're so close. Feet away. Boys, I could really use your magic spell right about now! But, no. I'm alone, and it has to stay that way.

A new fact strikes my mind, as true as humans needing oxygen. He's won. It's shocking. All that planning. All that fear. Maybe if we had just found that screw one day sooner. We could have summoned him on Saturday. Or Sunday. I thrash on the bed, tangling the cotton sheets and choking back the tears. Try to steady my breath. I remember he lives for the fear of his victims, and at least I can deny him that. Have my tiny shred of power. I pray with all I've got that Mom, Frost, and Maggie will be okay without me. That he won't ever use his power to hurt them again.

"Aw, she's gone quiet," he says with an exaggerated frown. "Giving up already, darling? I thought you'd have more fire." He cocks his head to the side as if contemplating how to stoke the reaction he wants. "Don't worry, it's not like you were going to amount to much anyway. Now, instead of acting like a vapid little slut, you get to be useful, just like your Daddy always wanted."

A whimper escapes me. Aunt Eva, my doppelganger, and I —we meant well, but maybe we just didn't have what it takes. Maybe I do deserve this. For a second there, I thought maybe I was more. I am glad it's me and not her.

Knox leans over the bed, stinking of rot. Just inches away, he examines my face and moans deeply. "I want," he kisses my cheek like it's a perfectly ripened peach, "to have," another kiss, "this power." He kisses my lips fully. I force myself not to react to his moldy taste, laying limply as a discarded dishrag. He turns and talks into my ear, lips brushing with every word.

"E-va," he drawls, "I don't want to rot and become like those disgusting Despairity wenches. And you are going to give me what I need to stay in this body forever. Thankfully, I found a silly little witch to tell me the ritual and," he licks my face from ear to mouth, "how to break your weak little sigils. I'm strong enough now that all I have to do is plow them with my magic till I find a weak spot. Then I'm in." He finally stands back up and adds quietly, like a doctor comforting his patient, "Now, we can play whenever I want."

He treads quietly across the hardwood to the dresser, where a framed picture of Frost and me with Maggie celebrating after I got my driver's license sits. He plucks something up—a dagger, long, twisted, and dull. I blink away the fear my eyes want to show him. My chest spasms, holding back a sob.

"It's simple, really," he drones on. "You used sigils to *try* to keep us out, now I use one little sigil to keep me in. A small pathway between our souls only the carver controls. Nice, right?"

"You love to hear yourself talk, don't you?" I force myself to sound bored. Mildly annoyed. "Can we just get this over with?" Uh, hopefully reverse psychology works on psychotic Blurred Ones? His nostrils flare with irritation.

"Let's see how this knife works." He grabs my tied up arm with one hand and with the other, plunges the dagger into my forearm. I forget myself and scream in pain, but it's cut short as he forces my voice to quiet again with the flick of his hand. My blood splatters onto his white shirt, melds into my crimson throw pillow. I don't hear any noise from the kitchen anymore.

"Now your mother will die. Eva, you really do need to be smarter." He wipes the rusted dagger on my chest, snagging the fabric. "At least you've got your spark." He clears his throat, and I can barely breathe. "The dagger is dull, isn't it? This is going to hurt a lot." His eyes glimmer with excitement and he grabs my upper arm, the lower part now burning with pain.

"*Spiritu*," he digs the dagger in slowly, "*tuo mea*." It bites through my skin, cutting and bruising where it struggles to slice. I can't scream. I can barely breathe. And my rescuers aren't even banging on the door like they were back in the Gunter. Mental note to not need rescuing *ever* again. "*Spiritu*," he turns the dagger, forming a curved line.

The sound of wood exploding rocks the room. Suddenly there's a hole in the door. The barrel of a sawed-off shotgun pokes through the hole and shoots again, this time hitting Knox in the shoulder, but he just flinches like he'd been stung by a bee.

"Eva?" Maggie's panicked voice yells into the room, but I still can't answer. I sob internally with relief that at the very least, I won't die alone. Knox throws a hand out, and I hear a thud I can only imagine is Maggie hitting the hallway wall.

"Pardon me just a moment, darling." Knox's raspy voice seethes, his face twisting with rage at being interrupted. He barely looks human anymore. "Let me exterminate a few pests." He cracks his neck and spits some salt onto the floor, still holding my arm. But Frost is running through the doorway, chucking a vial of holy water on Knox. Knox bellows in pain, skin sizzling with smoke like a sulfur experiment gone bad in Chemistry. She reaches the bed, eyes wild as she throws herself between Knox and me. He grabs her arm, wrenching it back, but freezes, arm in the air, like someone just did his own body-controlling trick on him.

Maggie's head pokes through the hole and I'm screaming her name, but the atmosphere of the room shifts, clicks, and Frost, Knox, and me, are ripped away.

The porch cracks with impact. My porch? With Leo, Raylan—and our porch swing, surprisingly intact.

No one told me that summoning spells can take more than one person. I guess because he's holding onto us?

Shards of ice feel like they've splintered my head—probably from moving through space like that—and Knox's iron-clad fingers squeeze both Eva's and my arms.

We're in a cage—a metal cage tall and wide enough for a very big horse-like dog. Below our feet is the spray-painted pentagram, and if Dad saw this graffiti on his front porch, he'd march us to the garage for the paint thinner, stat.

The three of us have landed so hard, the entire wooden porch has split in half, maybe one and three-quarter inches through the wood, so not fully in half. One side of the painted star's nearly severed, though. Knox will continue the break and escape the trap.

His once handsome face ripples with anguish. "Send me back! Send me back." He pants, out of breath.

Eva and I lock eyes. Try to twist in his arms, but it's like moving in a box of concrete. *Are you okay,* I want to cry, but the fear on her face tells me she's not. Reminds me of the time she prematurely took off her helmet while rollerblading and sliced her head open on a landscaping rock.

I think Knox will maybe hold me so close he'll break my arm, but he releases me and shoves me at the locked gate of the cage like a rabid dog.

He wraps his arms so tightly around my sister, I want to throw up.

Veins bulge from his neck. He's losing his grip on his plan. "*Spiritu!*" he snarls. Like he can return to that room and finish his bonding ritual. Break the pentagram.

I'll spit in his face, pound his head so hard his brains spill out, but now Leo's reading something aloud from a book. *Latin*. He's saying Latin phrases that I've never heard, and the fact that Knox hasn't re-disappeared tells me this summoning spell and pentagram will keep holding him for now.

"Aren't you all a treat?" Knox spits, still holding a trembling Eva to his chest. She might be going into shock. She could pass out, but she jerks her head to take a bite out of his arm.

He slaps her—hard.

I hurl myself at the demon.

I connect with part of his arm and graze Eva's hair, just the fringe. He slams me so hard into the cage that I taste metal on my teeth and wires slice through my nose and hands.

Knox eyes the drill and duct-taped screw in Raylan's steady hand. He gives a joyful whoop. "So you mean to use that fine hunk of metal to bind me now? It's what I've been hoping to do all along."

Raylan snarls, "Not with Eva, you won't."

Knox chuckles as he glances at the almost broken line of the pentagram. Narrowing his eyes, he tries to finish off the break of the pointed side with his power, but Leo grabs a can of paint and sprays the breaking part without missing a breath of his Latin.

"*Nos hic captionem*," he says, "*malum daemonium.*"

Will the line hold? It's impossible to tell.

I need to shove Knox so hard that he'll have to release Eva. He might snap my spine just like that, but I reach for my Sig strapped to my ankle and raise the barrel.

My hands are shaking. My aim's as unpredictable as Maggie's hunting lessons. I might skim Eva's legs, but it's worth it to slow him down.

With one flick of the eyes, Knox sends it flying from my grip.

"Come out, come out, my little girls!" Knox cries. But his Despairity are hovering over by the oak trees like they're unsure whether they want to get involved or not.

They don't seem to like the idea that Knox can be summoned at the drop of a hat.

Raylan prowls toward the cage like he'd love nothing more than to roast Knox over a fire for lunch. Pointing the drill at the demon's face, he says, "I'm going to enjoy this. A lot."

"You'll never get close enough," Knox spits.

Raylan looks like he'll have no problem fitting the screw end of the drill between the metal of the cage. Problem is, Knox still has Eva like a fly in his web.

Scooting a little closer, Leo places his finger halfway down the page of his spell book and primly says, "'Our birth is but a sleep and a forgetting.'" He's quoting one of my premortal realm books. Wordsworth's *Immortality Ode*. "'Not in entire forgetfulness, and not in utter nakedness, but trailing clouds of glory do we come. From *God*. Who is our home.'"

"You don't want God." Knox scoffs. "He doesn't want *you*, Leonardo."

Leo's gaze falls to his Latin. "I simply wanted to put

things in perspective." His gaze raises to Knox's again. "What if I said he told me I could be born?"

"You can't talk to him."

"One of his messengers, then."

Knox squeezes Eva's arms so tightly she cries out. Her face is pale. Sweat drips from her neck and chest. I'll take him back to the Gunter. Drag him back to our room and introduce that meat grinder to *him*.

And yet, a little part of my mind is whispering, *Leo can be born*? He never said that. Is it true? I want to believe him. I want to scream for joy, but murmur, *stop*.

If he's born, he'll have a life like I have—with too-big shoes and geometry tests.

I'll never see him, but he'll have a way to progress.

Knox throws himself, Eva in his grasp, against the thin wires of the cage like sheer force will get him out. We tilt like a shaken globe to the side. We're on a roller coaster. It's designed to be fun. But the pentagram beneath our feet is working. Prevents us from rocking out.

I think we might be winning—Leo might stand a chance —when blood runs from Leo's nose and his spirit bleeds out of his vessel. Like a cloud. His body is dying. So is the real Leo I love.

Worry rips apart my throat. "Leo, you need help." But I'm stuck in here and Raylan doesn't have the powers of a Blurred One. And the Despairity, still hovering over there by the oaks and ferns, seem unwilling to get into the fight. Are they only willing when the kill is easy and obvious?

Leo continues murmuring his Latin, but now he doesn't even look at his book. He's repeated the phrase so many times, he's memorized it. His cheeks strain to continue saying the words—an invisible resistance from Knox. Blood drips from his ears, and my heart squeezes in my gut.

"You need to feed on me!" I scream as three dark spirits

trail toward us from the woods. They sense that we're losing. They'll take Knox's side now.

Leo's skin is so green that it's amazing he's even standing up. I need to reach him, hold him up. So I grip the wires of the cage, which singe my palms like the racks in an oven. *Hot.*

Sucking in a breath, I whip my head around to face Knox. Wish I still had my Sig. He's raising one of his hands. Heating the cage with his mind. The metal's glowing so orange that steam hisses as it sinks into the porch wood.

Like it's made of plastic, it melts. It won't hold us long. Flames burst up from the metal, and I inch away from the heat toward Knox. Maybe I can knock away his hand or disrupt his concentration—when a hand reaches through the burning cage and yanks me out.

I stagger, roll to the splintered ground. I nearly careen into Dad's chair but duck just in time. Leo staggers away from me, a mess of a wrinkled polo and sweat. He must have just pulled me out. But his arm's burnt, charred. Black. And an angry burn mark singes across the length of my arm. Leo continues reciting his summoning spell, but he's slurring the words. He staggers toward the porch swing, which creaks in the wind.

Raylan's ducking through the flames to try to find a path to Knox's head, but Knox continues to hold Eva like a shield to his chest, protecting her from the melting cage like her body is already his.

Release her! I want to gouge his eyes out, but the more I remind Knox of what I'm trying to do, the more he'll hold on.

The wind tears at my face, my hair, batting at the painted lines of the devil's trap.

"You are not good," Knox tells Leo. His smile is horrific.

Leo's spirit contorts inside his vessel like he's tempted to believe Knox.

Knox will take Eva. "Feed on me!" I scream again. "Now!" I need to force him somehow. I reach for his arm.

But he backs away as his body sags. He wants to beat Knox, but how can he when Knox's power has been amplified by all the spirits he's fed on?

Leo throws all his energy into the metal cage with a hectic grunt, and the fire slips so low, all that's left of the cage is a rim of red glowing ash. Knox extends a fingernail and physically scratches at the thinning line of the pentagram.

He'll break through in mere seconds.

"*Leo!*" I scream again. I duck my head against the power rippling in waves between Knox and him and force myself to crawl toward those plain brown shoes not so firmly planted on the ground.

Splinters embed into my palms. My shoulder stings from Leo yanking me from the cage. My knee's shrieking like someone's just stomped it flat. The whole porch rings so hot it feels like a furnace, and Raylan has more holy water to throw on Knox, drill whirring in his other hand.

Knox swipes at the drill, which flies from Raylan's hand. It lands inside the pentagram.

Having made it to Leo's brown shoes and starched pants, I wrench his arm so hard it actually slams into my already throbbing kneecap.

"Do it."

His eyes skirt to mine. *But I will never do that to you*, he seems to say. Panic.

"If you don't," I scream, "my sister's dead."

His resolve is gone. He can't quite form the Latin. So I do what he refuses to do—

I slap his palms on my cheek and chin.

There's a *crack* like thunder. Electricity surges inside my eyelids. I knew he had power, but I had expected more of a dull throb.

Volts of power surge from the top of my spine to my feet and back up to my tailbone. I'm a ruin of flesh.

I know he needs to feed on my fear and despair, but all I can feel are his thoughts probing like tentative fingers, hesitant. He doesn't want to be cruel, but I give him whatever he needs.

Feed on.

A bitterness of cold runs over my head like an ice bucket. I'm seeing myself sticking that ax in my father's back.

I'm doing it once. Again. And, despite what I never wanted to see, what I never wanted to acknowledge, I *enjoyed* it.

You hurt Eva. Not just once, but again and again. I'll do this to you. Stab you every single time you hurt her.

You're a disgrace to who you should be. A sorry excuse for fatherhood.

There's a truth to this, I know. And lies. How is it that misery is so full of truth that we're so willing to overlook that nasty last, twisty and wicked, one percent?

The ax in my hands is heavy and full. I like it. Loathe it. *It's an extension of my hand, and I want to sink it into the pinkest part of his flesh, because it gives me the power I never had.*

I'm just lifting that blade, about to place it for the sixth time into the meat of his back, when Leo shouts something sharp into the back of my mind. A warning. *Stop.*

But he needs to beat Knox.

A whirlwind of memories twists within my head.

He turned Eva and me into slaves. *I'll enslave him.*

He complained about Mom's cooking. *I'll poison him.*

It's all too much. Must. Make it. Stop. I reach my icy fingers round my throat because it's the only way. The only way to make it end. Somewhere in the back of my mind, I know killing myself isn't right, but what if it's the only way? The only way to make sure Eva isn't dead?

Deep, deep down, though, where thoughts aren't so much as thoughts, I see a single symbol.

Like a snowflake. White.

Frost. Leo had said. *You are like that.* Because he thought I was beautiful and pure.

Am I?

I successfully killed my Dad. I killed my own father. There's no greater evil than that.

Yesss, another voice hisses. In my mind, I look sharply to my right. A dark figure. Ruined. More rot.

The decay is so foul I can feel it on my own breath. It's Knox—Knox—reaching for me through Leo's, and then my own, mind. He's telling me I *am* evil and, like he's the black petals of a decaying rose, I can see him for the first time.

Rot, stink, gunk.

He cares so much for worldly pleasures. And himself. Uses them at the expense of others. Likes killing people when I do not.

It was all a lie. I *didn't* like killing my dad. I may have liked killing that part of him that hurt Eva, but I never wanted to steal his life.

Dad tickled Eva and me. Right between the ribs.

Read to us *Green Eggs and Ham* when we were sick.

Told us he loves us several times a week. All growing up.

Knox is a pathetic excuse for a soul. Leo's weakened him enough. And now Leo can use my positive memories because he isn't evil but good.

I can feel Knox wilting. The rose is falling to ash.

All we need is the screw.

I force my eyes open and lock my gaze on Leo's. "Stop."

CHAPTER 44 - EVA

Knox laughs, but it's hollow now. They've weakened him enough that he can't break the pentagram trapping us, but he's still strong, and I'm trapped in here with him. I twist again and try dropping my weight all at once, anything to lessen his grip. Get away from him and let Raylan finish the job.

Knox grabs my arms, one hand on the first stab wound on my arm. Effer. He wrenches them painfully, twisting me back against him. "Really, Eva?" he chides. "You haven't learned by now?"

Dark forms bleed through the wall. Great. The Despairity have finally decided to join the party. But they just hover closer, watching with their caverned eyes. I gulp and try to assess the situation. I search for Frost. She's staring at them like she's about to jump them and not like Leo just did some giant mind suck on her. He's chanting again, bolder, like he just hit the nitrous oxide. Raylan's got his shotgun now and has it aimed at Knox's face, waiting for a shot.

I glare at Knox. "You get off on being the big bad man?"

"I do," he says, grabbing a handful of my hair. He shoves me down to his side so I'm crouching near his waist like a loyal puppy, then pulls my hair back till I'm forced to look at him. He licks his disgusting lips. "I'm going to cut you in so many places, but never enough to die. Then I will taste every bit of you."

Even as he threatens me, though, he isn't as intimidating as before. Whether he's weaker or I'm just getting used to him, I'm not terrified anymore. He's been preying on unsuspecting victims for so long, he doesn't know how to handle a fair fight.

I elbow him as hard as I can between the legs. He pulls my hair harder, but that brings my face close to his arm. I lunge and bite into his moldy-tasting forearm as hard as I can and grind. He howls and stumbles back, nearing the broken pieces of our porch swing.

Screeching tires wail down our driveway. A dusty Buick driving like a bat out of hell—Maggie's here. She'll know what to do.

As she tears out of her car, Knox turns toward her. "Another one to die. Sisters," he says, jerking my hair again, "help me." He's surrounded and his bag of tricks is running out, but the Despairity are all facing Frost now. Returning her dirty looks or something?

As Knox focuses on Maggie, Raylan runs up behind him, finally seeing his opportunity.

The *boom* of his sawed-off twelve gauge shotgun blasts my ears, and something wet sprays my face.

Raylan keeps the gun trained on Knox, cocking to reload. The back of Knox's head is missing. He's a face plastered on a mess of tar, and his throat must have been hit too, because he's making a wheezing, gasping sound. He pulls me up to my feet, and I'm scared my neck will snap, but it's what I've been waiting for. On my feet, I can move. I throw every ounce of my not-tiny body into his nasty self, pushing him to the edge of the pentagram we're trapped in.

Off balance enough to let me go, Knox coughs again, and I grab the porch swing's chain that's now just dangling from the ceiling, wrapping it around his neck, pulling it tighter. It pinches my hands and he scratches at me, but I throw every ounce of energy I have left into it, and after three loops, he can't move.

The hovering Despairity draw closer, forgetting Frost. Knox's pain is a riptide, pulling them in.

"Sisters!" Leo yells, but he's hoarse. "Wait!" Their blurred faces flicker to Leo like they're annoyed by this interruption. They pulse against the brim of the trap, and the air inside grows frigid.

Frost bolts to my side, screw ready, but Knox's arms still flail, trying to get free. Maggie tosses me the drill and pulls out her wicked brass knuckles.

"You're about to get what's comin' to ya," she snarls, storming to us. She pounds Knox in the stomach with her brass spikes. Frost shoves Knox's jaw to clamp it shut. Like practiced surgeons, Frost puts the screw on his philtrum and immediately, I begin to drill.

The bolt is dull and slow, but I reckon that's good riddance and I'm pissed enough to get it done. I push it slowly through first the skin, then the bone. The skin rips and shreds, and this body Knox has possessed spews tar-like blood. He just twitches, too weak to put up much of a fight.

"It's in," Frost gasps, and I throw the drill down. Maggie grabs Frost and me.

"Get out," Leo shouts, so she hauls both of us out of the trap. As soon as we're free of the circle, I feel the warmth of the outside air, and Leo crumples to the ground.

Frost is at his side and in the same instant, the Despairity fall on Knox like dirty water down a drain. They gasp and heave, muffling Knox's weak screams as they drink in his despair. They don't even stir when Raylan slides Maggie's metal cage next to them.

Maggie shoves what's left of Knox's vessel into the cage, and the black forms cling to the outside like gnats. But he's inside, stuck in his vessel with no power, the cage offering an extra barrier. The Despairity don't give us a second look. Maggie pulls me farther away, just in case.

I'm surprised, when I finally look away, to see the bright blue sky and beautiful foliage. Like it shouldn't exist next to our demolished porch and these dark spirits. It reminds me of Dad for a second, how he had so much good but his actions made it so hard to see his goodness inside. I think he'd be pretty dang proud of me right now though.

"Holy Hades," I pant. "That's it, right?" I reach over and knock on the porch beam that's now lying on the ground next to me. "Is Leo okay?"

"Are you?" Maggie asks, eyes wild. She grabs me by the chin, looking into my eyes and stealing worried glances at Frost and Leo. "He will be. Just spent, I suppose."

I sag in relief. "Fine. I'm fine. I ain't nobody's plaything."

Raylan, assured Knox is secure, races over and pulls me into a hug so tight I choke. It makes me feel lighter than I've felt in weeks. Almost light-headed. We did it. Knox is done for and we're okay.

I hug him back as tight as I can, letting his strength ground me, but he lets go much too soon. I'm fixin' to say so, too, but his hands are on my face, holding me, examining me like Maggie, but *no,* not like Maggie. Instead, he pulls me in and kisses me like he couldn't wait one more second.

Fingers cradling my face, he moves his lips on mine like I'm the last drop of water in the desert and he wants every last bit. He tastes just like I've dreamed about since our first kiss, maple and apples. And this kiss is, impossibly, better. I could freakin' die right now.

"Y'all gonna keep carryin' on much longer?" Maggie booms, and we freeze, our lips still touching. "Or can we dispose of the evil demon now?"

I can feel him smile, and it's like I've just conquered Everest.

"Yes, ma'am," he murmurs, kissing me like I'm his perfect treasure. He moves his mouth next to my ear and whispers sternly, "Don't *ever* scare me like that again."

*L*eo pulls me past a boy wearing a sleeveless shirt that says, THE CONSTITUTION GIVES ME THE RIGHT TO BARE ARMS. Half a block later, we tread past a sign that says, GOT FAR WOOD. I think of my classmates—how they willingly wake up at four in the morning to go hunting, but on a school day, half don't even bother showing up until noon, many of them hung over, smelling of campfire or tobacco.

I squeeze his fingers as he pulls me toward Mr. Harris' trailer. "Don't leave me," I whimper, spotting a trio of kids in matching camo who've decided to smoke something adventurous.

Leo smiles gently at me, like *I'm* the one who's charging into the unknown, while pulling me up to the library trailer.

I squeeze his fingers again, willing myself to speak. *You won't forget me?* It's not supposed to be sad, that he wants to be born.

Before reaching for the door's handle, he pulls me into a hug as my neck presses against the metal fastener of his suspenders. How will I go on not being able to touch this?

Two of the kids duck behind a grouping of trees, whooping something about fart jokes, and it's like I'll never be around the class and sophistication of someone like Leo again.

A bird perches on the porch rail and I feel like sobbing into his shoulder. Eventually, I say, "When you're born, you won't remember any of this."

"I'll never forget you, Frost."

It's not true, but I laugh anyway. Maybe I'll tell Mr. Harris to forget about being the liaison between Leo and the messenger from God. I shrug like none of it matters. "Maybe you'll be born after I'm long gone."

He tilts his head.

"I'll visit and be your invisible friend," I tell him.

Tears shine in his eyes, and I pretend that tears aren't burning in my own vision. He pulls me into another hug where the cotton of his white shirt is a warm blanket. My head fits, snug, in the crook of his neck, and there's a pulse, but I know it's not even his. It's his vessel's. The kid's a drug dealer, or so Leo says, but it's better that Leo allows him to make his choices again.

"Any pointers for when I don't like my parents?" He searches my eyes with his.

I almost say, *Don't kill them,* but instead I lighten it. "Make them scones and put on puppet shows for your sisters."

He plays with the watch on my wrist. "What if I get into booze and girls and stuff?"

"Then I'll hunt down your butt and slap you until you swear it off."

"That's if you die before I'm born."

"I can still hunt you down as a little ol' granny and make you listen."

He lifts his chin. "How will you know who I am?"

At this, I pause, watching the truant kids smash beer bottles into a rock, catcalling each other like they're winners of the Olympics. I wish I knew that answer, so instead I say, "You'll do all right." Tears dribble down my neck.

He hugs me once more, and the somberness in his eyes tells me that he's going in alone. This is the last time. I hug him for the way he made me feel, for the way he bonded with Eva. I run my hands over the back of his thin cotton shirt, wondering if I can ever love somebody like this again.

"Thank you for helping me," he whispers, "for pushing me to believe in myself." Pulling away, he locks eyes on me, and I try to memorize their love and confidence. Slowly, he drops his gaze with a weak squeeze of my hand.

"I love you," he says. He doesn't look back.

CHAPTER 46 - EVA

Raylan and I stand over our abandoned mine, listening for Knox's cage to hit the bottom, but it's far too deep. Despite disposing of a body, the pink and orange sunset is hella romantic. I consider stealing a kiss while we wait but restrain myself. Not quite there yet. We hear a few muffled clangs, but then he is so deep no one will hear anything from this sicko.

"Too bad we couldn't actually kill him." I lean as far as I dare over the hole in the grate we temporarily pried open wide enough to wedge him through.

"Who knows how long he can survive like that?" Raylan throws a burning rag down and watches it fade. "But he can suffer there for years and it won't make up for what he's done."

We tried to get rid of him two days ago when we trapped him, but wouldn't you know it, Wade was here with his latest frizzy-haired conquest, throwing flaming chunks of cow manure down. Then Leo *left*, so there was attempting to console an inconsolable Frost. And Mom decided she was going to start being crazy protective. But I didn't mind leaving Knox out in the woods for a bit to get eaten alive by ticks and chiggers. Jerk's healing way too fast though. He was starting to get mouthy. It was time.

"It doesn't feel as good as I thought it would," I say, then shove my hands in my pockets so I don't grab Raylan.

"That's because you're a good person. You don't enjoy even truly evil people suffering." He tucks a strand of my hair behind my ear, and I hold back a shiver. "But *why* are you so far away from me?" He grabs me by the waist and we walk-slash-stumble back to his truck.

My heart is falling for this guy like Knox down that mine shaft, and it's just about as scary. "So, you've decided I'm not some immature airhead?" I keep my arm around him but start fiddling with my hair with my other hand.

"No, you're not. I'm sorry if I ever made you feel that way."

"Eh, to be fair, I can be sometimes."

He jerks to a stop and pulls me in front of him, demanding eye contact. His eyes are so open. A soft, slate blue, like that day back on the couch at Maggie's. He could tell me the moon is made of barbeque ribs and I would believe him.

"Eva, no. You are fearless and carefree." He wraps his arms around my waist so his face is only inches from mine. "I haven't been carefree a single day since my parents died. I kinda thought it meant you couldn't take things seriously. And I took things too seriously. You're smart, you're funny, beautiful, you kick butt, and, you're a really good kisser." He never talks this much, so I keep my reply to a minimum, drinking it in.

"Yeah, I am," but I can't keep his eye contact. The other shoe must be about to drop, right?

"You are." He squeezes my waist. "And you make me feel

like it's *good* to enjoy life. I can keep being a hunter and still maybe be happy."

"You can for sure." My heart leaps at the thought of him being happy. It's so different from his closed off, brooding side, but it reminds me I don't have to be just one thing either. "I'm going to keep working on just being *me* because you make *me* feel like that's not such a bad thing."

"No way. You're amazing. Also," he flashes a wicked grin, "if you don't mind, Maggie invited me to stick around for awhile. I can't let you keep running headfirst into trouble —alone."

"Seriously?" I yelp so loud it echoes all the way from the mine shaft. He laughs, loud, rich and free.

"Seriously." His eyes twinkle ocean blue. "Leo's gone, my sister is always off hunting, and honestly, I just can't leave you."

I can't take any more. I throw my arms around his neck and kiss him fiercely. I twist my hands around in his thick, always messed up hair, holding on for dear life, since this has to be a dream and I'm gonna wake up any second.

But he's kissing me back, and his hands are all over me. If he weren't so solid, I'm sure we would have fallen down by now. I slam my back against the driver's door and melt. The heat of the metal matches the heat of Raylan's body. Only him pressing against me keeps me standing.

He pulls back just an inch and grabs me by the back of the head, cupping my face with his giant, calloused grip, fingers tangled in my hair. He kisses me three, four times, and we're gasping the same air. Five, six more times, then he pulls back and looks at me again, eyes alive like a hurricane.

"Eva, I can never leave you."

CHAPTER 47 - FROST

 om hasn't said a word the entire drive over to
Maggie's. In fact, her already infrequent
words have become pretty near obsolete ever since I
killed Dad.

Still, when she pulls into Maggie's gravel drive and puts
her car in park, Eva and I both say, "Thanks for driving us."

Mom's eyes look more brittle than ever as she somberly
looks at me from where I sit at shotgun. "You saved Eva
from Knox."

It's obvious, but it's like she needs to say it.

"Guy went ka-boom!" Eva smiles and reaches out from
the back seat to give Mom a sideways hug.

Mom pats her arms, a little lacking of spirit, but what do I
expect? She lost her partner in life. But, we did stop Knox
from taking an Eva.

I reach for the cool fabric of my sleeping bag. "Are you
sure you don't want to come with us?"

For once, Mom doesn't reply with a sigh. "I'll stay in with
a movie tonight."

She's discovered *Wives and Daughters*. Told us when we got

in the car that she wants to be more a part of our lives. There would be no time like the present, but she needs time to heal. With Leo so newly gone, I get that.

Eva grabs her sleeping bag and shoves her door wide open. "Sure you don't want to stay for s'mores?"

The exhaustion in Mom's face tells us to leave her alone tonight.

Out back, Maggie welcomes us with new bottles of root beer and hot dog pokers. The sky's just gone dark enough that the fire glows red with comfort.

I'm just hunkering low into my sleeping bag's slick polyester when part of me quasi-believes the past few weeks never happened. I never met my imaginary best friend or fell for him all over again. Eva never met Raylan, a keeper. Though Raylan's technically "here," inside Maggie's house, he seems to know the sanctity of a ladies' night.

Eva keeps stealing glances at the house, though, which is putting quite the damper on getting our conversation flowing.

Maggie grabs her bag of marshmallows and throws it so it lightly smacks Eva on the side of her head. "Stop looking for him."

Eva cringes. "Sorry! I'll take a lecture, it'll last longer." She rips open the bag and sticks a big, fat marshmallow in her mouth.

"Point is to *cook* them first," Maggie says.

"Sorry!" Eva says over the marshmallow.

I chuckle as Eva hands me the bag and I quietly stick my own marshmallow on my poker.

It's a little unsettling how every single object I look at resembles a weapon now. I imagine jabbing it into Knox's eyes for *ever* going after my sister. I glance at Maggie's fanny pack, because maybe she has some other bare necessities in there.

"Know your girls' problem?" Maggie accepts the bag of marshmallows. "You haven't heard a ghost story in a great long while."

I fight the urge to say, *We've been living one instead.*

But Eva waves the poker in her hand. "Ooh, what about the patriotic Wendigo that accidentally appeared in Mexico?"

Maggie laughs. "Ah, yes. He couldn't understand how a Canadian would ever want to veer from home." The laughter shines from Maggie's eyes as she finds the seriousness of her voice now. "Know what I figured out?" She grips her knees with focus. "You girls are growing up."

Eva drops her poker and not so gracefully tromps over the weeds and gives our oldest friend and staunchest ally a big, fat hug. "Thanks, Mags."

Maggie snort-laughs. "I sort of bought into the idea that, because I'm not officially part of your family and I'm a hunter, I'm somehow lower on the totem pole, but your Dad never treated me like that." Tears shine in her eyes. "I can trust you both to do more, and you can trust me to measure up."

I'm just bending my knees to give her a hug of my own when Maggie pales. "Forgot to tell Raylan to pull the cobbler out of the oven."

"Cobbler?" Eva squeaks as she reaches for another marshmallow.

Maggie gives her the stink-eye, obviously knowing my sister's not only tempted by her famous dessert but the lure of Raylan. "No going inside my home."

"What if I have to pee?"

"You know I have a latrine right over there." Maggie waggles her pointer finger deeper in the woods before strolling back over to her house.

The fire crackles and spits as I turn my marshmallow over the flames, content to be with my sister.

I wonder what Mr. Harris' contact did to send Leo wherever he needed to go. Did he first need to return to the spirit world or would he be zapped and planted directly into a baby's empty vessel inside a womb?

He could be a baby, pooping into a diaper in a few months.

I robbed the cradle, and I didn't even know.

I can feel Eva's eyes on me, dissecting what's going on inside my head. "You two really did make the cutest couple," she says.

"Only next to you and Raylan." I offer a small smile.

Eva sighs that monstrous sigh she could only learn from Mom, but one that's infinitely happier. It promises to break *all* the rules. I think she's going to ply me with the sordid details of their entire romantic history when she sensitively says, "I am *so* sorry he had to go."

I pull my marshmallow from the fire since I can't look her in the eyes without tearing up. My marshmallow's perfectly browned anyhow.

"Know what I think?" she lightly asks. "I think you'll see him again, and things will turn out better than any of us could ever hope."

I want to mutter that it's all well and good for her to be in a good mood—*her* guy gets to stick around—my guy's a freaking demon who decided a couple of millennia too late to be born. Still, I'm glad that he changed his mind. That he wanted to. And I'm being selfish, believing the only way to happiness is keeping Leo when doing that would pretty much ruin any chance he has to progress.

So my mouth curls into a small smile, because Leo gets to do that.

"Plus, I noticed Wade was looking mighty fine earlier," Eva quips, and I chuck my marshmallow at her.

She hands me the bag, and I grab another.

"Know what?" Eva almost sounds wise except for the fact that she's picking marshmallow out of her hair. "You don't need to leave anymore."

I stare at the orange and blue flames as they lick at my new marshmallow.

"You always wanted to go to college, and you still shall," she takes on almost a mock scholarly tone, "but there's a community college down the road. You leave, and you'll be turning your back on the best kind of education to be found. How many people can get an education on how to hunt the scariest demons in the world?"

A fit of yelling comes from the house and something crashes inside. Eva and I lock eyes with worry until the sound of Raylan and Maggie's laughter all but shakes the house. She yells at him again, and he laughs so high, his laugh is like a girl's.

"They're getting along well," I say.

"And so will you." Eva moves to her feet from her sleeping bag and snuggles up to where I'm sitting. Her cashmere lotion wafts over me, and it feels nice to have her so close. "You belong here with us." She quickly adds, "But only if you want to."

I think about my ambitions—how I always wanted to be a doctor, because I felt that it *was* the most ambitious thing I could do. But it's not like I exactly have deep pockets now. I killed my own father, true, but now's the time to honor his memory. Improve on it, too. I'll protect Eva just like I always have, but take a step back. Give her a little room to grow. And, even though learning the truth about the Blurred Ones didn't go the way I'd hoped, at least now we know what we're dealing with. To think how much more prepared we'll be when we happen upon more in the future.

"I wouldn't mind killing some demons," I say.

"Don't you know!"

"*You* have to finish high school."

Eva harrumphs like I'm the meanest sister in the world. Pulling the sleeping bag over both of our laps, she quietly adds, "I don't need you."

Eavesdroppers would think I should be offended by her tone, but she's telling me she's going to be okay. That she doesn't need Big Sister to look out for her. No one's going to slap her around. Not anymore.

At the same time, she snuggles up close, laying her cool cheek on my shoulder. It makes me feel content. Nice.

"But I sure want you to stay around," she finishes.

Pulling my marshmallow from the fire, I slide it onto the cracker and chocolate Maggie laid out on a log. Always so prepared, Mags. Eva hasn't managed to cook her own marshmallow yet, so I break my newly-made s'more and hold it out for her. "You are the most fantastic person I know."

Shyly, Eva takes her half and nibbles on it. When she's polished off her half, she gently nudges my shoulder. I think she's going to say something deep or even argue when she wordlessly plucks the other s'more from my hand and eats that, too.

THE END

If you enjoyed Hush, Now Forget would you please do us a huge favor and write a review? Our goal is to qualify for a BookBub to help with our marketing efforts, which means we need to get 50 or so reviews. We would really appreciate it. Even one line helps. You can leave one at any book review site or retailer online. We are a small independent publisher and honest, positive reviews can majorly help us compete with the Big Dawgs. Thank you!

ACKNOWLEDGMENTS

Thank you, dear reader, for reading our book! Storytelling isn't even close to being complete without you.

We want to thank God for putting this story in our hearts, and for our review team who agreed to read and review early copies of our book.

Thank you to anyone who reviews or buys any of our books!

Thank you, Katie and Vanessa, for supporting Monster Ivy every step of the way. Thank you Kelly, Travis, Brian, and Jerusha for being our beta readers and helping us see big picture stuff. Thank you Tamara Hart Heiner for being the best editor we could hope for. And thank you to our husbands and children who put up with our artsy ways, including going on vacation—which is really code for researching our next book!

DISCUSSION QUESTIONS

1. Eva and Frost are frustrated when Maggie and their parents refuse to share the truth about the Blurred Ones. If the girls hadn't gone to San Antonio seeking for answers, do you think the truth would have caught up with them eventually? Why or why not?

2. Eva loves to mix up cliches. Why do you think she does this? Ask each book club member to create a mixed up cliche of their own and share with the group.

3. Frost refuses to acknowledge her true relationship with Leo when they first meet up. Why do you think she reacts like this?

4. After a bit of a tumultuous beginning, Maggie and Raylan bond pretty quickly. Why do you think they're able to find this dynamic?

5. The Sisters of Bloodcreek series explores the idea that we

not only live after we die, but our spirits existed before we were born. If you believed this ideology and accepted that you came to earth to gain a body and experience, how might that change how you live?

6. As Leo can attest, sometimes we choose the wrong path and think there's no way of changing or going back. Does Leo seem redeemable? Why or why not?

7. Character duality is when a character feels two emotions at once. Since Eva and Frost have a complicated relationship with their parents, what two strong emotions might they feel toward them at the same time? When have you felt this in a relationship?

8. Eva and Frost get along for the most part, despite not always being in agreement. How do you think they're able to be loving toward one another while still standing up for their own beliefs and opinions?

9. To thoroughly research the book, the authors visited San Antonio. Highlights of their trip included staying in the Gunter, attending a ghost tour, eating at a barbecue restaurant on the riverwalk, and floating the sloth-like Comal River. Which of these tourist destinations would you be interested in visiting, and how do you think this in-person research helped with the creation of the book?

10. What kind of a hunter would you be if you were forced to live the "hunter" lifestyle? Would you put up a facade, like Maggie, and hang up animal furs? Would you embrace the cloak and dagger mischief like Eva, or keep a detailed diary, like Raylan?

*Enjoy delving deeper? Join the Monster Ivy Book Club Facebook Group, where we read and discuss our latest releases with live Q&A sessions, host giveaways, and offer insights on how to host your own perfect book parties.

ABOUT THE AUTHORS

Mary Gray balances dark and twisty plots with faith-based messages. Some of her best ideas come when she's lurking in the woods, experimenting with frightening foods, or pushing her kids on the tire swing. She is a contributor to The Faithful Creative Magazine, a co-owner of Monster Ivy, and the membership chair of Indie Author Hub.

Cammie Larsen loves all things creative, especially something that tells a fantastic story. She's doing what she can to bring more beauty and insight to the world while building her own life's story. For now, that includes helping run Monster Ivy Publishing, volunteering at her local church, and hanging out near and far with her hubs, kid, and two giant dogs. She's an editor, graphic designer, and contributor to The Faithful Creative Magazine.

To learn more about our publishing company, please visit:
monsterivy.com

ALSO BY THE AUTHOR(S)

SLEEP, DON'T FRET (SISTERS OF BLOODCREEK #2) - The Abram sisters head out to New Orleans to contend with witch doctors and Raylan's ruthless sister.

OUR SWEET GUILLOTINE - a young executioner falls for the daughter of a woman he had to kill...

HER DARK FANTASY: A PREQUEL TO OUR SWEET GUILLOTINE - A short story prequel to French Revolution-era novel, OUR SWEET GUILLOTINE. Young Tempeste witnesses an executioner break apart her mother's feet in an attempt to extract a confession.

THE DOLLHOUSE ASYLUM - a group of teenagers are granted asylum from the apocalypse, only to be forced to reenact some of the most famous, tragic literary couples... or die.

THE DEVILS YOU MEET ON CHRISTMAS DAY - a short story anthology about the outliers, the murderers, the misunderstood, and the forgotten, penned by editors and friends of Monster Ivy Publishing.

HOW TO WRITE FAITH-BASED MESSAGES FOR A SECULAR MARKET - for secular writers who hope to incorporate messages of hope and faith.

HOW TO WRITE CLEAN YET SCINTILLATING ROMANCE - bodice-rippers are some of the most lucrative books in the industry. So what if you don't write books that aren't as steamy?

Clutching the steering wheel like a purple-haired granny, I slam on the brakes. I narrowly avoid hitting a rusty delivery truck that's just decided it owns this tiny road. "Come on, New Orleans!" I wail. "You're supposed to be better than this."

So many one way streets. And people. Drunk people. Walking every which way to dodge piles of trash. I guess I'm not sure what I expected, but I think it has something to do with being somewhat . . . classier? Bigger? Definitely a little cleaner.

"You said it was the best yesterday," Frost argues, all sassy with her chin tucked into her plaid collar. I stick my tongue out at her, but through the corner of my mouth so I can focus on this monstrosity of a neighborhood.

"That's because yesterday was awesome," I concede. "City Park was awesome—and we had the boys and Mags with us." Those big ace trees, friendly people, a gorgeous gazebo to cuddle with Raylan in? Those were all hard to be mad at. "But this French Quarter is madness."

Some dude in the debonair mixture of a beret and

Hooters shirt steps right in front of Betsy. I brace myself and slam on the brakes again, as I had finally reached the speed of like five miles an hour. "Really, dude?"

Frost holds her hands up like I've somehow blamed her.

"Tell me it gets better," I demand, but lightly. She's taken on so much responsibility since Dad died, I try to remember to not need anything from her.

It's true we've been in the French Quarter for a whole three minutes, so I probably shouldn't be making such definitive accusations about the place, but still. Give me potholes and roadkill to dodge, not drunk pedestrians and speeding trucks. It's enough to make me, the usual designated calm driver, spaz.

"Google says to turn left up here," Frost says. "Two more minutes to your love-ah." She lets me vent, so I assume for now that she agrees with me. "Saint Mary. Turn."

"Yes'm. Here we go because I cannot see anythi—" I end in a shriek and slam on the brakes again as a taxi speeds down Saint Mary street. "This is the worst." But I risk glancing up for a half second, and I'm digging the intricate green and black iron work on hundreds of balconies. And the different blue, green, white and red stucco, even if it's all mossy and faded. "Cool architecture, though."

Frost gives a dainty snort as she tucks a gorgeous strand of blonde hair behind her ear. "The worst, with cool architecture." She looks back at her phone for directions. "Got it."

"Oh, hush up your mouth." I wink at her sideways, not really caring if she sees. She knows I love to play on Mom's way of saying "shut up," and she knows I sound way more irritated than I am. It's still an adventure in a new city, and she actually took two days off work to be here. No way I'd actually be mad. "Two more minutes till we're re-u-ni-ted!" I sing like a hairband singer from the eighties.

"And we test out our hunting skills," Frost sings less

dramatically, but the fact she's singing back at all proves she's almost as excited, even if we're both still a smidge nervous.

"Watch out world!" I hold my ringed fist out for her to bump.

"Darn straight," she agrees while bumping my fist.

I reach a stop sign and glance at my sister. My heart feels good when I see her self-satisfied grin instead of the usual weight-of-the-world emptiness she carries most days. She must be getting into the excitement of the hunt.

"Now pull into this parking lot. Grab a ticket over there." She points to a ticket machine across the lot. "We better hurry, it's getting dark."

"Look at you, getting better at directions, Sacajawea." She has enough she can tease me about, but I'll never let her live down how she forgot her way to chemistry five times in our two-hallway school.

Finally able to see that this road is free of taxis and renegade pedestrians, I gun it across the street to the parking lot. "Yeah, we just need some handsome men and our dear friend Mags back to enjoy this city." I roll down my window to grab a parking pass and take a breath of the Deep Southern air but end with a cough, like my body has sampled this air and rejected it as poison. "Ugh! It smells like puke, pee, and poop put together! For crying out loud."

Frost gets a wicked grin on her face that I usually see in the mirror. "All the better to hunt down evil, my sister."

*Available now